NIGHT AFTER NIGHT

Books by Joan Elizabeth Lloyd

THE PRICE OF PLEASURE

NEVER ENOUGH

CLUB FANTASY

NIGHT AFTER NIGHT

Published by Kensington Publishing Corporation

NIGHT AFTER NIGHT

JOAN ELIZABETH LLOYD

KENSINGTON BOOKS

KENSINGTON BOOKS are published by

Kensington Publishing Corp.
850 Third Avenue
New York, NY 10022

ISBN 0-7394-5767-5

Printed in the United States of America

This book is dedicated to Meg and Annelise,
always supportive and positive;
John S., always helpful and creative;
and Ed, always.

Chapter
1

"I'm going to write a book," Marcy Bryant said to her twin sister Jenna as they settled in the living room of their house in Seneca Falls, New York, after a leisurely Easter dinner. "About Club Fantasy." The mid-afternoon sun shone through the open windows that let in surprisingly warm air for upstate New York in April.

"You're going to what?" Jenna's shocked expression was priceless. Marcy had found out about Club Fantasy the previous January, and since then she'd been incredibly curious. Writing a novel would give her a reason to delve more deeply into the high-priced bordello dedicated to fulfilling gentlemen's sexual fantasies that Jenna and her friend Chloe had founded the previous summer. Maybe she'd even learn to understand her sister. And herself.

"Write a book." Marcy popped a grape jelly bean into her mouth and chewed slowly, trying to sound confident. "I've been spending a lot of time in the bookstore looking over the erotic fiction section. I've even read several books of short stories and three erotic novels. I think Club Fantasy would make a wonderful setting."

"You're nuts. You can't do that."

"Not only can I, but I've already written a few short stories.

I changed the name to the Eros Hotel. Isn't that a fabulous name?" She knew she sounded like a lunatic but this project had become important to her.

"Marcy, you don't know anything about what I do. You couldn't understand what it's like."

"Why not?" Marcy said, working very hard at keeping her voice bright.

"You're, well, you're just you."

Marcy's face darkened. Although they were as close as sisters could be, sometimes she resented her twin's city mouse–country mouse attitude. "If by that you mean that I'm a repressed, thirty-one-year-old, dried up, old prune . . ."

"Calm down. I don't think that at all. I just meant that you haven't got a lot of experience."

"You don't have to be an egg to make an omelet." And she didn't have to be a *femme fatale* involved in kinky sex to write about it. She sighed. "Okay. Mixed metaphor or something. But I'm a good writer and I've written professionally."

"I know that. But just because you wrote a few short stories that got published doesn't mean you can write erotic stuff."

Marcy grabbed a handful of pages from the end table. "Here. Read this and if you don't think it's a good idea I'll abide by your decision." She paused, tightening all the panicked muscles that wanted to snatch the story back and hug it against her more than ample bosom. "But I don't think it'll be necessary because I know you'll like it."

Marcy handed the pages to her sister, wondering how she'd react and trying to still her stomach full of kangaroos. What the hell did she know about good sex? The story was about her, a woman who'd never had a real orgasm and didn't really know much except what she'd read in stories on the Internet.

Her sister was the one with the bordello. Her sister was the one with the incredibly active sex life and the wonderful boyfriend.

She looked at Jenna, so confident, so poised. Slender,

shapely, such a contrast to her own soft, blobby body. They were twins, at least it said so on their birth certificates, but in so many ways they were worlds apart. Except for their gray eyes, changeable from steel to fog, and their hair, soft brown, they were so different. As Marcy looked at her sister, she realized that even her hair had changed, now highlighted with lighter streaks and cut in a stylish shape to her shoulders, curled to frame her face.

Marcy pulled the barrette from her long ponytail, combed it with her fingers, then refastened the metal tightly. She looked at her nails, bitten to the quick. No, she'd never be her sister, but she could dream, couldn't she? And what made erotic short stories good? Dreams. Club Fantasy was built around them and she knew dreams. Well.

She saw the trepidation on Jenna's face as she took the pages. They were pretty good, Marcy knew that. Jenna would like them, and then Marcy could do what she'd always wanted to do, write. And maybe even get paid for it. The money had become important too. It was all so complicated.

She watched Jenna curl up in her typical position, legs tucked beneath her, and begin to read.

LOVE LESSONS

"So you guarantee that I'll have an orgasm," Melissa said.

"I don't make guarantees," the representative of the Eros Hotel said. "What I said was that if you're not satisfied, you will be granted a refund."

"Doesn't satisfied mean that I'll have an orgasm?"

The woman's voice was clear and cultured. "Only you will be the judge of what that word means. We guarantee satisfaction to each of our customers for every visit." She typed a few sentences on her computer, printed out a sheet of paper and handed it to Melissa. "Read this carefully and, if you're comfortable with all the terms, sign at the bottom."

Melissa read. The agreement said very little, just that she was going to spend an hour with some man who would make every effort to see that she was "satisfied." There was that word again. *Oh, well,* Melissa thought, *for a thousand dollars I'd better be, and if not, I'll get my money back.* The contract stated that in very clear language. She signed.

"I'll set up a time for you, at your convenience of course, and get in touch."

As Melissa left the Eros Hotel, she considered what she had just done. She had just celebrated, if that was the right word, her thirtieth birthday, and had finally admitted to herself that she hadn't really climaxed in all that time. Oh, she'd had lovers all right. Quite a few. And they were talented in bed. But she seemed unable to climb over the edge, make the electricity, the fireworks. The earth hadn't moved. Ever.

This guy better be good, she thought. *For a grand, he'd better be more than good.*

At five minutes to eight on the arranged evening, Melissa arrived at the Eros Hotel and was escorted to Room 6 by the same woman she had met with several days earlier. She knocked and the door was opened by a tall, slender man with wire-rimmed glasses and a slight overbite. He had soft, sandy hair, hazel eyes, and slightly larger than necessary ears. Melissa was deeply disappointed. She had pictured some dark-haired, dark-eyed, Greek-god type with a gorgeous body and great, talented hands. *Well,* she thought, looking down, *his hands are really great.* Maybe that's all that matters.

"This is Justin," the woman said, "and he's here for your pleasure."

God, Melissa thought, *he's a male prostitute.* She'd never really thought about that aspect of it at all before. About the guy. He must service several women each week, maybe several in a night. Ugh. Maybe not!

"It's really all right," Justin said, taking her hand. "It's really not as bad as all that. Since I'm engaged for you for as long as you want, we can just sit and talk for a while. Then you can get a refund and be on your way." He pulled at her hand gently and guided her into the well-furnished room. The door closed and, as they settled on the sofa, Melissa felt very alone.

"I've been told about your desires and I'm only happy to try to help. I understand that you've never climaxed. A lovely woman like you should have had a bevy of lovers, all able to please you."

His voice held such sincerity that Melissa relaxed a bit. "I've had lovers," she admitted. "And they were all good. But I've never . . ."

"How do you know they were good lovers?"

"Excuse me?"

"You heard the question," Justin said, gazing into her eyes. "How do you know they were good lovers?"

"Well, because . . . Well, everyone said that . . . Well . . ."

"Did any of them ask you what you wanted?"

"No."

"Did any of them play and tease and kiss?"

"Kiss? Of course we kissed."

"Like this?" Justin slid his arms around Melissa's shoulders and lightly touched her lips with his. His tongue slowly licked the joining of her lips until her mouth opened. Melissa was surprised when he didn't push his tongue into her mouth. Instead, he nibbled at her lower lip, licked her upper one, then moved to her jaw. He placed a line of kisses along her jawline until he reached her earlobe. He nipped at the soft flesh until she almost cried out.

When he sat back, he asked, "Like that?"

"Well," Melissa said, "not quite like that."

"And did you ever tell them what you wanted?"

"Of course not."

"Why not? Don't you know what you want?"

"Well, of course I do, but it's not my place to ask."

Justin laughed. "Why in the world not? How are they supposed to know what you want unless you tell them?"

Melissa was speechless. How indeed? But this wasn't her fault, was it? Men were just supposed to know.

"For example," Justin said, his mouth now close to Melissa's ear, "what do you want right now?"

I want your hands all over me, Melissa thought, but she couldn't say it. It just wasn't her place to say. "I don't know?"

"Of course you do," Justin said. "You're like so many women, taught to be silent during lovemaking. Never ask. Well, now you'll have to tell me." When she hesitated, he said, "I'll make it easy. Do you want me to kiss you?"

Her body was humming, needing. She'd worked herself into quite a state waiting for this evening and she wanted him to get to it. She did want kissing, but more, she wanted his hands. And his body. She wanted to know, to stop worrying and wondering.

"Do you want me to touch you?"

"Oh, yes," she said. "Please."

"Good," Justin said, sliding his hands up her arms. "I love touching beautiful women."

"Let's get one thing straight here," she said. "I'm not beautiful. I'm an ordinary-looking woman with quite a few extra pounds, and I don't want to be lied to."

"You are such a silly woman," Justin said as he opened her blouse and slipped it off her shoulders. "Every woman is beautiful. Are you a movie star? Of course not. A beauty queen? No. But you are warm and soft and anxious for loving. That's beauty, and anyone who doesn't think so is crazy."

As Melissa started to protest, Justin's hands moved to her breasts. She had always been particularly sensitive there and her dates usually found that out quite quickly. A few pinches and sucks, then whammo. Not now, she cried silently. Not this time!

Slowly Justin tossed Melissa's blouse aside and unfastened and removed her bra. He lifted her ample breasts and played with her nipples. "Do you like what I'm doing?"

"Oh, yes," she said.

"Would you like me to continue or do something else."

She couldn't speak.

"Tell me." He leaned down and took one hard nipple into his mouth. Gently he sucked it deeper, increasing the pressure until she thought she would explode. "I know what you like," he said. "It's obvious to anyone who cares, but I want you to begin to control the lovemaking. Tell me what you want."

"More."

"Of what?"

Melissa swallowed hard. "Suck me like you did."

"Good," he growled, taking possession of her other nipple. As he sucked, he rhythmically squeezed the other. Melissa could feel the rhythm echoing through her body and deep between her legs.

For long minutes he played with her breasts, lightly biting, pinching, teasing, until Melissa felt hungry for more. "Tell me," he whispered. "You will have to tell me."

"I need more," she whispered, barely recognizing the sound of her own voice.

"What do you need?"

Melissa almost cried. "I can't."

"You can't tell me yet," he said, taking her hand. "So show me. Where do you want me to touch you?"

Again, Melissa swallowed. Then she took his hand and slid it down her belly and between her legs. "Good," he said. "So good. I know that was hard for you, but you will see how much easier it will become to ask for what you want, what you need."

He began to stroke her through her slacks. She was getting wetter and wetter, her legs opening wider of their own accord, her hips moving to increase the pressure of his fingers. Needing more direct contact, Melissa unbuttoned her slacks.

"I'll do that," Justin said, moving her hand away from her pants, "but you have to ask."

"Take them off," she groaned. "Please."

Quickly he removed her slacks and her panties. "Do you want me to touch you, or use my mouth?"

She wanted it all. "Touch me," she whispered.

"Good girl," he said, sliding his fingers through her wet folds. His fingers seemed to know where to rub and stroke to drive her higher. This was where she usually lost it, the excitement slipping away, dissipating like smoke. Not this time. Please, not this time.

"Do you want my mouth?"

Although she had showered just before she came to the Eros Hotel, she knew she was no longer sweet smelling. She could smell the odor of sex. "No," she said, although it was a lie. A date of hers had had a hot tub and they had played in it. That time she had felt good about the odor.

Justin inhaled deeply. "I love the smell of an aroused woman. The scent alone is almost enough for me to climax." He took Melissa's hand and placed it on his bulging crotch. "Feel what you do to me."

He was so hard, Melissa realized. Can he mean what he's saying? He flicked his tongue over her hard clit. "Tell me. Does that feel good?"

Good? It was heaven. "Yes," she admitted.

"Then let me love you with my mouth."

"Let you?"

He chuckled. "Please."

"Oh, yes."

His mouth covered her clit, slowly sucking until the pressure was almost unbearably erotic. Then he released, and again sucked. She felt his fingers playing with the folds at the entrance to her channel. "Oh," she hissed. "Oh, God."

Higher and higher until she could almost reach the top. Almost. Almost.

Then he plunged three fingers into her and she came. "Oh, God, oh, God, oh, God. Yes, yes, yes."

He kept sucking and driving his fingers into her until she was drained. Slowly her body relaxed and his motions slowed. "I never realized . . ." she whispered.

"I know. And there's so much more. You are a grown woman, yet there is so much more to learn. So much I can teach you."

She could barely make her mind focus. "More?"

"Shall we make another date here for next week?"

He was a male prostitute, yet he had helped her to feel so much. Maybe he could teach her. More? "Oh, yes." It was more than worth the tuition.

As her sister read her story, Marcy considered all that had happened during the previous year. Jenna, her always-reliable sister, had gone to New York City and opened a brothel. There was no other name for it. Club Fantasy, as it was known, was a brothel, entertaining wealthy clients with scenarios right out of their deepest desires. Marcy hadn't learned about it until just a few months—had it only been three months?—earlier and had freaked, at first. Now she thought she understood. Well, if she were being honest, she didn't really. But she accepted and for the moment that was enough.

The book. What had ever possessed her to think about writing a book? Well, why not? Club Fantasy was a great setting, although for safety sake she'd changed the name to the Eros Hotel. She was a writer, after all. Well, it had only been a few articles and stories while she'd been in college, but those had been really good. She could do it. It would be good money and maybe, if she hit it really big, Jenna would give up the "business" and move back to Seneca Falls, marry Glen and they'd all live happily ever after.

She'd always been the one to try to set the example for

Jenna, and maybe she could just guide her into doing the right thing, for her and for Glen. He was such a doll, and since he'd returned from spending a few days in the city with Jenna, they'd been all lovey-dovey. If only she'd agree to return home.

Why was she writing a book and getting involved in Jenna's life? Hell, she wasn't sure she could sort it all out, nor did she want to right now.

"Okay, Marcy," Jenna said as she finished reading her sister's story. "You win. This story is really good. How did you learn to write erotica?"

"It's amazing what you can learn from books and the net," Marcy said, releasing a long breath and curling her legs beneath her, unconsciously duplicating her sister's pose. "I read a few books on writing novels and lots of short stories on the Web, most of which were awful. I think I've learned what makes a good erotic story, and I thought I could do it. So I did." Bravado, but she felt her heartbeat slow.

"You sure did, Sis. This story's great, but it isn't a novel. You need a plot, characters, like that. You need much more for a novel then you do for a short story."

"I know that and I've got the setting. The Eros Hotel. Like Club Fantasy. So many things can happen there. There's loads of material." Marcy grabbed a key-lime jelly bean and popped it into her mouth, trying to believe everything she was saying. Writing was easy and she'd read hundreds of novels over the past twenty years. Nothing as erotic as what she was planning, of course, but she was bright and creative so it couldn't be that difficult. Her sister's skeptical expression merely deepened her resolve.

Jenna leaned forward. "You need characters, a hero and a villain."

"I don't think it will be that kind of book. Maybe just a coming-of-age thing with lots of hot short stories thrown in for the reader to enjoy. The sex alone should sell it. Everyone loves to read erotica, especially when it's not called erotica."

Jenna considered, then said, "Okay. That might be true and I'm not poo-pooing your ability to write, but what do you know about the Eros Hotel? You'd have to have details about the business, too, wouldn't you?"

"You can tell me whatever I need to know. I wouldn't need to include much about the running of it, and you can tell me about all the people you've met, the fantasies they've acted out."

Jenna shook her head. "Not a chance, Sis. That won't work. It would be like trying to write a book set in Paris from Yakima, Washington. It will never seem real enough."

Marcy heard the honk of an automobile horn from outside and assumed it was Glen, picking Jenna up for an evening out. "I can do it."

"Who are you trying to convince, you or me? Let's both give it some thought over the next few days and then we'll see what we can come up with." Jenna stood and grabbed her purse. "I'm off," she said, heading for the door. "Glen and I are going for a drive. Wanna come?"

Marcy waved, then grabbed a jelly bean. "No thanks. Say hi to him for me."

"Will do. And I'll think about that book idea and see what I can do to help."

"So you don't think it's such a bad idea? You'll teach me about Club Fantasy?"

Jenna let out a long breath. "It's not a bad idea and I think you'll do fine. But getting a book published is a lot more difficult than you realize, I'm afraid. And I just wonder when you'll find the time to write."

"I've got oodles of time."

"Okay, Marce. See you later."

Find the time? Marcy thought as Jenna closed the front door.

Finding the time wasn't her problem. She really did little other than work as a translator at AAJ Technologies.

She replayed her conversation with her sister and wondered how much of what she'd said about her personal motivations had been true. Why had it suddenly become so important to write a book when she'd never had literary aspirations before? Why now? As she told her sister, the Eros Hotel sounded like such fun to write about. But there were other reasons. She wanted to understand her sister's world. Was she also using the book as a reason to climb out of her small-town rut, if only on her computer screen? She was in her thirties and hadn't had much of a life. Did she want to lead Jenna's life, if only vicariously? Perhaps.

Did she want to earn a lot of money so she could lure Jenna home, back to Seneca Falls, to Glen and what Jenna always called a white picket fence life? Perhaps.

She didn't understand her reasons any more now than she had when she'd first come up with the idea for the book. But did she have to understand? No. She'd just forge ahead and do it. Why not?

As she headed down the front walk toward Glen's car, Jenna wondered about her sister's sudden desire to write a book. Why? Oh, she had written a good erotic short story all right but that didn't translate into a novel. She could put in months of work and, in the end, have nothing to show for it. Was there more to this than met the eye? *Oh, well*, she told herself as she climbed into Glen's Honda and kissed him hello, *it's not my job to lead Marcy's life. If she wants to try writing, who am I to second guess her?*

Chapter
2

Over the next several weeks, Marcy read more books on writing novels and penned three more short stories about the Eros Hotel. Sadly, when she reread them later, they all seemed a bit wooden and the sex didn't turn her on. If it didn't turn her on, how could it turn on a reader? Unless the heat in her writing improved, the book thing wasn't going to work after all. But it had to.

The more she thought about it, the more she realized that much of her desire to write was driven by her need to get Jenna out of the prostitution business. Would the book do that? Would Jenna come home if Marcy had a lot of money? Maybe not, but she had to try.

Prostitution. Much as she tried to understand, and as often as she replayed her conversations about how it hurts no one, Marcy hated it. Hated it. Hated it. Her sister was a whore. Okay, a very well-paid, well-dressed, high-class whore, but a whore nonetheless. She mentally slapped herself. Stop being so hard on her! She's not really that different from the woman she'd been for over thirty years. Marcy sighed. It was all so confusing.

Instead of writing short stories, Marcy tried to concentrate on the story of the Eros Hotel. How had it begun? Just as Club

Fantasy had, two women who slipped into it, slowly, inexorably sliding down the slippery slope of selling sex. It all seemed innocent enough, beginning as it had with taking videos of lovemaking. But when it evolved into fulfilling men's fantasies, the business became the whorehouse it is now.

Marcy tried to incorporate into her writing what her sister had told her. It was a crime without a victim. Men wanted something so Jenna and her friend Chloe provided it and the men paid for it. What was wrong with that? She wrote it, but she didn't really believe it. Was that why the novel part of the book came out so stiff? She sat at her computer and reread the first chapter she'd written. Actually rewritten was a better word. She'd edited and reedited, but it still didn't come off. Was she going to have to give it all up?

She thought about the writing she'd done in college and since. She'd written about her town, about the surrounding Finger Lakes region. She'd penned a great series of articles on the wineries and another on the Lakes themselves. One late spring evening after work, she took out her scrapbook and read the articles. They were good, really good. Why couldn't she make the Eros Hotel live the way the places and characters in her articles did?

She continued to write for a few hours each evening after work, but she finally had to admit that she was getting nowhere. It was June and the late spring flowers were slowly fading. Two months after she had told Jenna that she was going to write a book the two women again sat in the living room. Since Club Fantasy was closed Monday and Tuesday, Jenna often flew up Monday morning and stayed until midday Wednesday. Although the sisters got to visit, Jenna spent most of her time with Glen.

Feet propped on the coffee table, Jenna was finishing reading the first chapter of Marcy's book and one short story. She'd kicked off her shoes and sat in a stylish flowered skirt and tailored rose silk blouse. As she looked up, Marcy said, "That's the best of it. I've rewritten chapter one a zillion times, torn up several short stories and not even finished a few more. I just don't know what's wrong." Marcy, her black-sweatpants-covered legs crossed beneath her, could see the indecision on her sister's face. "Spit, Jen. I know it hasn't got the spark that the first story had."

Jenna heaved a long sigh and looked decidedly uncomfortable.

"Really, Sis," Marcy continued, pushing the sleeves of her black sweatshirt up to her elbows, "I want to know, so hit me as hard as you need to. Please, if I can't get an answer from you, I don't know where else to turn."

"You've put me in a terrible position," Jenna said, twisting to curl her legs beneath her. "I don't want to hurt your feelings or come on like I know something about writing." She hesitated, then said, "But I know what I like to read and this just isn't it. Maybe I do know what's wrong, though."

Marcy sighed. "I can guess. I just don't have it to become a novelist. I've suspected it all along."

"That's not it," Jenna said, shaking her head. "You're fabulous when you write about things you know. That first story, the woman who'd never had an orgasm. That's you, isn't it."

Marcy felt herself blush to the roots of her hair. She'd had boyfriends, and been sexually active since college—even before if she wanted to be truly honest—but most of the time it hadn't been very good. Was that story her? Of course it was. It was a fantasy she'd had and honed over the past few years. It had become even more detailed since she'd learned about her sister's business.

"You don't have to say anything. It was pretty obvious from this story." Jenna shifted so she sat beside her twin, and circled her arm around her shoulder. With a hug, she said, "Marce, you aren't any different from the person I was a year ago. I didn't know good sex from the mediocre. When I told Glen I couldn't marry him, sex was a good part of the reason. I felt I would be settling for something less than I wanted. I learned and eventually found what I was looking for, and with Glen I can now have it all."

"I'm so happy for you, Jen," Marcy said.

"You write great stuff when you write about your own experiences or your dreams. This story," Jenna said, holding up one of the sets of pages she'd just finished reading, "isn't based on your own experiences. And the first chapter is a bit flat and difficult to believe."

"Write what you know," Marcy said, feeling like the dream of writing a book was slipping away. Jen was right. It wasn't going to work. She didn't know about good sex, or about Club Fantasy. "That's what all the books on writing say. What do I know about running something like Club Fantasy, fulfilling fantasies? I don't even have fantasies worth fulfilling, except that first one. I guess I'll have to give it all up. It just isn't going to work." She felt her heart sink.

"That first story you gave me was fabulous," Jenna said. "You have talent, something I always wished I had." She squeezed her sister's shoulders. "If you really want to write the book, you do have another option."

"Don't say it," Marcy said, already knowing what her sister was going to suggest. It was all so obvious, but she had been avoiding thinking about it.

"I *will* say it, only once, then I'll shut up if you want me to. Marce, if you want to write it, you have to live it."

"No way. The 'city mouse' isn't going to convert the 'country mouse' into someone who fucks men for money." When Jenna raised an eyebrow, Marcy felt even more embarrassed. "I'm sorry, Jen. I didn't mean that the way it came out."

"Actually, you did. I know you don't approve of what I do for a living, but I love you and I think you're jumping to a lot of wrong conclusions. Sadly, I can't help that. I do make love with men for money.

"If you want to write this book, however, you don't have to

go nearly as far as I do," Jenna said, her voice low and serious. "You could come to the 'big bad city,' talk to some of the people I work with and learn about the business, and sex." She paused. "And about yourself."

Marcy found tears prickling the back of her eyes. "God, you sound like a shrink."

"Marcy, I don't want to fight with you." Jenna let out a long, deep sigh. "I've adjusted to the fact that I probably can't ever make you understand, but it does make me sad." When Marcy tried to interrupt, Jenna held up her hands, palms out. "Don't deny it. It is what it is. I said I'd say something once, then let it drop. Forget the book. Forget the sex. I won't mention it again."

Marcy deflated. She didn't want to forget the book. Somehow she knew she could write the plot part. It could be a great book. It would have everything, a great story about two women founding a business the ended up earning tens or even hundreds of thousands of dollars each year and trying to get their friends to understand why it happened. But how could she write that when she truly didn't understand? And then there was the sex part. She couldn't write it, at least not as well as she wanted to. Damn.

She wouldn't be a whore just to write a book, however, and that was that. "I can't be you, but I want to learn. I want to do this book." Was it the book, or the sex, or learning about her sister and thus about herself? Trying to figure out her own motivations was making her brain hurt.

"Sis, you wouldn't have to do what I do. That would be wrong for you, at least for now. But why don't you take a couple of weeks off and come down to the city. Stay with me and collect stories from some of the people who work for Club Fantasy. They aren't weirdos or monsters, they're just people. You've spent time with Chloe and she's not a monster, is she?"

Marcy thought about Jenna's friend and business partner. Tiny, with tremendous eyes and a twinkle that made her look like she knew everything about loving. Marcy had noticed it when she'd visited the previous Labor Day weekend and had wondered briefly what it was that made Chloe light up. Now she knew. She was a prostitute, too.

Jenna hugged her sister again. "I'm not a monster either."

"Of course you aren't. I love you, Jen," Marcy said, hugging her sister back. And Jenna was right. She could learn about the business of fulfilling fantasies without becoming a whore, with her honor intact. It would just be a visit. "Maybe I could take a week's vacation."

"How much vacation time have you got saved up?"

Marcy grinned ruefully. "Several months worth."

"Great. So take a week or two to start. I know you have pre-conceived notions about Club Fantasy but try to be neutral. Come down with an open mind and see what develops. You can stay with me in my apartment and just take it all in. I'll tell you everything about everything, then you can spend time with Chloe and a few of our employees. Maybe Erika will be in town. I'd love you to meet her, too."

"Who's she?"

"She was in the—entertainment—business before I was and has helped me a lot. She's retired now. She and her husband live way out on the Island and they travel a lot. She's the one who helped me to understand it all. She could give you her slant on everything and possibly explain it all better than I can. Please. Just try not to prejudge."

Another hooker. She pictured a woman with too much makeup and tight, revealing clothes. "She's married? With a husband?" Like real people?

"Sure. I've met Stuart several times. He's a lawyer and he loves Erika to pieces."

"He knows she was, as you put it, in the business?"

"He got her into it actually."

Marcy was aware of her jaw dropping and snapped it shut with a click. This was all too much. Jenna and this Erika person seemed to be treated like regular business women. But they were madams. Successful ones, but madams nonetheless. "Okay. It's all bizarre and beyond anything I can understand right now. Let me think about coming down to stay with you, but I'm not sure I'm ready for all this."

Jenna leaned back and looked seriously into her sister's eyes. "I'd love to have you, but this isn't a gotta-be. You're the one who wants to write the book. And to write it, you've got to understand it."

"Let me think about it, okay, Jen?"

"Of course. You're welcome any time."

"You didn't really mean all that stuff you've been saying about understanding, did you?"

Marcy sat across the restaurant table from Glen Howell, Jenna's fiancé, a few days after Jenna's return to the city. Since his trip to New York to confront Jenna several months before, Glen seemed to have accepted what she was and appeared to be all right with it. The couple was even talking about setting an actual date for their wedding. Tonight Marcy and Glen were having dinner together, as they did often, as friends. She had told him about her invitation to stay in the city for a week to learn about Club Fantasy. "Of course I meant it. I do understand. It's just difficult for me to think about getting involved."

Glen reached across the table and took Marcy's hand. "Marcy, she's your sister. Since you found out about the Club, to an outsider at least, your relationship with Jenna has been as it always was; but to me, who loves you both, there's something not quite right. You're warm and loving as you always have been, but there's a wariness, like you're being careful not to get too close. It's not catching, you know."

"Don't be silly. There's nothing like that going on." She gazed into his deep brown eyes and saw the hurt there. Pain because they both loved Jenna, and he knew something was wrong. As he raised an eyebrow, Marcy said, "Really."

"Marcy, you protest too much, but that's between you and Jen. It just bothers me to see a wall between you."

Marcy sighed. "Okay. Maybe I'm a little afraid of everything. If she's like that, what does that say about me?" *Would I go lust crazy, too?* Another complication. "Does she feel that wall you're talking about?"

He nodded. "But she understands. She knows it's a big bite to swallow, and Jen being what she is she doesn't say anything negative about you. Relax. I think spending a week or two in the city is a great idea. No one's asking you to get involved in her business, just be an observer. I think you've got a lot to learn, about the business, about Jen and about yourself."

She realized that knowing herself was a part of all this, but she was afraid of it, too. She knew the story of the beginnings of Club Fantasy, but deep inside, she had no idea how her sister could have become a prostitute or why she kept it up. And why could Glen so readily accept everything. Maybe their kind of love meant putting up with a lot of things you didn't really like or understand. She huffed out a small breath. "I don't get it, Glen. We've been friends for a long time, aside from your being engaged to my sister. How can you just sit there, knowing that she's probably entertaining—" Marcy smiled a small, embarrassed smile. "Entertaining, that's a small, weasel word—entertaining one or more men right now, even as we speak?"

"Listen, Marce, I'm not necessarily thrilled with it all, but Jen and I have talked and talked about it and I really trust her. No, that's not the word. Of course I trust her, but that's not it. I respect her and know that she's telling me the truth when she says this is just a job. Sure, she likes the men she deals with and she's charming and very social, and they are sharing sex. For her it's just a one-night thing, no love, just mutual caring and doing her job."

"Aren't you jealous?"

"At first it ate me up inside but now it just is. She could be in sales, making nice to customers to sell a product, and then I might worry about her giving away sex in return for commissions, behind my back. This way I know what's going on. She's not lying to me about anything and I guess that's the most important thing to me."

"I hear what you're saying, but I just can't absorb it."

"You don't have to, you know. She'll always be your sister and you'll love her anyway. Forget this book stuff."

"I want to do this. I want to learn."

"Do you want to write or is this just an embarrassed excuse for getting to know what kinky things Jenna's doing every night?"

At first she let out an embarrassed giggle, then thought about that aspect, too. Was that part of what was going on in her head? It was all so convoluted. "I don't know, Glen. I really don't know."

"You know Jenna's friend Rock was a big help to me in learning about Jenna. He once told me to make a decision and stick to it and stop making it over and over again."

Marcy remembered Rock, a huge brute of a man she'd met briefly when she'd arrived unexpectedly at the brownstone that housed Club Fantasy. He lived there as a combination male prostitute and bouncer. "Is that what I'm doing?" she said, playing for time. Go to the city, live with Jenna for a short while and delve into Club Fantasy or give up her plans for the book. She didn't want to make this decision.

"Yup," Glen said, his face in an obviously innocent grin, the dimple in his chin deepening.

"Okay. I guess I give up. I'll take a week's vacation, fly down to the Big Apple and take a bite."

"I think that's the right way to go, if my opinion makes any difference. I've been there a few times and I know you'll find things are a bit different from what your imagination has concocted."

"Well, we'll see."

* * *

She had to go and find out. She arranged to take four vacation days the week of Fourth of July so, on the Saturday before the holiday, Marcy arrived at LaGuardia Airport in late morning and found her sister waiting just beyond the security checkpoint. Jenna was wearing a pair of trim white linen pants and a deep gold shirt with full sleeves. Over the blouse she wore a soft, buttery yellow leather vest. On a hot July day she looked like a vanilla ice cream cone. "You look fabulous," Marcy said, considering her unchanging attire, black sweatpants and a black tee shirt. In the winter the uniform top became a black sweatshirt but otherwise she wore little else when she had a choice. Of course, she wore more formal clothes to work at AAJ, but they were also usually baggy and made of dark-colored fabrics.

"You look just like you," Jenna said, wrapping her arms around her sister, "and that's great."

"No, it's not, but that's the way it is." How was it that, although identical twins, they were so different in looks? Jenna looked like a million dollars and she looked like ten cents—in a big, lumpy sack. She remembered several years earlier when she'd last worn jeans. She'd overheard someone in the mall refer to her rear view as looking like two pigs wrestling under a blanket. From then on her clothes became baggier and baggier.

"Let me take this," Jenna said, grabbing her shoulder carry-on. "Did you check a suitcase?"

"No. After all, how much room does a week's worth of tee shirts, underwear and socks take."

"Great. Maybe we can do some shopping while you're here. I've found lots of great little shops."

"I don't need clothes, Jen," Marcy said, her hackles rising. Jenna was always trying to change her look. "I like myself just the way I am."

Jenna put her hands up, palms out. "Hey, Sis, back off. It's me you're talking to here. I love you, whatever way you want to be."

Marcy let out a long breath. "I know. Sorry I got so defensive."

Jenna smiled warmly. "No prob. Let's go and find a cab."

Jenna started off toward the ground transportation doors of the airport, chatting idly with her sister. *What am I going to do with Marcy?* she asked herself. She could be so much more if she just took a little pride in her appearance. She wore no makeup other than a little pale lipstick. And she had such lovely eyes. Of course that was a bit egotistical since they were identical twins, but she'd learned at an early age to make the most of her looks and Marcy had buried herself from the beginning. Was it from the beginning? She remembered that in high school Marcy had been much slimmer and had used cosmetics. What had changed her? Maybe during this week she'd make an effort to find out.

Although the sisters had always been very close, Jenna realized now that she'd never really taken the time to get to know what made her sister tick. She'd always assumed that, beyond the obvious differences, they were pretty much alike. She thought about that while their taxi made its way toward Manhattan and they shared gossip about their hometown. Did she really know her twin? Interesting question. Maybe she'd become more aware of people's true desires since she'd been part of Club Fantasy. Much of what she did was to ferret out what a client really wanted, even when he, or increasingly often *she*, wasn't able to be completely candid.

They arrived at Jenna's apartment on the Upper West Side of Manhattan and dropped Marcy's bag on the hall table. The apartment was large with a comfortable living room, a full kitchen and a bedroom large enough for a queen-sized bed. "You've redone the place," Marcy said. "It looks great, and thanks for having me, Sis. Are you sure I'm not in the way?"

"Not a bit," Jenna said quickly, meaning it. Maybe this trip could help bring back the closeness she'd missed for the last six months.

Jenna remembered their last encounter here, when she had told her sister all about Club Fantasy. After her initial shock and pain, Marcy had been thoughtful and seemed accepting, but Jenna knew she hadn't really understood. For now, however, acceptance would have to be enough. After an hour of small talk, Jenna finally broached the topic on both their minds. "About Club Fantasy, I thought you might want to meet one or two of the people I work with."

Marcy looked slightly like a deer in the headlights. "I guess."

"That's what you came here for, isn't it?"

Marcy squared her shoulders. "It certainly is."

"Good. Why don't we start by having brunch with Chloe tomorrow morning and we can swap war stories?" When Marcy nodded, Jenna continued. "Shall I invite Rock to join us?"

"I think I'd like to stick with just us girls at first."

"Okay. I understand. But you'll have to spend some time with him. He's quite special and you can learn a lot from him." Rock was such a sane person and Marcy could learn a lot about the business and about Jenna herself. He knew her in ways no one else could. She smiled inwardly at the thought. They'd made love a few times but now that she and Glen were engaged Rock was merely a dear friend and coworker. Coworker. Business-office words sounded so silly when applied to a brothel.

"In time," Marcy said, her voice a bit hesitant.

Jenna continued. "How about I give you the grand tour of the brownstone this afternoon so you can get the feel of the place? We've made quite a few changes since you were here six months ago." Jenna tried to choose her words carefully but soon realized it was hopeless. She'd just have to say what she meant and let the chips fall . . . "I've got a client at seven, but we could grab a bite before." Client, the best word she'd been able to come up with.

She watched her sister take a deep breath. "Sounds good."

Jenna looked at her watch. "Okay. Let me give Rock a call, but I don't think there's anyone booked in the house until after six. That gives me a couple of hours to show you around, then we can have dinner. Will you be okay taking a cab back here after we eat?"

"Sure." Another deep breath. "Sure," she said, sounding resolute if not totally comfortable with everything.

Chapter
3

Visit the brownstone. Marcy reflexively tightened her stomach muscles. She hadn't been in the building that housed Club Fantasy since the evening in January when she had just showed up, worried about her sister and found out what sort of business went on there. So many memories and so much to deal with. She'd always met problems head-on, and now she vowed to do no different. "Let me just wash my face while you check with Rock and Chloe."

As she entered the bedroom and closed the door behind her, she thought about both Rock and Chloe. It was difficult not to color her memories of Jenna's best friends with the knowledge she'd gained since their last meeting. She'd spent a wonderful Labor Day weekend almost a year before with Jenna and Chloe and she'd liked the tiny woman. She'd been a bit more outgoing than Marcy cared for, but on the whole their weekend had been delightful.

Rock was a different story. She'd only spent a few moments with him on that fateful evening when she'd discovered the truth about Club Fantasy, but looking back he now scared the daylights out of her. At the time she'd noticed only his bulk and the surprisingly soft-spoken tone of his voice with its slight Southern twang. His head was completely shaved, his skin dark with amazingly blue eyes and a small diamond stud winking in his ear. Thinking about him since that evening and knowing that he was a male prostitute terrified her. Had he been with her sister? Did he think of her as being exactly like Jenna? Would he think about sex with her? She swallowed the lump in her throat. Did he turn her on? Nonsense. She straightened and headed for the bathroom.

An hour later Marcy and Jenna got out of a cab in front of the simple-looking brownstone on East Fifty-fifth Street. A four-story building with a simple front entrance, it gave no hint of the strange goings-on inside. Jenna took out her key and opened the front door, quickly punching a security code into a very elaborate panel just inside.

Almost immediately Rock emerged from a door in the hall-way near what Marcy knew to be the kitchen. "Marcy," he said, extending both hands to grasp hers. "It's so good to see you again. Jenna's been looking forward to your visit." He held her hands in his huge ones, then pulled her toward him so he could kiss her on both cheeks. "Jenna said she'd be giving you the cook's tour, so I'll get back to what I was doing downstairs." He looked at Jenna. "Just a few new goodies," he said with a wink and disappeared through the basement door.

Rock was an amazing presence, Marcy thought, all charm and friendliness. Maybe her memories had been colored by the knowledge of what he did in that building. Now she got the feeling that if you were his friend he'd defend you against all comers; and if you got on his bad side, he'd pummel you either verbally or physically. Although he still overwhelmed her a bit, she was glad that her sister was protected by his presence in the building.

"Coffee?" Jenna asked. "Or are you ready to see the place."

Get the guided tour of a house of prostitution, in which fantasy fulfillment was the gimmick. "Let's wander first."

Jenna took her up to the second floor. "We use the living

room downstairs as a waiting area. We serve drinks and munchies for folks who arrive early. Sometimes the anticipation is part of the pleasure of the fantasy."

It was time to throw away her doubts and hesitations and ask the questions she'd have to answer in the book. Book, be damned. She was curious. "How do you know that's the way they feel?"

Jenna stopped in the hallway. "I spend quite a bit of time getting to know my clients," she said. "We sit over coffee in a neutral location and I've learned how to get them to open up and tell me exactly what they're looking for in a fantasy. Although guys don't specifically mention the waiting as part of their dream, I can usually tell that just contemplating making it reality is very arousing. It all comes from observation. I've learned a lot in the time we've been doing this."

"Observation?"

"Sure. I see how nervous they are and exactly which part of the discussion makes them most uncomfortable. That's usually the part they want to avoid most."

"Sorry. You lost me. I would have thought that if they were nervous, that's something that scared them."

"I thought that way, too, at first. Now I think I understand that it's a sort of delicious fear. They are afraid that I'll discover their deepest desires and judge them. I don't, of course."

Marcy's curiosity was overwhelming. "Like what?"

"Okay, let's say I'm sitting with a guy and the subject of a threesome comes up. He begins to stammer, or play with his napkin. Maybe his eyes won't quite meet mine. Slowly I begin to talk about the topic nonjudgmentally. He usually opens up just a bit so I can create a fantasy exactly like the one he's been using to masturbate to for years."

The whole discussion was making Marcy a bit uncomfortable, but she didn't want to reveal how deliciously exciting it all was too. Why not? Probably for the same reasons that the guys whose fantasies Jenna fulfilled felt. She understood that perfectly. What did her excitement level say about her?

Jenna opened the door to one of the bedrooms on the second floor. "This is a general, all-purpose room, the second one we have. The first is called the motel room. We use both of them for hooker-in-the-hotel, burglar-in-the-bedroom scenarios. We can dress the room up with flowers and paintings for more bedroomy stuff, like virginal bride or masterful groom. With a few more mirrors and a room spray with the scent of magnolias, it becomes the southern mansion from which the daughter has to pay off her father's gambling debts, in the obvious way."

Jenna crossed the hall and opened the door to another room, one that looked like something out of the Old West. "This is the sheriff's office. I never would have imagined how many men have the desire to be the Gary Cooper–John Wayne type of western hero but this room is used at least once a week. There's also a harem room. We covered the floor with sand and have a sort of tent-thing so guys can be chieftains or women can be captives." Women? Captives?

Jenna opened the bathroom door. "We have lots of fun in here, too."

"I'm not sure I'm ready for bathroom sports," Marcy said quickly, shaking her head.

"Not that kind," Jenna said, laughing. "I guess some of my employees do that sort of thing but not me." She squeezed Marcy's shoulder. "No, I meant that the shower plays a part in lots of fantasies. Notice the clear shower curtain? Men like to watch a woman touch and lather herself. Lots of acting, of course, and some feigned embarrassment at being watched if that's what the guy wants." She giggled. "It's really good clean fun, as we say."

When Marcy laughed along, Jenna said, "Pardon the little joke. I hope you realize that I'm not making fun of my clients.

I play with things that arouse a man and sometimes it's difficult to be aroused by all of them. It's fun to watch a guy get off but it's not always sexually arousing for me. Sometimes it's just a job, one that pays very well. At other times, of course, it's sexually stimulating and satisfying."

"Oh," was all Marcy could say. This was all so far beyond her ken.

A bedroom on the third floor looked like the "motel room" on the floor below. "This is the first room Chloe and I created. The difference between this and the one below is this." She opened a closet to reveal a jumble of electronic equipment. "We have state-of-the-art photographic equipment so we can film everything that goes on in here."

Marcy gasped. Incriminating videos? Blackmail.

"Don't even think it," Jenna said quickly. "Any filming in here is because the client wants to take a movie away to relive what happened. No one is ever filmed without his or her permission and the client takes the only copy. Guaranteed."

Relieved, Marcy said, "Thanks. I will admit I wondered. Not about you, but about some of your employees." The Jenna she knew could never be involved in anything crooked. But this Jenna? How well did Marcy know her?

"Not a chance. We're very tight about privacy. That's one of the things our customers value about Club Fantasy."

Across the hall Jenna showed Marcy a room done up like a doctor's exam room. "This is another one of our popular rooms. Playing doctor or patient goes back to childhood for many men, and women too for that matter, and in adulthood it becomes a deeply erotic fantasy. It's a game of either power or surrender and really delicious."

Marcy peeped into the room and was amazed. It looked exactly like her gynecologist's office, complete with cabinets, a small sink and a table in the center with stirrups. Playing doctor. Although Marcy hated to admit it, she'd often had quite vivid dreams about it. She'd be the patient, dressed in one of those gowns one wears tied in the front, seated on the edge of an exam table. She'd dreamt this one so many times it was crystal clear in her mind.

The "doctor" would arrive, not her usual female gyn, but a handsome, well-built man of about thirty, with a totally bald head, flashing dark eyes, a devastating smile and a diamond stud in one ear. "I'm sorry, but Dr. Hemmings was called away to deliver a baby. We called to reschedule but you had already left your house."

"The nurse didn't tell me anything."

"I'm so sorry. If you like, we can make you another appointment. But, since you're already undressed, I could do the exam. It's just your annual and it's no big deal."

No big deal? She felt herself getting wet gazing at his large hands with their short, blunt fingers. Exam? Well, she'd feel like a fool calling it off now. Fool? Chicken?

"Sure, let's just go ahead."

"Great. I'm Dr. McKay. If you'll just lay back, we'll do this as quickly as we can."

She settled against the slightly raised back of the table and straightened her legs. She was trembling in anticipation of those wonderful-looking hands on her body, yet terrified that her excitement would show and embarrass her. She would not be turned on by this. She would not!

"So how long has it been since your last exam?" the doctor asked, opening the front of her gown to begin the breast exam.

"A year," she said, proud that she was able to control her voice.

"Good. I'll just be a minute." He began manipulating her right breast, pressing, kneading. It was purely professional, yet it felt sooo good. He moved to her nipple, pulling, squeezing, making her usually small nub hard and erect. As she closed her eyes, she thought she saw him smile. He took quite a while playing with one breast. Playing? No, not possible. This was a doctor.

Trailing his fingers across her chest, he moved to the other breast. The nipple was already erect and her vaginal tissues were swollen and damp. Eyes still closed, she felt his knowing fingers press and pinch until it was all she could do to keep her hips still. "Good," the doctor said. "Everything seems fine. Let's move on."

He lifted each foot into a stirrup, pressing against the insides of her knees to open her legs completely. Then he moved his wheeled stool between her feet and touched his gloved hands on her pubis. "No need to be nervous," he said softly. Was there a slight purr in his voice? Of course not.

Then one finger found her entrance and slowly penetrated. It was as though he knew exactly where to touch to excite her still more. A second slippery finger followed the first, then a third until she was stretched and so aroused it took all her concentration not to writhe beneath his hand. "I'd like to test your reactions," he said, his voice almost a whisper. "I can feel how ready you are and it will only take a moment."

"Ready? For what."

"Why, to come, of course."

"What the hell?"

"You're so aroused you're like a firecracker ready to explode. Let me help you to one of the best climaxes you've ever had."

"No. This is just an exam and you're a doctor."

"Right, but you want it. You know you do."

She did. So much. "No."

While still rubbing her vaginal channel, he touched her clit with his other hand, knowing fingers stroking the sides, deep in the valleys, driving her still higher. It was so wrong. He was a professional. Professional what? Doctor? Lover? He leaned over and touched the tip of her clit with his tongue and she exploded, unable to control the spasms that consumed her. She was on fire, quaking with the fulfillment she had secretly desired.

"Marcy," Jenna said, closing the door to Club Fantasy's medical exam room. "Hello?"

"Sorry," Marcy said, slowing her breathing. Reliving her fantasy had only taken a moment and suddenly she was back on the third floor of the brownstone. She didn't like to think she had sexual fantasies, but she had to admit that she did. Damn, she could certainly understand men wanting to live them out. "I guess I drifted off for a moment."

"No problem. Let me show you a few more rooms."

Jenna continued the tour for another half an hour but was interrupted by Rock. After a quick whispered conversation, Jenna said, "Would you mind if I stood you up for dinner? Rock just took a call from a long-time client of mine who wants to make an appointment for six-fifteen." She looked at her watch. "That only gives me a few minutes to get ready. He's only in town for tonight and . . ."

"Listen, Sis," Marcy said. "I don't want my being here to mess with your business." She had been more shaken by her fantasy than she cared to admit, even to herself, and thus was just as happy to have a little time to think through her reactions. "I'll just stop somewhere and get some dinner by myself and go back to your place."

"I'm really sorry about this."

"Stop apologizing. It's fine. It will give me time to think about the book and make some notes about stories and stuff." *Maybe I'll write about my fantasy.* Or would that be too personal?

"Thanks for understanding. Make yourself at home in my bedroom and I'll crash on the sofa." She raised her hand to forestall any response. "Don't argue. We'll get the sleeping arrangements straightened out in the morning." She leaned over and kissed her sister on the cheek. "Thanks again, sweetie. See you tomorrow and we'll talk at length. Brunch with Chloe at noon?"

"Sure," Marcy said.

As she walked down the stairs behind Rock, he said, "I'd love to take you to dinner myself, but when we have customers I'm always here. We've never had any trouble, but maybe that's because of me. Who'd mess with this?" he said, flexing his thick arm muscles, easily visible beneath his short-sleeved, navy tee shirt. "Since we're closed Monday and Tuesday, maybe we can get together one of those evenings."

"That would be fine," Marcy said, surprised at how intimidated she was by this seemingly comfortable, soft-spoken man. Intimidated, but deliciously so.

"Jenna told me about the book," he said with a warm smile, "and I think I can give you lots of good insights and stories."

The book. Right. She'd been so involved in her fantasy, which usually featured a guy with blond hair and a short beard but this time featured a man who looked suspiciously like Rock, that she'd completely forgotten why she was here. "I'm sure you can. I look forward to hearing some war stories."

"War stories," Rock said. "An interesting way to look at it."

Marcy walked out of the brownstone toward the corner of Second Avenue. She didn't want to go back to Jenna's apartment just yet, and she realized that she was hungry. She hadn't had anything to eat since lunch, and she hadn't even had her usual supply of jelly beans to maintain her blood sugar level. She recalled a small restaurant with a quiet bar just down the block where she and Jenna had eaten on her trip to the city the previous Labor Day weekend. She walked into George's Bistro and the hostess seated her in the corner.

She was still a bit shocked by the vividness of her fantasy and by the fact that she remained wet and aroused. She was also shaken by the ease with which Rock slipped into her dreams. *Okay, relax. It doesn't really matter. I'll calm down. Eventually.* "Can I get you something to drink?" She wanted a glass of wine, but wasn't it unseemly for a woman to drink alone? *God*, she thought, *I'm such a small-town girl.* "I'd like a glass of white wine."

"We have a nice Chardonnay, a Pinot Grigio or a Chablis."

So many choices. "What would you recommend?"

Holding his order pad, the waiter smiled. "I like them all. It's just a matter of what you like."

What did she know? "I guess I'll have the Chardonnay."

A man's voice interrupted from the table behind her. "If you don't mind a suggestion, I would recommend the Chablis instead."

She whirled around.

"I'm sorry," the man said, and she became aware of a slight German accent. "I didn't mean to startle you."

He was about forty, with soft brown eyes, unruly brown hair with a cowlick on the top of his head and a small scar on his prominent chin. He was dressed in brown slacks and a short-sleeved, brown-and-beige-plaid sport shirt. Was he trying to pick her up? Nah. Just helping her decide about the wine. "Thanks for the suggestion." To the waiter she said, "I'll have the Chablis."

"Of course, madam," the waiter said, and scurried off.

"Good choice," the man said. "Are you always so willing to take advice?"

His open, easy smile took any sting out of his words. She automatically smiled back. It was difficult not to. "When I know nothing on the topic I'm pretty easy." Damn. Why had she said it like that? *Now he'll think I'm trying to pick him up.*

His slight chuckle was warm and friendly. "Are you waiting for someone?"

She wasn't totally stupid. He *was* trying to pick her up. Why, she couldn't fathom. She was no bargain, fat, not terribly attractive. Why? She should discourage him right off. *No, I'm not waiting for anyone, but I'm happy just being by myself.* She should say that, but after spending an hour in a brothel, she found herself saying, "No, I'm not waiting for anyone."

"Would you care for some company?"

Again he was giving her an opportunity to say no, but they were in a very public place after all and she didn't have to give her full name or anything. He was just a nice, probably-lonely man who wanted some company. Why not? "Why not?"

He grabbed his newspaper along with his menu and wine-glass and shifted to her table, settling across from her. "I'm Steve. Steve Franks." He reached out as if to shake her hand.

She couldn't refuse without being outwardly rude, so she took the proffered hand. "Marcy." She wasn't comfortable giving her last name even though she wasn't known here at all.

"Like in Peanuts?" he said, with a twinkle. "Peppermint Patty's best friend."

"Of course, sir," she said, using that Marcy's favorite phrase with the character's inflection from the cartoon movies. She noticed that his eyes twinkled when he smiled.

"Delightful. I hope you don't mind that I accosted you like this, but I do hate eating alone."

"Do you do it often?"

"More than I'd like," he said. "I hate cooking and I've learned to hate peanut butter sandwiches and canned baked beans. Sometimes I get take out, but more and more frequently I find myself here."

"Do you live around here?"

"On Fifty-sixth between Third and Lex. You?"

"No, I'm from upstate. I'm visiting my sister who lives here now." She told him that Jenna was her twin, that they were from Seneca Falls, New York, that they had no other siblings and that their parents had been dead for quite a few years.

"You're visiting, but your sister left you alone tonight?"

How could she explain without really explaining. "She works evenings. In this neighborhood."

"Ah," he said. "So you're on your own in the big city."

"Do I look like a hick?"

"No, of course not," he said with another chuckle. She noticed the deep laugh lines around his mouth. "I guess what I said didn't come out the way I intended. It's just that I've never seen you around here before."

The waiter arrived with her wine and she sipped. It was cool, crisp and delicious. "Thanks for the advice. This is really good."

"Would you care to order now?" the waiter asked.

"Not just yet," Steve said, turning to her. When she didn't object, he continued. "Give us a little while."

They made small talk for several minutes and Marcy found out that he was in sales, originally from Bavaria, then the mid-West. He had been divorced for only a few months and had two college-aged children, one going to the state university in Albany and one at Brown. She quickly calculated that that probably put him in his late thirties or early forties.

"Where in Bavaria?" Marcy asked in German.

His eyes lit up. "Where in Germany are you from?" he asked. "No, you said you were from upstate."

"Sadly, I've never traveled outside the United States."

He looked puzzled. "You speak German like a native."

"My sister and I both have an ear for languages. Other than English I speak five fluently and several more to a lesser degree." Was she bragging to impress this man? Maybe.

"I had such trouble learning English, even though I came here when I was fourteen."

"It's not anything I can take credit for," Marcy said. "My ability to pick up languages is a talent I guess my sister and I were both born with. Other than German, I speak French, Italian, Spanish and Portuguese. They're so similar that moving from one to another wasn't too hard. I think that English is one of the most difficult languages to learn and I admire you for doing it."

"I didn't have much choice. I was put in an English language school and it was sink or swim. There were times when I think my history teacher tied an anchor to my feet. Everyone else knew so much about American history just from living here. Not only did I have to pick up the language, but everything I'd missed in my first fourteen years."

Over a simple dinner of chicken and vegetables, accompanied by another glass of Chablis, they found that they shared an interest in politics, although they were of opposite beliefs, and spent considerable time discussing solutions to the latest Middle East crisis. Over slabs of chocolate cake they found another interest they shared, vintage TV shows. They did some of the dialogue from *The Dick Van Dyke Show* and *The Mary Tyler Moore Show* and laughed as they recounted their favorite episodes of *I Love Lucy*. "The chocolates on the conveyor belt," he said.

"The one where she locks herself in the freezer."

"The one where she tells Ricky she's pregnant. She couldn't say pregnant in those days so they had to say 'having a baby.' She looked tremendous for months before she told Ricky."

"I loved that one, too."

Finally, Steve ordered creme de menthe for each of them and, replete, Marcy realized that she hadn't enjoyed a dinner this much in quite a while.

"Marcy," Steve said, "I know you're visiting your sister for just a few days, but I'd love to show you around. I mean show you both around."

"Thanks, Steve," she said as the waiter placed the check on the table between them, "but let's just chalk this up to an enjoyable evening and leave it at that."

"I hate to give up on something that was so enjoyable. Would you give me your phone number so I can at least chat with you?"

"I'm not really comfortable with that." She looked at the amount of the check and pulled her wallet from her purse.

"I sense a 'yet' at the end of that sentence. I'd give you my card but I know you'd never call me, so let's leave it this way," he said, taking her hand loosely across the table. "I eat here almost every evening about this time. If your sister's working and you're interested in a tour of the city, or visiting a museum, stop in and you'll probably find me." The twinkle that usually lived in his deep brown eyes changed to become a very serious expression. "I'd really like that."

"Thanks for understanding and giving me the space I need." She grinned as she stood and counted out bills for her half of the check and left them on the small plastic plate. She looked around and realized that it was already dark. She'd been enjoying this man's company for almost three hours. "And you just might see me here sometime in the next week."

"I hope so," he said, remaining seated.

Marcy walked outside and hailed a taxi. She'd had a wonderful dinner and Steve was a charming and nonthreatening companion. Maybe she *would* meet him again. She gave the driver Jenna's address and let her mind drift as he wended his way across town.

All their lives, Marcy had been trying to separate herself from her twin. Their late mother had started the efforts. Always different clothes, different teachers, different friends. And Marcy had continued, using every activity she could think of to bring out their differences. Of course, in college they had both studied languages but that was only natural. It was in their genes. But they had traveled in different circles of friends and barely saw each other outside of class.

Marcy had always been the organized one, the cerebral one, while Jenna had been the friendly one. Since their return to Seneca Falls after graduation, Marcy had always tried to set a good example, handling the twins' finances, caring for the house. She'd bargained for and purchased every car either of them had ever owned.

Things had changed now. Jenna ran a business, kept books, schedules, client lists and profiles. Were they really so different? She had to admit to herself that the major difference was still in their sex life. Jenna had done everything with everyone. Marcy had done very little with only a few men with whom she'd had more lengthy relationships. She wasn't interested in kinky sex the way Jenna was. She wasn't. Not at all. But what about her fantasies? They were only dreams and would stay dreams. She'd write the book without any personal experiences. After all, she reasoned, she could write, and people who write novels about nineteenth-century England haven't been there. They just have good imaginations, and hers was as good as anyone's. Wasn't that all that mattered?

Late that evening, Steve stood beneath the shower thinking of Marcy. She was the first woman he'd been brave enough to talk to since his divorce, and the evening had been wonderful. She'd looked at him as if she cared what he thought and had listened when he spoke. She wasn't terribly attractive, but her personality and caring made up for everything. He felt drawn to her. As he soaped his chest, he thought about how he'd have liked the evening to end.

She'd have said, "I gather you enjoy fine wine. If you like brandy, my sister has a wonderful bottle of Armagnac that I think you might like. Would you like to come up to her place and sample a bit?"

"I'd love to," he'd say.

As he let his soapy hands slide over his arms, he lived the fantasy.

They were in a small apartment and she was pouring the fiery brandy into two snifters. "My sister works until the wee hours so we have quite a bit of time to get to know one another."

"That's wonderful." They settled on the sofa. "So tell me more about yourself."

They talked for several minutes. Then Marcy said, "This fireplace isn't real. It works with propane, but it's kind of pretty, would you like me to light it?"

"That sounds great."

She motioned toward a stereo in the corner of the room and to the rack of CDs beside it. "While I do that, why don't you pick out a CD from her collection? I'm sure you can figure out what goes where."

God, he thought, *I know what goes where but it has been so long.* Marcy's sister had a great collection of classical CDs so it took a few minutes for him to make a selection. "Is Vivaldi okay with you?"

"Wonderful."

By the time he had the CD playing, the volume low but audible, Marcy had the fire lit and was seated back on the sofa. "I love a fire," she said, sipping her brandy.

"Me, too," he said.

He finished his brandy while they talked, then set the glass on the small end table and started to rise. "Oh," Marcy said. "I hope you don't have to leave just yet."

"Well, I thought . . ."

As he settled back onto the sofa, she said, "Don't think." She put her glass on the floor, then leaned forward, eyes closed. He didn't have to think twice. He met her lips with his, the kiss long and soft. As he backed away, she opened her eyes and gazed at him. "You're thinking," she said.

"I'm wondering."

"About us?"

"Yes."

"Stop wondering." She put her hand gently on the back of his neck and pulled him toward her. Their lips met again, but this time the softness was replaced by heat. Her mouth opened beneath his and their tongues slid together. She was warm and pliant in his arms as he held her close against him.

Slowly, lips still pressed together, they leaned back until he was almost on top of her.

He was hot, hungry, and she met his heat with her own. She pulled his shirt from his pants and her hands slid beneath it to clutch at his back. He felt her hips arch against his and he thrust back against her.

She made little purring noises as the angle of their kiss changed over and over. He couldn't get enough of her and she seemed to feel the same. She unbuttoned his shirt and he pulled hers off over her head. Her skin was warm and so soft. He tangled his fingers in her hair and placed kisses along her jaw, down her neck and across her collarbone.

"Inside," she said, breathless, her voice hoarse and needy.

In the bedroom they quickly undressed each other and fell onto the cool sheets. She smelled of light perfume and woman and he couldn't get close enough to her. He filled his hands with her breasts, then leaned down and filled his mouth. Her nipple hardened between his lips as he licked and suckled, first one, then the other. He was in heaven. He felt the length of her body against his and then she parted her legs and thrust her hips upward, as if reaching for his penis.

He was hard and his erection slid into her wetness. Her legs twisted around his waist, dragging him more deeply inside. He pulled back, then thrust over and over until they were both screaming.

In the shower, Steve's soapy hands were on his cock, stroking until he came, spurts of semen landing on the tile floor to be washed away by the streaming water. He quickly turned off the faucets and dropped onto the edge of the tub to catch his breath.

Oh, Marcy. I haven't felt like this in a long while. It's wonderful.

Chapter
4

Early the following morning Marcy opened the Dunkin' Donuts bag she'd brought home the evening before and devoured several munchkins with a big glass of orange juice. Then she poured herself a cup of coffee, made some notes for the book, and quietly read a romance novel in the kitchen until Jenna awoke several hours later. Her sister had always been an early riser, but Marcy guessed that the late nights Jenna spent at the Club had changed her sister's sleeping schedule.

Dressed in an oversized sleep shirt with a fluffy bear emerging from his hibernation cave on the front, Jenna wandered into the kitchen just after eleven o'clock. "We're meeting Chloe at noon," she said, stretching and heading for the coffeepot, "but I need a cup of coffee first."

Since they had a few minutes until lunch, Marcy popped another jelly-filled munchkin into her mouth. "That sounds fine," she said, chewing. She extended the donut bag to her sister. "How was your evening?"

"Let's just say it was adventurous," Jenna said, hesitating, gazing at the sweets, then shaking her head. She took her Garfield coffee mug from the cabinet and filled it to the brim.

"Do you think I'm a prude?" Marcy blurted out.

Jenna stared. "Where did that come from?"

Marcy tucked one leg beneath her and grabbed a mango jelly bean from the bag she'd bought at a neighborhood market. "I don't know, but you seem to treat me as though I wouldn't understand sex the way you and Chloe do it. An adventurous evening. It's like you don't want to tell me stuff. After all, it's pretty simple. Put tab A into slot B. I've read a lot of stories about the more unusual stuff, too, so you won't shock me." She hesitated, the added, "I read the tales as research for the book."

Jenna's laugh was genuine. "Research. Right. Sweetie, let's just understand a few things. Plain vanilla sex can be wonderful. It completes a person, feels good, isn't fattening and, if you do it with someone who isn't married to someone else, neither illegal nor immoral. But what Chloe and I do usually isn't plain vanilla. Most of the time it's about as far from plain vanilla as cheese is from chalk."

"Good. That's the kind of stuff I need for the book. Firsthand experiences, not just stories off the Internet." Many of those stories, Marcy reasoned, were just wishful thinking on the part of the author. Real people didn't do that stuff except at Club Fantasy.

"Well, you'll get that from Chloe. She's about as outspoken as they come. It's not that I think you're a prude at all. It's just that I don't know how much *I* want to share. After all, you are my sister, and it feels a bit awkward to tell you about my sexual exploits."

With a chuckle, Marcy admitted, "I feel the same with you. Maybe I need to get my information from other folks. It feels weird talking to you about kinky sex."

Jenna's shoulders fell and she looked a bit more relaxed. Until this moment, Marcy hadn't realized how stressed her sister had seemed since she had arrived the previous afternoon. "That's really good. I was afraid you'd be hurt if I didn't 'tell all.' " She reached down and hugged Marcy's shoulders. "Let me shower first and then we'll be off." Jenna started toward the bathroom.

As Marcy's eyes dropped to her book, Jenna turned. "There's one thing you need to know about me and all this. I hadn't done any of the more kinky sex stuff before last year." She referred to her moving to the city and sharing space with Chloe. "This was all new to me then, too. Plain vanilla is nothing to be ashamed about."

Startled, Marcy said, "I'm not ashamed." Was she? Up till now all her stories had been straight sex. No bondage, no spanking and that's the way she was. Other folks probably enjoyed the off-center antics but she was content. She needed that kind of story for her book, however. "Okay, I'm not very experienced, but I don't need to have experienced stuff directly to write about it, after all. Chloe's stories and those I can get from other folks should be enough." She thought about her previous efforts to write sex stories for her book. They weren't very good. Did she need to experience the more unusual stuff to write about it? She hoped not. She had to admit, however, that the prospect of hearing about it titillated her. She couldn't wait to hear Chloe's stories.

Just before noon the two sisters walked the few blocks to the small restaurant called Eat At Joe's. On the white tile floor, the tables and chairs were also white, with cushions in hot primary colors, complimented by the geometric paintings in the same colors that covered the walls. The benches in each booth were done in a hot color as well.

Jenna had warned her sister that they might have to wait for a table, but they were surprised to find the restaurant practically empty. "I forgot that it's a holiday weekend and everyone's probably out of town," Jenna said as they spotted Chloe seated at a kelly green booth in the back and wended their way between small tables packed tightly together. "This place was much better before they tried to cram as many tables as the fire code allowed in here. It used to be comfortable but, sadly, it got trendy, the death knell of a restaurant for me."

Marcy understood what she meant. Despite being half empty, the place was noisy, with waitstaff zigging and zagging around chairs, tables and people, carrying trays high above the seated crowd. The sisters finally dropped, side by side, on the bench opposite Chloe.

Chloe Whitman, the woman who had lured Jenna into the business. Stop that, Marcy said to herself. Lured is a loaded word and it wasn't like that at all. The two women had needed to earn extra money to support the brownstone and pay the taxes, so, slowly but inexorably, they slid into the business of fulfilling fantasies for wealthy men. She'd weave the story more deeply for the book.

Dressed in a bright blue halter top with a sheer flowered blouse worn as a jacket, Chloe half stood and leaned across the table to kiss Marcy on the cheek. "It's great to see you again, Marcy." She looked her best friend's sister over, then said, "You look nice." Turning to Jenna, she said, "I'm glad I got a booth. I thought it would give us a bit more privacy." She looked at Marcy. "I'm so excited about your book." She almost squealed.

Chloe was positively glowing. Marcy realized that if she ever got down about the idea of writing, she could just call Chloe. Obvious enthusiasm radiated from her fabulous eyes like flashes of lightning. "You can even use my real name if you want," she said in a loud stage whisper.

"No real names, not even the real city," Marcy said, propping her elbows on the table. "I've given that part a lot of thought. I'm not going to risk embarrassing anyone, clients or employees. Or innocent bystanders for that matter."

Chloe looked a bit deflated. "Of course not. I hadn't thought about that. It was just so exciting to think of people reading about me and knowing my name."

"Sorry, love," Jenna said. "I completely agree with Marcy."

"You're right," she said, clearly disappointed. "Anyway, how was your trip down?"

They chatted for several minutes until the waiter arrived. Jenna and Chloe shared a Western omelet, while Marcy, after spending considerable time reading the extensive menu, decided on eggs Benedict. "And mimosas all around," Chloe said. "I wish I could spend the day showing you around town and swapping stories, but I've actually got a client this afternoon. We're driving to northern Westchester."

"How come so far?" Marcy asked. "Why not in the Club?"

"Originally his fantasy was to do it in the park. Right out in the open. When I balked at that—we could get arrested, I told him—he suggested that we cover ourselves with a blanket. Needless to say I wasn't too keen on that either, so he imposed on a friend with a big backyard and we're going to use that instead." She grinned. "I don't think I've ever done it in the sunlight before. Sounds delightfully kinky, actually."

"Yeah," Jenna said, "it does. I'm afraid I have to work tonight, too. Again I'll be leaving you to your own devices."

"No problem." She thought about Steve. She could drop into the restaurant and see whether he was there. It wouldn't really be a date. She'd considered telling Jenna about him over coffee earlier but she found that she wanted him to remain private, for a while anyway.

"Actually maybe you can help me change the motel room around for tonight, Marce," Jenna said. "If you don't mind."

"That would be terrific. I can see how you do things."

"After tonight we'll have two days to play together."

"Yeah," Chloe said. "Weeks are backwards for us. We work weekends, but are off on Monday and Tuesday. It makes for a strange life."

Strange. Right. "I've been wondering," Marcy said, "isn't it expensive, keeping the place closed for two days? Why do you do that?"

"Because we can," the two women answered simultaneously, then laughed. Jenna continued. "When we got so successful, we decided that if we didn't reduce our schedule, we'd work seven nights a week and collapse from exhaustion."

"But don't you let your other—"

"Employees?"

"Right. Employees use it?"

"Nope. It's closed up tight. We won't let anything go on without Rock around just in case, and he needs time off, too. So we don't allow anyone to book time Monday or Tuesday."

"Oh yeah, about Rock. Is he an employee or what?"

"Or what," the two women said, giggling.

Marcy suddenly felt left out. Chloe and Jenna obviously shared many inside jokes about people and situations she'd never be part of. "I'm sorry, Marcy," Jenna said. "That was so rude of us." She must have sensed Marcy's sudden discomfort. "I never want us not to be able to share stuff. Rock isn't an employee. He's our bouncer and referee, our bodyguard and doorman and we won't entertain anyone without him there. He uses the place, especially the basement, for his own pleasures and with his own clients. In exchange he lives in the ground-floor bedroom."

"You've got a basement? You didn't show me that part yesterday."

"I know, and I'm sorry," Jenna said. "I was just a bit reluctant to tell you about the really wild activities that go on down there. The basement is where some of the bondage games are played. It has evolved into quite a room."

"Oh," Marcy said, picturing Rock, stripped to a pair of leather pants, whipping a bound prisoner. She shivered.

"I gather Jenna showed you around yesterday," Chloe said, breaking an awkward silence.

Happy for the shift of topic, Marcy said, "It's quite a place. What do you do if you don't have the right room for someone's fantasy? You obviously can't cover all the possible scenarios."

"You'd be amazed at what we can create with props and costumes and stuff," Jenna said as the waiter put mimosas on the table and hurried away.

"Wow," Marcy said. "These aren't glasses, they're small fishbowls." She took a sip and sighed. "What a way to begin a morning."

"Setting up for a new fantasy isn't as easy as you might think," Chloe said, sipping the combination of champagne and orange juice.

"Tell me about it," Marcy said, taking another swallow. God, she could really get drunk on drinks that tasted as good as this. And she never got drunk. Ever. "This is the stuff I need to know. Go through a client from the beginning."

"Okay," Jenna said. "Let's say that someone new calls. First of all, the only way we will even talk to him is if he's vetted."

At that moment the waiter returned and put plates in front of the women. When the waiter left, Marcy said, "You were talking about men getting vetted. What the heck does that mean?"

"It means that someone we trust knows him—let's assume it's a man since I would say about seventy-five percent of our clients are men—and he's been recommended. We don't take calls from anyone we don't know. That's a firm rule."

"Sounds sensible," Marcy said. "I guess there's always a danger it's a cop."

"A cop or a nut or a snoop," Chloe said. "We don't want any of those."

"It took me quite a while to make Chloe understand the risks we'd run if we weren't careful," Jenna said. "That's all behind us now. Amazingly enough, we've never had a problem."

"Yeah," Chloe continued, "partly thanks to Rock. He's quite an intimidating presence."

"A lover and a fighter," Jenna said, "and a damn nice guy." She turned to Marcy. "You really need to get to know him.

He's someone really special and will be able to add quite a different slant on things."

She thought about the basement and her fantasy in the doctor's office, then said, quickly, "Okay, so the guy's vetted. Then what?"

"That's the trickiest part," Chloe said. "Either Jen or I meet with him to find out his wildest dreams. It often takes an hour or more to get the guy to finally tell us what he wants."

"Either that," Jenna said with a grin, "or you can't shut him up. I've had lots of guys who seem to only want to talk about exactly, precisely, what they want. That can be even more difficult."

"Why?" Marcy asked, mopping egg yolk from her plate with the English muffin from beneath her Canadian bacon. "I would think that would make it easier."

"When a guy has a fantasy that's lived in his mind for a very long time, it's difficult to get our version perfectly in tune with the image he's built. He knows exactly what the characters say and do, so he's bound to be disappointed with our reality."

Chloe said, "Sometimes I have a guy write an actual script of who says what and does what. I warn him, however, that he also has to roll with the punches. We don't want it to be a let down for him."

"And the woman or man he wants won't look like the one he's dreamed of. We try to match body type but that's as far as we can go. Of course, makeup and the occasional wig help, too."

"What if he is disappointed?"

"If he stops things before anything happens, no sex, then he can have his money back, minus expenses of course."

"Expenses?" She realized that she was sounding like an idiot, but this was all so strange.

"We rent costumes if necessary," Jenna explained, "hire extra people for guys who want threesomes or performances.

We might have to rent furniture or accessories, too, although that's getting less and less necessary as we acquire stuff."

"Chloe's a flea market and tag sale junky. It's a way she's found to harness her desire to shop, although now she has the money to do as she pleases. She's constantly picking up valuable goodies for the Club at garage sale prices."

"Of course," Chloe continued, "if the guy's actually had sex then the money's ours."

"Okay, I'm really curious. How much do you charge?"

Chloe had finished her half of the omelet and pushed her plate away. "We charge a client anywhere from one to two thousand dollars for a fantasy lasting up to two hours. Plus expenses, of course. We have a few employees and they get fifty percent of the proceeds and sometimes contractors use the facilities for their own clients and they get seventy percent. Of course, when we do it ourselves, it's all ours."

"Sometimes Club Fantasy has as many as a dozen clients a night."

"Holy . . ." Marcy did a quick calculation and her mind boggled. No wonder they can afford to keep the place closed two nights a week. The numbers were astronomical. So much for the proceeds of the book getting Jenna out of the business. If she wanted out, she probably had enough money in the bank to do it herself. Marcy sighed. She still wanted to write the book, of course. For the fun of it, to learn about the business, and now to learn about herself and her sister.

The waiter cleared the dishes, and when he dropped the check on the table Jenna grabbed it. "Business expense," she said, putting down an American Express Gold Card. "We have some of the most unusual business expenses. I can't wait to be audited."

"That would be really embarrassing, wouldn't it?" Marcy asked. "Isn't what you do illegal? How would you explain it all?"

"We're in the entertainment business," Chloe said with a giggle. "We create scenes for customers. There's no proof that anything more goes on unless someone gets inside and that won't happen."

"I guess," Marcy said. "So the guy outlines his fantasy. Then what?"

"If it's something easy and we already have a room set up, we're in business. Sometimes the guy doesn't mind if the person he met with is in the cast, sometimes he's got a different type of woman, or man, in mind."

Jenna continued. "We warn him that he's not going to get the woman of his dreams and they have to accept that or not do it. Once I explain it specifically so the guy won't be let down, some decide to go for a different type than the one they've been thinking of. Others are willing to settle for 'close enough.' A few have such specific requests that we can't oblige. So be it. I'd rather have someone go away disappointed after the initial meeting than be annoyed at our failure to meet his needs."

"You talk about the rooms already set up. I've seen most, the Western room, the harem, the doctors office," she almost stumbled over that one, "the motel room, but it's a limited supply. What other fantasies can you do? I'm looking for ideas for the book."

"I think I told you about burglar and victim, that's a really popular one. It's control or lack thereof, combined with the fear of getting caught doing something naughty. Chloe? What else have we done?"

"Several times we've turned one of the 'motel rooms' into a child's room for a guy who wants to ravish a young girl."

For the first time in quite a while Marcy was shocked. "You don't use girls, do you?" she said, her eyes widening.

"Of course not," Chloe said, patting her hand. Then she lowered her eyes and looked at Marcy through her lashes, dropped her shoulders and stuck her index finger in her mouth. "We don't have to," she said, her voice now several tones higher, her body stooped to de-emphasize her breasts. "With plain cotton underwear and a school uniform, I've fooled a lot of guys. Actually it doesn't fool them, since we make it quite clear to every man that his partner for the evening will be of age, but it's amazing what makeup and such can achieve. Guys quickly forget that I'm over thirty."

"That's amazing."

Chloe giggled. "I do it so well that I've got a few regulars who like to take me to the zoo or out for ice cream. For a fee of course. It's a funny world, all right."

Jenna signed the credit card receipt and the three women walked out onto the street. They wandered over to Riverside Park, found a bench and sat under the hot, hazy summer sky. "What other kinds of fantasies do you do?" Marcy asked, intrigued.

"We do quite a bit of period stuff," Jenna said. "Lots of men like the Victorian 'master-of-the-house' scenario, and many women love to reenact scenes from a favorite romance novel. We do costumes, props, all the items to help everyone get into the right mood."

"I remember one guy. I played an old-fashioned English maid, complete with uniform. I even tried a bit of an accent, but it wasn't really necessary." She smiled. "Then there was the guy who wanted me in a wedding dress."

"Are most of the men satisfied with Club Fantasy's services?"

"Amazingly, yes," Jenna said. "We've only had about a dozen who've asked for a refund. Oh, and one or two guys have rejected the charge on their credit card and we don't fight it. But that guy's *persona non grata* from then on and most men don't want to risk that. It also gets back to the person who referred him, not a good thing either."

"You get a lot of repeat business?"

"You bet," Chloe said, turning her face up to the mid-

summer sun. "I would say more than half of our clients are
regulars. Right?"

Marcy knew that Jenna kept the books. "Probably closer to
seventy percent. Our clients seem satisfied and they come
back month after month, sometimes for the same fantasy,
sometimes for a different one."

"Why would a man want the same fantasy over and over?
Isn't there a danger that it will be diluted the second time?"

"I used to think that, too," Jenna said, wiping the gathering
perspiration from her forehead. "But I guess it's not a problem
for them. Sometimes men actually want to hone the actuality
so it gets closer and closer to their dreams. 'Can you get a
blonde?' Or 'I'd like more mirrors.' We try to accommodate.
Actually that's some of what I have to do this afternoon."

"Chloe, I was interested in your guy who wants to do it outside."

"He's a sweetie. We've been together several times doing it
in different setups. For this one, he want's the illusion of possibly being discovered or watched. I'll play it up. You know,
'Do you think someone might be behind those bushes.' He'll
love that."

Jenna asked, "Have you decided how much you want to do
this week? Would you like to chat with some of the women
who work with us?"

"I've gotten a lot just from this chat," Marcy said, "but if
there's someone specific. Maybe a man, too, for a different
slant. You employ men, too, right? Besides Rock, I mean."

"Several." She looked at Chloe. "Maybe Zack would be
able to give you some background and stories. We met him
through Erika, the woman who used to run Courtesans, Inc."

"What's Courtesans, Inc.?"

"Courtesans, Inc. was an escort service right here in the
neighborhood that catered to a very wealthy clientele. She
was a great help when we were getting started and she urged
many of her ladies to use our rooms. We took a percentage and

that cash saw us through some of the lean times at the beginning. A number of those people still use our facilities from time to time."

What had happened to Erika and to Courtesans, Inc.? Marcy's heartbeat suddenly quickened as the risk of running a brothel in the middle of Manhattan struck her anew. Police, weirdos, drunks, so many dangers. Maybe they don't want to talk about it. "I gather she's not in the business any more," Marcy said gently. "Did she get arrested or something?"

Chloe and Jenna laughed. "Not at all," Chloe said. "She got married and settled down way out on Long Island."

"Right," Marcy said, feeling her heartbeat return to normal. "You've mentioned her a few times."

"The three of us used to get together from time to time, but those lunches are getting fewer and farther between." Jenna shook her head. "I never thought she'd be happy anywhere but Manhattan, but she's blissful and doesn't get into town much any more."

Chloe giggled. "Would you believe? She's even growing vegetables."

"Next time we get together," Jenna said, "if you're in town, you have to meet her. I guess she's sort of my idol."

Marcy could see why. Maybe Jenna and Glen could eventually have a normal life like this Erika had.

They talked for another hour, then Marcy and Jenna left Chloe to get ready for her client, and walked to the brownstone through the heavy, humid New York July air. By the time they arrived, part of Marcy longed for the cool and quiet of upstate New York. Jenna rang the doorbell. "Just in case Rock is here." He wasn't, so Jenna used her key.

"What do you need to do this afternoon?" Marcy asked.

"I've got a guy coming tonight who loves mirrors, so I'll adapt one of the motel rooms to his taste." They climbed to the third floor and Jenna dropped her pocketbook on the plain, hard-mattressed bed. As Marcy looked around, she began to picture her sister in here, having sex with some anonymous man. She closed her eyes, then opened them again.

"I see that look and I can still read your mind. Doing what I do may be illegal but it's not immoral."

"I know you've said that a number of times, and part of me understands what you're saying. But another part still has a hard time with it. After all, the bible calls it fornication and adultery."

"The church, and society in general, still has a vested interest in keeping married folks monogamous. It's so much simpler that way. No worries about whose kid is whose." She sat on the edge of the bed. "Think about it. If I want to have sex with some guy, who's hurt?"

Marcy considered seriously, then said, "Society."

"Nonsense. How can society be hurt if two people do something that feels good, even if money changes hands?"

"Marriages are hurt."

Jenna stood and started to fuss with the room. "I'll admit that sometimes that's true. But is it any less true when a guy goes to a bar and picks up a woman? Dinner, a movie and a roll in the hay. Is that so different? I know the husband or wife sits home and doesn't get theirs and that's a shame but that's not my problem, any more than it would be if he picked me up in a bar and we went up to my place.

"Often people come here to do things they don't think their wife or husband would be interested in. Sometimes that's hogwash. They just don't have the nerve to ask. I encourage them to take their ideas home, but most of the time they're too embarrassed to, and we make money because of it."

"You keep talking about women using your services, too. Are there a lot of those?"

"Some. It's less common than men, but we have a flourishing business with women who want more out of sex than they're getting."

"Does Rock take care of that part of the business?"

"He has quite a few women clients, and we have several more men who use our facilities for their ladies." Jenna thought a moment. "I really want to introduce you to Zack. You'd like him. He's great to look at, charming and interested in everything."

Marcy was fascinated by the idea of women paying for sex. "I guess I always thought women were different. They don't need sex the same way men do."

"Who says? Women are entitled to great sex the same way men are, and Zack and Rock and Vic and several more guys can attest to that. We also have women who want cultured men to escort them to parties, concerts and such, men who they can show off.

"Women often outlive their husbands, or are left behind when hubby dearest goes off with some trophy wife. They're interested, and sexually active. We still live in a couples culture, so for many of the things they want to do, sex aside for a moment, they need a partner. We supply them, with or without the bedroom afterward."

"Quite a concept for a poor country girl to understand."

"Poor country girl my foot."

While they'd been talking, Jenna had replaced the slightly industrial-looking bedspread with a brightly flowered one and added lots of coordinated throw pillows to the bed. Now she was removing the simple white cotton curtains from their rod and hanging brightly colored ones that matched the bedspread. "Come give me a hand," she said, walking across the hall. "There's a great standing mirror in here that I could use help with."

The women took the sides of the pier glass and carried it into the "motel room." "The room looks so much softer somehow," Marcy said. "Not so industrial."

"This is such a great room, so adaptable." She pulled a large vase filled with straw flowers from the shelf in the closet and placed it on the dresser. Then she adjusted the tilt of the mirror so it pointed at the bed. "Let's get a few plants from across the hall and then we're almost done."

As they brought the plants back and put one on a bed table and two more on the dresser, Jenna said, "I'd love to mirror the ceiling of this room, but when it's a motel room that would ruin the mood."

Marcy considered. "I'll bet you could rig up a sort of horizontal window shade that you could pull over the mirror so it would look like just a cloth-covered ceiling when you don't want the mirror to show."

Jenna stared at the ceiling and grinned. "You know, that's a great idea." She walked around the bed and wrapped her arms around her sister. "Thanks, Marce. That's wonderful. I knew I brought you here for a reason."

As Marcy hugged her sister, she felt a bit of the closeness that had been missing for the last few months.

Chapter
5

They spent another half hour puttering around the brownstone, then Marcy and Jenna took a walk around the city, enjoying being together, talking about nothing of any importance. Reveling in a level of comfort with each other they hadn't felt in quite a while, the two women stopped at a small Italian restaurant and shared supper as they had so many times before in Seneca Falls.

Afterward, they hailed a taxi and, after dropping Jenna back at the brownstone, Marcy went back to the West Side. She had heard a lot of stories from Chloe and her mind was filled with images of what might go on inside her Eros Hotel. She booted up her laptop and began to type.

ANONYMOUS

"I want to make love to an anonymous stranger; someone I've never seen before and will never see again," Monica said to the interviewer for the Eros Hotel. "I want to be able to try things." She found she was embarrassed to say what things.

What things? Oral sex, for example. She'd read about it in sex manuals, she'd seen it in movies, but she'd never actually done it. Well, she'd never really done much, and she wanted to. At almost thirty she wanted to know. How could she expect some guy to be interested in her if she didn't know a thing about sex? Never happen.

She'd meet some guy at work or at the laundry mart and they'd get to talking. Maybe they'd have a dinner or two and eventually he'd say something like, "How about coming back to my place for a cup of coffee?" She'd go, then, as they entered "his place," he'd make the grab and she'd chicken out.

Not that she was a virgin, of course. She'd done the deed a few times; one-night stands that never went any further. She was totally uneducated and hated herself for it. So now here she was at the Eros Hotel, trying to form the words to tell the woman what she wanted.

"It's okay," the woman said. "I do understand. I can offer you several different scenarios." She discussed three, then came the right one. "You could be in a hotel room, without any lights on and a guy comes in. He's a bit drunk and ready for anything. He's also willing to show you how he likes things done."

"Dark? He'd have no idea who I was?" It sounded a bit silly, but she wanted this badly.

"Exactly. You'd be totally anonymous. Would that feel right?"

Heartbeat increasing, hands shaking, she said, "That would be perfect." She gave the woman a few bills and was told to return the following evening.

Now she was here. The room was dark and she was lying beneath a sheet, naked. And terrified. She wanted to know, but did she want to learn? Yes, she told herself over and over.

The door opened and a shaft of light stabbed the darkness, only to disappear when the door closed again. She heard the rustle of clothing, then someone slipped beneath the sheets beside her. "Monica," a very masculine voice whispered, "I'm glad you're here waiting for me."

It might have been awkward, but instead his breath was hot on her cheek and she relaxed. "I'm glad, too," she said.

His hand found her thigh and his fingers brushed her skin, causing a shiver to echo up and down her spine. For several minutes he lay still, softly caressing the skin of her arms, shoulders and legs. As his arm moved over her, she realized that he wasn't wearing a shirt. Then, his lips almost against her ear, he purred, "Your skin is soft, like satin." His breath smelled slightly of peppermint.

She wanted to say his skin was soft, too, but she'd been lying so still she didn't know whether it was true. She reached out and stroked his bare arm and shoulder. His skin was covered with crisp hair. "You feel good," she said hesitantly. She wanted to explore more so she allowed her palms to roam over his body, naked, at least from the waist up. She'd never really felt a man before. Not slowly and freely.

She ran her hand over his chest. He must have been quite well built because his muscles were hard and seemed well developed. At first her hands had been driven by curiosity, now it just felt good to touch him. "You feel really good," she said, meaning it.

His hand found her breast and played idly with her nipple while she explored his body. Not his crotch, of course. That was still too scary and he was probably wearing briefs or something. His stroking slowly aroused her, but her hands continued to glide over his skin. She wanted to feel his penis, know whether he was getting excited, but she didn't know how. She knew there was a right way and a wrong way to touch a man, and she didn't know the secret.

"Like this," he whispered, his breath hot in her ear. He took her hand and guided it to his cock. No briefs. Nothing.

He was very hard but the skin over his erection was very soft. She sensed he was holding himself tightly in check as she fondled him. She rubbed the head of his erection, feeling a

little sticky fluid, then slid her hand down and found his testicles. Cupping him she heard him hiss. Was he getting really
excited? From what she was doing? Wow!

He flipped back the sheet and lay stretched out on his back.
"I would love it if you would kiss me there," he said gently.

Panic! She didn't know exactly where or how. She'd seen
movies, but she knew she couldn't do that deep throat thing.
She knew she'd throw up if she took a man's cock into her
mouth. He took her hand and guided it to the shaft, showing
her with one finger where to kiss. "Just one kiss. Right there,
lightly. It would feel so good."

She bent over and touched her lips to his skin. She had
been worried about the smell of a man's genitals, but he
smelled slightly spicy. And the heat of him. He almost sizzled.
As she kissed him, she heard his sharp intake of breath. He
quite obviously liked it, so she did it again. Her hand was still
on his testicles, so she squeezed very gently. His moan told her
she was doing something right.

She wanted to do more, so she kissed the head of his cock.
Merely kissed him. Slow, sweet kisses. He moaned and grasped
her wrist tightly as if to hang on. He groaned, and as he did his
excitement gave her courage. She extended her tongue and
flicked it over the tip, tasting the slightly salty fluid. As she ran
her tongue over him, his hips jerked slightly. This was great.
She was aroused, but well under control. He was telling her
with his body that he was flying.

"Would you take just the tip in your mouth?" he asked, his
voice hoarse and raspy. "I promise I won't come." When she
hesitated, he said, "Just the tip. Please? It would feel so good."

Would she! He didn't want deep throat, just a little of her
mouth. He'd promised that he wouldn't fill her mouth with
semen as the guys always did in the stories she'd read.
Enjoying his seeming agony of pleasure, she played with him
in her mouth. Then he held her hair and pulled back. Had she
done something wrong?

"I promised I wouldn't come in your mouth," he said, trembling, "but you're making that almost impossible. Would you like me to make love to you?" Again she hesitated. "I'd like it if you'd do it for me with your hand instead. I'll take care of your needs later, but I'd love it if you'd make me come while I feel your fingers on me."

Shit. Do him with her hand? She'd no idea what to do. He must have known about her, probably from the interviewer, so he took her hand and wrapped her fingers around his shaft. With his hand over hers he showed her how to stroke from base to tip, then from tip to base. "Touch here too," he groaned, taking her other hand and putting it back on his sac. She used her hands together, faster and faster until he jerked his hips and cried out.

She could feel his orgasm beneath her fingers, the spasms and twitches. She actually felt it. She'd done it for him, given him all this pleasure. She heard him get tissues and felt him clean himself up. Then she rested her head on his chest and listened to the pounding of his heart and the harsh sound of his rapid breathing.

When he calmed he pulled her close and she lay beside him, enjoying the closeness. As he started to play with her breasts, she gently pushed his hands away. "I don't want anything more. This was better than I ever dreamed."

"I understand," he said, cuddling her.

Eventually he stood and, from the rustle, she knew he was putting his clothing back on. "That was really wonderful," he said. "You knew how to please me, and what you didn't know, you learned really quickly."

What could she say? She hadn't known much, but he had taught her, as much by his reactions as with his words and gestures.

"Good night," he said, opening the door. "If you come back, ask for Barry. I'd love to be with you again."

As the door closed behind him and the room went dark, she

considered coming back. He'd asked her to request him next time. He must have enjoyed it. She laughed at herself. Of course he'd enjoyed it, and he wanted to do it again. That was his business. But he'd also gotten off. That much was obvious.

She could afford it, and she might just come back. She did have a few more things to learn, and she was sure that Barry could teach her.

Marcy reread her story. Was this another autobiographical story about her own problems? She decided not to dwell on that aspect of her writing.

She concentrated on the fact that the story pleased her, and the knowledge that she was incredibly turned on. Her panties were soaked and her lower lips were itchy. She hadn't masturbated often in the past, thinking sex wasn't necessary for her. She had always believed she didn't have a lot of sex drive but now she wasn't so sure. Maybe if she had an outlet . . . ?

She wandered into Jenna's bedroom and stretched out on the bed. She remembered her words to her sister. *I guess I always thought women were different. They don't need sex the same way men do.* What she felt now was need. She slipped her hand beneath the waistband of her sweatpants and panties, and touched her sopping vagina.

She felt her breathing quicken as she raised her knees and rubbed her now-prominent clitoris. She found that by stroking the left side her arousal level increased, and she rubbed herself toward climax. She was so aroused that she came almost immediately, then pulled her hand back. Need. For a woman. When she'd masturbated before it had always been like an itch she wanted to scratch, not something that was driving her, like this evening. The more she delved into Jenna's life, the less she understood her own.

The following morning was Monday, a day of leisure for the people of Club Fantasy. Marcy sat in the kitchen reading and munching on an apple and spice donut when, before nine, she heard the phone ring twice, then stop. Five minutes later Jenna stumbled in and filled her Garfield mug from the pot of coffee Marcy had made half an hour before. "Something wrong, Sis?" Marcy asked, seeing her sister's troubled face.

"I've got a problem and I've been trying to decide what to do. Rock's dad had a heart attack last night and he's leaving this morning to go back home to be with his mom. I've known him since last Thanksgiving and he's just always there. It's strange to think of him having a family. He never talks about them. Despite what he does, he's really a very private person."

"I'm sorry," Marcy said. She had only seen him briefly twice before, but it was obvious that her sister was really bothered. "That's really tough."

"I'm not concerned only for him. It's a bit selfish, but it's a real problem for Chloe and me, too. Rock's presence in the house is what makes us all feel protected. Without him there I don't think we can open Wednesday, and we've got several bookings."

"Can't you get someone else? Hire a bodyguard type for however long you need?"

Jenna chuckled. "Can't you just see the want ad. Wanted: Big, well-built guy to be the bouncer for a brothel. Salary negotiable. Fringe benefits not included."

Marcy laughed. "Yeah, I see your point. Don't you have anyone who works with you who might do?"

"Zack maybe. Technically he used to work for Erika, but now, since she's retired, he's freelance, and very busy. I don't know whether he would be willing to take time off. I mean he'd have to give up all his Wednesday through Sunday evening appointments, for as long as Rock's gone." She took a swallow of her coffee. "It might not be too long, I guess. Or maybe just until I can think of another solution."

"So ask him. The worst he'll say is no. What does Chloe think?"

Jenna sighed. "She's sleeping and she's turned her phone off, as usual." Marcy heard a trace of bitterness. "Sorry. That sounded nasty." Jenna took several swallows of her coffee. "It's just that Chloe has essentially turned everything over to me. She works with clients, of course, and does lots of interviews about the desired fantasies. But I field all the phone calls and do the initial reference checking. I also do all the bookkeeping, except what I pay an exorbitant amount to a payroll company to do. I keep track of clients, employees and the folks who use the rooms and pay us a percentage. I reconcile the credit card receipts and charges. I do pretty much everything, and I must admit that it's beginning to get really old. Even when I'm in Seneca Falls, I spend part of every afternoon making calls and telnetted to my computer here."

"Sounds like a lot of paperwork. It never occurred to me that you paid payroll taxes and had health insurance. It's like a real business."

"Yeah," Jenna said, refilling her mug and dropping again into a kitchen chair, "and since Chloe's not into any of that stuff, I get to be COE. That's chief officer in charge of everything. I love the business, but this paperwork is killing me." She sipped. "Sorry to dump all this on you when there's really nothing you can do. I'm just venting."

To change the subject and ease the strain she saw in her sister's eyes, Marcy said, "I've been wondering. You don't seem to take phone calls a lot, but people must call for appointments and stuff. How does that work?"

"We have a private phone number that hooks to an answering machine. The word is around that you can only get a call back, nothing direct. I check that answering machine every hour or so. That's a real drag, too."

"Sounds like it. Well, let's tackle what has to be tackled, and that's the Rock problem. When can you call Zack?"

Jenna glanced at the wall clock. "I wouldn't dare call him before eleven."

"Okay, then. Why don't you tell me about the mundane business side of running Club Fantasy? I need that for the book, too."

For over an hour, Jenna showed Marcy some of the record keeping she did. She showed her the desktop computer in the portable workstation Marcy had noticed in the corner of the living room. Booting it up and entering several passwords, Jenna showed her the files she kept on each of Club Fantasy's clients, complete with credit card information, details of their fantasy wishes, what they'd played out and when, which women or men they'd been with, and any notes on what to change next time. She had records indicating who'd recommended them and who, if anyone, they'd recommended. She also had meticulously kept files on both employees and consultants with personal information, work history, dates and pay rates.

Jenna. Keeping records. It was all Marcy could do not to scoff. "God, Jen, I'd never have thought you could come up with all this."

"Actually, I didn't. This system is Erika's from her Courtesan, Inc. days. I just maintain our records in it."

"It looks like a lot of work."

"Believe me, it is. I spend hours in front of this damn machine."

"Maybe I can take some of it off your hands," she said. She'd always been the organized twin with a carefully structured day runner and carefully maintained information on everything that might possibly come up. This was right up her alley.

"Don't think I haven't thought of that," Jenna said. "It would be just as difficult, however, to send you the information as it would be for me to enter it here." She sighed. "It isn't as bad as I make it out to be. Just a mild pain in the ass. I'd gladly pay someone to do it, but this stuff is so highly confidential that there's no one I would trust."

"Yeah. I can imagine."

"So I do it, like a good girl." She clicked to turn the machine off, stood up and pushed the chair beneath the small desk. "But not right now." She glanced at her watch. "It's close enough to eleven that I think I'll call Zack. You up for lunch with the two of us? I'd love for you to meet him."

"No. You two need to talk business. I'd just be in the way."

"But . . ."

"Stop," Marcy said, holding her hand up, palm up. "My lower lip's not stuck out."

"Really, Marce. The business stuff will only take a few minutes. You'll really like him."

Marcy raised an eyebrow. "You fixing me up with a date?"

Laughing, Jenna said, "Not a chance. I stopped doing that when I set you up with that guy in our senior year in high school. What was his name?"

"You mean Ty?"

"Ty. That was it. He was so adorable. How was I to know he would ask you for a threesome with me?"

Tyrone Lynch, the center on the basketball team and one of the most sought after boys in school. Marcy had thought he really wanted to go out with her and was devastated when he intimated that he'd really only wanted a fling with the unavailable Jenna. Marcy winced, remembering the hurt, and said, "God, that was not one of my better moments."

"Right. You belted him. I wish I'd been there. I'd have nailed his other side. Or should I say his other face."

Marcy could laugh with Jenna about it now, but at the time it had been a deep wound. Had she always felt like she came out second best in their innocent competition for dates? More and more she was realizing how complex her feelings about her twin were.

Jenna grabbed the phone off her desk and dialed a number from memory. "I didn't wake you, did I, Zack? Good. I'm fine. Listen I need to talk with you about something serious. Can we meet for lunch somewhere? Okay, breakfast then. And I want you to meet my sister, too. Great. Noon? See you then."

An hour later Jenna and Marcy sat across from each other in a small luncheonette in Soho, sipping more coffee. Marcy saw her sister's face light up and turned toward the door. Crossing the small room toward them was the hunkiest guy Marcy had ever seen outside a movie theater. He was about six foot two, with hair that any woman would envy. Sable brown and worn slightly longer than shoulder length, it curled at the ends and gave Marcy the urge to run her fingers through it. His eyes were deep blue-gray, but with a warmth that kept them from looking predatory. His arms and chest were well developed, muscular without being muscle bound, and were shown off in a short-sleeved, red tee shirt and hip-hugging jeans. It was all Marcy could do not to salivate. She reflexively smoothed the sides of her hair, wishing for once that she'd put on a bit of makeup.

But it was the eyes that really got to her. She'd read the term Bedroom Eyes and now she'd seen a man who epitomized the idea. Languid. Deep. Sensual. Sexy. His eyes made her think about lying in a huge bed with red, satin sheets, all warm and satisfied after making love. She knew at a glance that this man was an asset to Club Fantasy and dangerous for her.

"Hi, Jen," Zack said, leaning over and bussing her sister's cheek, then turning to her. "And you must be the famous Marcy." He leaned over and kissed her cheek, too, and she had the desire to cup her hand over the spot. *Stop it!* she told herself. *You're drooling like a teenager.* He's just a guy. She paused. No, he's not just any guy, he's a male prostitute. And he probably has all the clients he can handle. Handle. *I even think in double entendres*, she mused. She brought herself back to reality as Zack pulled out a chair and sat down between her and her sister.

"Marcy, this is Zack McGee."

"Nice to meet you." She caught the quickly suppressed look that said, "you don't look like your sister."

The waiter arrived almost immediately with a cup of steaming coffee that he placed in front of Zack. "The usual?"

"Yeah, Tommy. Ladies?" Zack said to them.

"I'll have a BLT on white toast," Jenna said, "and a club soda with a piece of lime."

Still unable to clear her mind, Marcy said, "I'll have the same."

"Marcy," Zack said after taking a large swallow of coffee, "it's nice to finally meet you. Jenna talks about you a lot."

God, not only gorgeous but charming. He probably needs a stick to beat off the women. "She's told me quite a bit about you, too."

"Don't believe it all, love." His smile was wide and seemed genuine, but it was his eyes that captured her attention. He had the ability to look at you while you spoke as though your answers to even the most benign inquiries were the most important words he'd heard all day.

"Enough of the charm, Zack," Jenna said, "and stop flirting with my sister."

"I'm not flirting," Zack said, winking, then turning to Jenna. "What's up?"

"Rock's dad had a heart attack last evening and he's in intensive care. He's taking off this morning to be with his mom."

Zack's face sobered immediately. "God, I'm really sorry. I met his folks once, several years ago. They're nice people." He paused. "So that's what the message was on my answering machine. All he said was that he'd be away for a few days and didn't give a reason." He huffed out a breath. "Shit." He reflexively reached for his cell phone, then stopped his hand. "He's probably in the air already."

"Where do his folks live?" Marcy asked.

"He comes from a small town in the middle of California,"

Zack answered. "Wine country. Moved here several years ago."

Jenna frowned. "California? I never really knew much about his background. He just moved in and we became family."

"Yeah, he's like that. He doesn't talk about himself much, but it's not that he's keeping secrets. He just compartmentalizes his life that way."

With a nod, Jenna said, "With him gone, I've got a problem with the Club. I can't entertain without someone in the building."

"If you're asking me for help, I'll do whatever you need."

Without a moment's hesitation, Marcy thought. Nice guy.

"I need a body like yours in residence when the Club is open."

"Sure, happy to help," Zack said, patting Jenna's hand. "No problem."

"It would mean Wednesday through Sunday nights, full-time."

"I realize that. No sweat."

"Don't you have other commitments?"

"I'll change anything I have to, and cancel the rest. I'm yours, Jenna."

Jenna looked incredibly relieved. "That's a tremendous load off my mind, Zack. You're a treasure."

Zack's face lit with a charming grin. "I know. And you'll owe me big time."

"No doubt. You'll be compensated, of course."

"We can work all that out," Zack said.

Marcy watched the two people interact. Zack oozed charisma from every pore. Was that something that he cultivated or did some people just "have it"? Whatever *it* was, she wished she had just a little bit. She watched her sister. Jenna had some of that natural ability to talk to people, too. *Why her and not me?*

Their meal arrived and Marcy buried herself behind her sandwich, wishing she'd ordered fries with it. Zack and Jenna talked for several more minutes, then Jenna stood, dropping her crumpled napkin on her plate. "Listen, guys, I've got some errands to run. Can I leave you together for a while?"

Marcy stood as well. "I'll just go back to the apartment and do a few things."

"Please stay," Zack said, digging his fork into a sausage. "I really wish you'd stick around. You've hardly gotten a word in edgewise, and I gather you want help with stories for your book. I'd love to hear about it and give you my invaluable expertise." He winked.

If he wraps his lips around that sausage, I think I'll faint. Stop it! Stop it! Getting to know him might just stomp on this feeling. Feeling? Lust. That was what she was feeling. Stupid! He's as phony as a three dollar bill. It's an act. Okay, he's really gorgeous. She glanced at the people at nearby tables. Ladies lunching, but many unable to keep their eyes off of him. Marcy was a firm believer in "beauty is as beauty does," however. *On closer inspection,* she told herself, *he's going to turn out to be an arrogant jerk and it won't take long for that to surface and relieve me of some of this worship I'm feeling.* She settled back into her chair. "I could really use some help with the man's point of view on all this."

"Great. Then I won't feel like I'm deserting you." Jenna headed for the door. "Later, Marce."

"See you later, Sis."

Chapter

6

"What made you decide to write a book?" Zack asked. Marcy considered how much to tell him, then settled for the stock answer. "I've done a bit of research on the book market and I think a well-written, contemporary novel with lots of sex could sell. I've done some writing professionally, and with everyone's help I think I can do it."

"Okay, what can I do to help?" Zack said.

"I want some stories about the Club from a guy's perspective. You entertain women right?"

He did it. He pushed the end of the sausage into his mouth and took a bite with strong, white teeth. *God*, Marcy thought, *I certainly hope he's a jerk. Otherwise I won't be able to think straight.* "What I do isn't too different from what Jenna and Chloe do. There are just as many lonely women who want company as there are men. I spend time with them, make them feel desirable and make love with them if that's what they want."

"You mean that you don't always have sex with a client?"

"Not always. Some women just want someone to take them to the theater or some business function. I guess I'm the male equivalent of a trophy date. If that's all they want, that's fine. I've been places I might not otherwise get into. I've been to several political dinners." He rolled his eyes. "Dull, dull,

dull." His grin was irresistible. "I've seen plays that should have closed the evening before I went, and concerts of ultra modern music that sounded like the rattle and clank of bags of trash as they're being thrown into the back of a garbage truck. I've been to numerous museums, art galleries and restaurants just so a woman can demonstrate to any and all that she's still attractive."

Marcy giggled at the picture his words painted as he continued. "But I've seen performances by The Stones, Yo Yo Ma, and the Three Tenors. Afterwards, I usually get to make love to wonderful, exciting, intelligent women and get paid very well for it. What job could be any better?"

Marcy realized that she could ask Zack questions she couldn't ask Jenna. "How do you do it?" When he looked puzzled, she continued. "You can't tell me that every woman you're with turns you on. How can you just—well—perform on cue?"

"I can't. But you're wrong about being turned on. I love women, every size, every shape, every color. I've always loved women. I was brought up in a house filled with them. I have three sisters, all married now, whom I love dearly. My father died when I was eight, so from then on my family consisted of my sisters, my mother and both my grandmothers. I was the only one who put the toilet seat up. I got used to it, then learned to revel in it. I loved their smell, the sound of giggling and soft voices. Not that I hate men, mind you, but most women can get me—well, let's say interested."

So far he wasn't a jerk, and that was too bad. She found herself listening to his words, and watching his sensuous lips as they formed them. She focused on the information she needed for the book. "So you can do it with anyone? At the drop of a condom so to speak?"

"It's not like that at all," he said, wiping his hands on his napkin. Nice hands, with long fingers and well-cared for nails. *Stop it!* Marcy thought. "I talk with a client and spend time with her first. Women seldom want a quickie, so I have time to warm us both up. After that, it's easy."

You could even warm up to someone like me, she thought. Would she ever think of hiring a male prostitute? Never! New topic. "What's your personal favorite fantasy?" *What a question*, she thought. *I'm asking about this gorgeous guys fantasies.*

Zack paused to consider, then said, "I've no idea. I have lots I've acted, most with one client or another."

Images flashed through her brain. Southern gentleman, street tough, prison guard. Prison guard? Where had that come from. She took a sip of water to moisten her suddenly dry throat. "Okay. Tell me about the most recent one you did at Club Fantasy?"

Zack's laugh was quick and easy. "That was one of the more unusual ones I've done. Her name was Libby and she wanted to make it with a biker."

"You're kidding."

"No. I've been lots of things to lots of women, but this one was a first. Rock and I wrestled his Harley up two flights of stairs to a room we'd emptied and put it right there on the bare floor. We left the windows open all day and added fans for wind and fresh air-scented spray. When she came in I was discovered, as they say in the movies, sitting on the bike, helmet under my arm, in chaps, a leather vest and gloves, boots and not much else." His face softened at the memory. "I even added a few fake tattoos and a huge gold hoop earring."

Marcy could easily picture it, and it was all she could do not to drool. He'd make a dynamite biker and she felt her nipples tighten at the thought. Since when was she the kind of mature, small-town woman who would consider making it with a biker? Maybe since now. "So what happened?"

"Libby was probably five foot ten and maybe that's why she wanted someone really physical. We'd given her a costume, so she was dressed like a sweet young thing in a swishy little skirt and halter top with very high heels—probably ones she never got to wear with any of her boyfriends. She had specifically asked for someone over six feet tall.

"So there I was, " Zack continued, "seated on this medium-sized Harley trying not to drop Rock's helmet, hoping I looked like I knew a clutch from a gas pedal. I've never been on a motorcycle, by the way."

Well, Marcy thought. *There goes one stereotype.* She'd have bet he'd owned one. She wondered whether he watched sports on TV and worked out for hours each morning. "That surprises me."

"I know. I guess I look like the biker type, but I'm much more the taxi and limo kind of guy." When her eyebrows went up, he said, "I do love to shake people up and you're just too easy." His grin was infectious and Marcy couldn't help the smile that relaxed her face.

Zack studied Jenna's sister. He'd seen pictures and listened to Jenna talk about her for months. It was easy for him to imagine how Marcy might be, eclipsed by her socially adept, charming sister. He was anxious to find out what lay beneath the loose black tee shirt and black sweatpants. The more he talked to her, even about small things, the more he wondered.

It must be her eyes, he thought. There's such life there, intelligence, warmth and caring. And, of course, the way she was looking at him, like a starving man might look at a T-bone. It was flattering and increased his desire to open her up.

He'd also watched her with Jenna. He knew the two were very close, but within Marcy he thought he'd caught a note of resentment, a jealousy that was easy to understand. Jenna had always been the outgoing, popular one while Marcy stayed behind, like a kid with her nose pressed against the candy store window.

He found himself intrigued by this overweight, slightly shy, introverted woman. He loved all women but had always had a particular affinity for birds with broken wings, especially those he thought he could help and she was a case in point. Just a small push and he knew he could change her life, and he found himself eager to give it a try.

He told her a few details of his experience with the "biker babe," as he called Libby, and watched as Marcy squirmed. *Oh, yes,* he told himself, *I really want to explore Marcy Bryant.* He winked at her and gave her his most charming grin.

Marcy had watched him throughout his storytelling. She wanted him to stop his obviously phony flirtation, but then again, she also found that she enjoyed it. Lord, he could charm birds out of trees, but she vowed not to become one of his victims. Or clients. "I'll bet it was erotic. I'm really curious about something," she said, keeping it all on a conversational level and trying not to stutter. "Can a guy get an erection even with someone he doesn't know or care about? I mean, you said you could get turned on, but really—"

"I really can, most of the time. As I told you, I love women and I love making love to them. Sure, from time to time a woman's attitude turns me off and I have to slip into a private fantasy, relive a recent encounter, something like that, to get an erection, but it's not usually difficult."

"You said attitude. Doesn't a woman's appearance sometimes turn you off? Like someone very fat." That last sentence had just slipped out.

"Not really. It's the facial expression that does it to me and that's usually dictated by a woman's attitude." He stopped and thought for several moments. "If I think back to the women I had difficulties with, it's the cold ones with the haughty expressions, who look at me like the hired help, who turn me off. It's like they're saying, 'Get me off, I dare you.' I remember one particular woman—I actually had to return her money."

"You couldn't perform?" Marcy said, astonished, but gratified that he was human.

"Not a wiggle out of my cock." He snorted. "And if you tell anyone I'll deny it."

Marcy laughed at his chagrined expression. "It will be our secret. It must have been embarrassing."

"That's a small word for it. I was mortified. I think she was, too, since I'd come—pardon the pun—so highly recommended by several of her friends."

"Was that the only time?"

"There have been a few others, but for the most part I can fake it if I have to." He took another bite of his breakfast. "Okay. You've heard my dirty secret—or one of them. Tell me a little about you."

"There's not much to tell. Jenna and I are twins, and I work as a translator for a company upstate." She paused. "That's about it."

"Jenna's told me that much, but there's got to be more. About the real you, I mean."

"Like what?" Marcy said, shifting in her seat.

"What kind of music do you like? Movies? TV shows? What do you do in your spare time, like on the weekends?"

What harm could this do? Marcy wondered. "I like romantic movies, you know, chick flicks, old half hour TV shows, and, on weekends, I don't do much. I garden and I often bring work home. I'm afraid I don't lead an exciting life the way you and Jenna do."

He chuckled. "In my spare time I play tennis, and I like to workout at the gym. Nothing particularly glamorous." Marcy pictured him in a tight tank top and shorts with a barbell in each hand. He continued. "I read adventure novels like Tom Clancy and I enjoy gourmet cooking, particularly Indian food."

"Gourmet cooking?" She figured him for a steak and potatoes guy. And he liked to read. One stereotype down the tubes.

"Yeah. Remember, I grew up in a houseful of women," he

said with a laugh. "We used to play board games in the evening and the loser cooked dinner the next night. It was either learn to play Monopoly better or learn to cook so everyone wouldn't make fun of me. I chose cooking. In high school, two of my sisters used to clean my room in exchange for taking their turn at the stove."

Marcy couldn't help being surprised. "You're different from what I might have expected, considering . . . uh . . ."

"You mean considering what I do for a living? I'm not just your run of the mill stud muffin." His laugh was infectious. "What are you hiding from?" he asked suddenly.

"I beg your pardon?"

"What are you hiding from? Your manner, your dress, the way you carry yourself, even your size. Pardon the amateur Freud, but you're trying to fade into the background. Why?"

Marcy sat up straighter. "I'm not hiding from anything, and even if I were, it's not any of your business."

Zack's expression became serious. "True. It's not. But it's a shame to see you in sweats, without makeup or seemingly any thought about what you look like. It makes me sad to see someone being so much less than she could be."

Shut up! She controlled her hurt and anger. "Enough. Thanks for the information for my book, but I think it's time for me to head back to Jenna's place."

"Chicken."

"I stopped taking dares when I was twelve and fell off the crossbar of my swing set."

He pointed a finger at her. "There, you see? You used to be adventurous. What happened?"

"I'm me. I'm who I am. I'm not Jenna, I'm just Marcy. And I'm out of here."

"Aren't you going to pay half the check? Tommy hasn't brought it yet."

When she reached into her purse for her wallet, Zack grabbed her hand. "Listen. I'm sorry I got a bit out of bounds," he said, his voice soft and genuinely apologetic, "but, as I said, I love women."

"Not someone who looks like me." That, too, had slipped out before she could stop it. Now she felt tears prickling her eyes. She'd only just met this oaf and he was already trying to run her life. She had been right to begin with. He was an arrogant ass.

"Of course someone who looks like you. You look fine, or would if you—"

"Lost forty pounds. It ain't going to happen and that's that." Not that she hadn't tried, but she was beyond redemption in the weight department. Weight Watchers, LA Weight Loss, the Atkins Diet, and many others had proved it. She knew she was a lost cause.

"I wasn't going to say that. I never tell people something they already know, and your weight's not your real problem. I was going to say that you'd look fine if you just cared about yourself."

She wasn't going to burst into tears. "Just stop, right now. I care about myself, and I'm happy just the way I am."

"This is going to sound cliché, but you're really quite lovely when you're angry."

He looked like a naughty little boy. A naughty, hunky, little boy. She couldn't suppress a glimmer of a smile. "Okay. Enough. The 'You're lovely when you're angry' line did it. I give up and I'm leaving. I surrender the floor, and the check, to you." She dropped her wallet back into her purse. "Jenna can reimburse you the next time you see her."

"Oh, Marcy, I'm really sorry if I hurt your feelings. That was the last thing I intended. Would you do one thing for me before you go, please?" he asked, sounding genuinely contrite. "Come around and sit here." He patted the chair next to him. "I promise I won't bite. Indulge me for two minutes."

Tempted to walk out the restaurant door, she thought better of it. She couldn't start a war with the man Jenna needed to help at the club. She took a deep breath. Her mother had drummed good manners into the twins from the cradle. Resigned to being polite, she moved to the chair beside him. "Okay, I'm here."

"Look out the window at the people going past." When she was staring at the passersby, he said, "Count how many look like you would like to look and how many look like ordinary people, with bad hair or big noses. How many are overweight, or underweight and how many are perfect? And remember this is a skewed sample from a pretty upscale area of Manhattan." When she started to object, he interrupted. "Stop second-guessing me and just count."

So she did. There were quite a few women who looked the way she wished she looked, but many more were just ordinary looking. Silently, she watched people go by and considered. More than a few of the women she saw were more overweight than she was. So what? Was that supposed to convince her that she wasn't unattractive?

"What did you see?"

"Lots of women who weren't my ideal of the perfect woman."

"Like Jenna?"

"She's not totally perfect."

"I'm glad you remember that. How about the men they were with? Did they look at their ladies with contempt for their size?"

At that moment a couple crossed in front of the restaurant window hand in hand, laughing and pointing. Obviously tourists, he had a camera around his neck and she held a map of the city dangling from her free hand.

"You see those two, right?" Zack asked.

She did and it was as though he'd choreographed the whole thing. The woman wore a full, multicolored summer dress and must have weighed fifty pounds more than Marcy did. The man with her wore shorts and sandals and wasn't much smaller than his wife.

"Point made?" Zack asked.

"Maybe," she said, more to be polite than anything else. "Why are you doing all this? You seem to have it in for me. Why?"

"I'm sorry. I guess I am coming on pretty strong, but the way Jenna talks about you it's as though I've already known you for ages. She gave me the impression that you are less than she wished you were, and it makes her sad. When I walked in here this morning, I saw what she sees, a quite lovely woman who doesn't want anyone to know it. So, as usual, I jumped in with both size twelve motorcycle boots."

He stopped, considering, then continued. "This isn't for public consumption, but I have a sister, Amber, who's always been in our sister Diane's shadow." Zack gazed off into space. "Diane is just eleven months older, and I guess they're kind of like twins since they resemble each other in coloring and build. Because of the way their birthdays worked out, they were always in the same grade at school and had many of the same teachers. Diane was always better at things, mostly because she had the advantage of those eleven months. Anyway, through middle and high school, Amber slowly just made herself disappear, fade into the background. I'm four years older and, of course, I was always wrapped up in my own stuff so I didn't catch anything. No one saw."

Marcy was fascinated by the look into Zack's background and touched by his obvious pain. "Anyway," he said, taking a deep breath, "when she was seventeen she attempted suicide. She took a whole bottle of my mom's sleeping pills. We lived in Brooklyn and I was commuting to Columbia. Luckily one of my classes was cancelled, so I came home and found her before . . . well, before. Whether she was really trying to kill herself or just yelling for attention doesn't really matter. Mom made sure she got lots of professional help and now she's in great shape—married, with a wonderful husband, a toddler and another on the way. In spite of that, I guess I still feel a little guilty for being totally oblivious."

Marcy put her hand on Zack's arm. "It wasn't your fault."

Zack's smile was forced. "My brain knows that, but my soul still feels like shit." He seemed to snap himself back to the present. "That's why I came on so strong with you. The problems of being a twin must be enormous. I can understand why you've done the same fading thing that Amber did."

"I'm certainly not going to kill myself and I don't think there's as much of a parallel as you're trying to draw. I love my sister."

"Of course you do. Amber loved Diane and still does, but that's not the issue." Using his finger beneath her chin, Zack turned Marcy's face away from the window. "Let me tell you what I see when I look at you."

Zack's intense gaze made Marcy's toes tingle, and made her aware of her breasts and crotch, but she held his eyes.

"When I look at you, I see a very attractive woman. You're not beautiful, and I won't shine you on by saying that you could be. What you could be is someone who's proud of herself and her looks. Someone who stands straighter, emphasizes her great breasts and de-emphasizes her hips. Someone who wears makeup designed to bring out those wonderful gray eyes and soft, smooth skin. Someone whose hair looks like she cares about it rather than just gets it out of her way."

Reflexively, Marcy reached for the barrette that held her hair at the base of her neck, then let her hands drop back into her lap. She wanted to deny everything Zack was saying, but in all honesty she couldn't. And it hurt. Was she trying to disappear behind Jenna? Jenna had always been the social one, the one with all the dates. She remembered her mother saying that, although Marcy might not have as many first dates as Jenna, she'd have more second dates. She'd always felt that was the way her mother tried to let her down easily. It hadn't worked. In high school, when she sat home on a Saturday night, while Jenna dated guy after guy, her mother's words had been of no help at all.

When had she begun to fade away? She recalled that she and Jenna had looked pretty much alike in junior high, so when had she begun to gain all the weight? When had she stopped wearing makeup? She remembered a conversation she'd had with Jenna just yesterday. Ty Lynch. Was that when it had all begun?

She told herself that it wasn't fair to blame it all on one thing and she realized that Ty had probably been the straw that broke her back, that made her give up. Was that really what she'd done? Given up in the dating battle all teenaged girls wage? Surrendered to her beautiful, outgoing sister? She returned her gaze to the window. Women walked by the glass, many fatter than she was. Some looked dumpy, some looked good despite their weight.

"Is that really what you see?" she asked, looking back at Zack.

He merely nodded. "The question is do you want to do something about it?"

"I don't know."

"Scared?"

Marcy realized that fear was exactly what she was feeling. Terror actually. It was one thing to be what she was, another to make the effort to be more, and fail. What if she failed? What if she made the effort to look better and then found that it didn't make a bit of difference?

"It will make a difference," Zack said as if reading her mind. "Not necessarily to anyone else but you, and in the end you're all that matters anyway."

"I don't know."

"You don't have to know anything. Just think about it. If you decide to make some changes, I can help. I'm an expert at clothes shopping, and I've got several friends in the beauty business."

She looked at this hunky guy and tried to picture him pawing through the racks at Macy's. "Clothes shopping? You?"

"Sisters, remember? Actually, when I get time to visit any of them in suburbia, they each insist that I help them pick their wardrobe. I'm a whiz at it, and I enjoy it. Give yourself a day or two to decide, and, if you want, I can give you a hand."

Marcy was touched by his desire to help. She remembered her initial reaction to him. Beauty is as beauty does. He was offering to *do* for her. "Let me think about it."

"I'm free during the day, or will be when I've rearranged my schedule for Jenna." He pulled a business card from his wallet and scrawled on the back. "I don't know whether I'll be staying in my apartment or in Rock's room at the Club, so here's my cell phone number. Don't you dare call before eleven, however."

With a nod of agreement, Marcy put the card in her purse. "Thanks for the offer. You've given me a lot to think about. I don't know whether you're right about me, but it's been quite an education."

"I'm glad."

Zack watched Marcy walk out of the restaurant. What would she be like if he could find the sensual person beneath the reticent covering? He could teach her what he liked. He spent his time being the masterful lover for all his clients. What if he could create someone who not only knew how to take, but how to give? He allowed his vision to blur.

He and Marcy were lying in the sun on the deck of a small boat. A cool breeze drifted over their heated skin and soft jazz wafted from a small CD player. There wasn't another ship from one dizzying blue horizon to the other. The boat rocked beneath his back as they sipped wine and talked. Marcy rolled onto her side, her body only inches away from his, her hand on his chest. She licked his ear, then nipped the lobe. "Don't move," she murmured. "Let me love you."

He lay completely still while her hand stroked his sweat-dampened chest, flicking her fingernail over his flat nipple. Shivers echoed through him. Why had no one ever done that before? She propped herself on her elbow and kissed his eyelids, his cheeks, his nose.

She lightly tickled his side, making him smile. "I like it when you smile while we're making love," she said, softly, and when he took a breath to say that he liked smiling, she put her finger over his lips. "Don't speak, don't move. Let me have my wicked way with you."

He let the breath out slowly as she kissed him. Sweet, soft, but with growing hunger. Her palm made lazy circles over his chest, then her fingers slid beneath the waistband of his trunks, just barely brushing the tip of his penis. His body reacted to her touch as she obviously knew it would. Then her hand withdrew.

He wanted her now, but was content to allow the pleasure to build. "Turn over," she said, and, when he did, she straddled him, sitting on his buttocks. His erection was hard against the deck of the boat. Her hands were expert on his back, kneading and stroking, scratching and squeezing. He was in a hurry and hoped she didn't take too long, but again he waited.

Her timing was perfect, asking him to turn onto his back and pulling off his swim trunks just as he was becoming impatient. He looked up at her, the bright sun behind her so she was just a silhouette, and watched as she removed the top of her suit. Her breasts were large with deep brown nipples and he ached to fill his hands and mouth with them. She crouched beside him, leaned down and let him take her into his mouth. As he sucked, she placed one hand on her other full breast and he pressed, kneaded and squeezed.

He thought he was complete until she placed her hand on

his cock and wrapped her fingers around it. She manipulated his erection, sliding her hand from base to tip, then back until it was difficult to hold back. "Not yet," she purred. "Hold back as long as you can."

She knew just how to touch him, and he was hot with need. Then she moved until her mouth was near his cock. "Let me fill my mouth with you."

Her mouth on his cock was heaven. She didn't devour him. Rather she licked the length of him, then flicked her tongue over the tip. She blew a stream of cool air over his wet skin, then took him in her mouth again, pulling back and sucking in.

"I'm going to come if you don't stop that."

"Do it," she said, then resumed sucking. He could wait no longer and came in her mouth.

As he sat in the restaurant, Zack returned to the moment. He'd take his time with Marcy but maybe, just maybe, she'd become something more than the women he entertained.

Chapter

7

Since the Club was closed and Jenna finished her errands quickly, Marcy spent the rest of the afternoon with her sister. They wandered through the city, doing a great deal of walking, giving Marcy plenty of time to think. She considered sharing Zack's conversation with her sister, but decided against it. This was something she had to consider herself, without Jenna's possible hurt feelings or guilt.

Marcy and Jenna had done many of the purely tourist things when she'd visited the previous Labor Day weekend, so now they took the subway to Chinatown and just poked around in little stores that sold everything from fake ivory fans to smoked pork. They stopped for spring rolls in a tiny hole-in-the-wall shop, then had gelati in Little Italy. Since it was Monday, the financial district was alive with people rushing from place to place, many in suits and ties or business-casual attire, some in brightly colored jackets.

"Floor traders from the various stock and commodity exchanges," Jenna explained. "Quite a few of them have been our customers. Our original connection was through one of Chloe's boyfriends. By the end of the day there's lots of pent-up energy in these guys and many of them have disposable green." When Marcy looked puzzled, Jenna added, "Money.

Cash that they don't want to tell the government about. So they spend lots of it with us."

Back in Chinatown the sisters had dinner at a restaurant that specialized in dim sum with varied fillings. As they sat, oriental men in crisp, white jackets pushed carts covered with little plates containing dumplings of every description. Jenna told her that a diner merely pointed and the waiter would put a plate on the table, or explain what was inside the wrapper. Jenna kept pointing and Marcy tried half a dozen different types and enjoyed all but one. "Sorry," Jenna said, making a very sour face. "I had forgotten about that one. I don't like it either."

"How do they know what to charge?" Marcy asked.

"Simple," Jenna said with a grin. "They count the plates. White ones are one price, yellow another and so forth."

"Ingenious," Marcy said.

Late Tuesday morning, Jenna got a phone call from Rock. His father was still in intensive care, but was expected to recover. He told Jenna that he anticipated being back toward the end of the following week, but he'd keep in touch.

Tuesday afternoon, Jenna had a meeting with a potential client, so Marcy stayed in the apartment. Jenna had tried to set up a few meetings with the women who worked with her so that Marcy could get some stories, but, because some had escaped the hot, humid, holiday week in Manhattan and others were otherwise occupied, no one was available. Marcy was disappointed, partly because of the lack of material, but mostly because it gave her time to think. The things Zack told her had been dancing around in her mind, but now she had time to seriously consider. Was he right? Probably. Did she want to come out of hiding as he'd suggested? She wasn't sure. What if she made herself more attractive and nothing changed? Somewhere deep inside she could say now that if she looked better she'd have dates, be more socially active. If she let Zack help her redo herself and it failed to change things . . . She didn't want to think about that aspect.

To quiet her brain, she decided to write a story for the book so she sat down at Jenna's computer and began to type. She decided to call the heroine Marcia. So like her own name? Autobiographical yet again? She wondered, but by the second paragraph the story had taken on a life of its own.

She became Marcia, slender, willowy even, with small, perky breasts. Marcy hated the word perky. Even before her weight gain, her breasts had been large and droopy. The man on the bike was Zack. She felt her fingers tremble as she typed.

THE BIKER

Marcia had dreamed of making love to a biker type ever since high school and now she had enough money to make it come true. She'd heard about the Eros Hotel from a friend who'd called and recommended her to the woman in charge. Marcia was tall, willowy, with a slender, reedlike shape, small, uplifted breasts with deep brown nipples. She met with the owner of the Hotel and told her all the details of her fantasy. At first it had been difficult to discuss her dream. It was hers, and very private, but the woman had been so gentle and easy to talk to that she ended up telling her everything.

Marcia arrived at the Hotel early one summer evening and was escorted to a dressing room where a card told her to re-move her jeans and tank top and exchange them for a full, flowery skirt and sleeveless, white, cotton blouse. She had known before the card told her not to wear underwear. That was the way she wanted it. Quick and somehow dirty.

She slipped back into her sandals and waited only a few minutes until the woman arrived to show her to the door of Room 17, where her fantasy awaited. As she reached for the doorknob, she wondered whether it could possibly live up to her expectations.

He certainly did. She couldn't tell how tall he was because he was seated on a gold and black, twin cam 88B with leather saddle bags and staggered, short, dual exhausts. The bike was beautiful, but it couldn't compare to the man who rode it. He was dark, with wonderfully sexy blue-gray eyes, fabulous shoulders and biceps she could almost feel. He had a tattoo of leaves and thorns around his left one and a heart with an arrow through it on the right. His black calfskin vest only partially covered his well-developed, lightly furred chest and his chaps were low slung. Although the leather hid his crotch, she somehow knew he wore nothing beneath. His black, calf-high boots had silver tips and the helmet under his arm had an eagle on the front. He was her dream. Perfect. Between the look of the man, the hot breeze coming in the open window and the smell of leather and bike, she was wet and throbbing instantly.

He smiled slowly, then put the helmet down and beckoned her over. As she started to mount the bike in front of him, he turned her so she faced him, then bent her backwards so she was stretched over the handlebars. When he opened her blouse, her breasts swelled to meet his fingers, her nipples yearning for his mouth. He obliged.

She closed her eyes and inhaled: leather, oil, exhaust and him, all smoky and musky, smelling of man and sweat. She let herself flow with it all as his fingers pinched her flesh and his teeth bit until she winced slightly. He seemed to know how and where she needed him. His hands traced a hot path down her belly, then up her naked calves. Up the insides of her thighs beneath her skirt those fingers traced, toward her center, the pussy she longed to have him touch.

His fingers invaded. He seemed to know that she couldn't wait. She wanted to make it last, but she needed. Now! Right now! His fingers filled her, while his other hand rubbed her clit until she came. She couldn't help it, spasms filled her, her body writhed beneath his expert touch.

"More!" she yelled, and he started the bike. The roar was tremendous, and, as the vibrations traveled through her, she came again. His hands left her only for a moment, then he positioned his condom-covered cock at the entrance to her pussy. He grabbed her hips and positioned her so she was sitting on him, his cock impaling her, the roaring bike between her legs. She thought she'd pass out from the erotic joy of it, but maintained enough sanity to ride him. The power . . . The joy . . . The need and fulfillment.

They came together, him for the first time, her for the third or fifth or tenth. She'd lost count and was beyond caring. She just rode the waves.

Eventually, the bike was still. He lifted her and carried her across the hall and tenderly placed her on a bed. Then he leaned over and placed a gentle kiss on her lips, and left her there, smiling, totally replete, realizing that her biker had never spoken. She dozed, then half an hour later she found her clothing on a side chair, redressed and left.

She'd be back to relive her fantasy with this fabulous man again and again, whatever it cost.

———————

Marcy was panting, her pulse pounding by the time she finished typing. She vowed that neither Jenna nor Zack would ever see this story. Never. It was too close to Zack's encounter and Jenna probably knew about it. She researched details about the bike on the Internet to calm herself and made a few changes in the description. As she finished, she heard the front door and Jenna's voice. "I hope you weren't too bored," Jenna called as the door closed behind her.

"Not at all," Marcy said as she pressed the save key, saved again on a floppy disk, then closed the word processing program.

Jenna walked up behind her. "Been writing?"

"Actually, yes. A good story I think, but it needs editing. I'll show it to you when it's ready." Never. Too close! "How was your interview?"

"Great. He made a date for next Thursday."

"What's his fantasy?"

"It's a messy one. He wants to watch two women mud wrestle, then join in. With the obvious ending of course."

Marcy couldn't help wrinkling her nose. "Mud wrestling?"

"Of all things. It's all that lesbian touching stuff that seems to turn men on. I tried to gently guide him to soapy showers, but he wanted mud."

"You tried to change his mind? Do you do that often?"

"Sometimes, especially when we have a ready-made setup that might work just as well. This mud thing will take a bit of arranging, but we've done it a few times before. Plastic on the walls and floor, a kid's inflatable wading pool, lots of dirt and water. Would you believe that I have to buy special mud-dirt if it's to be the slippery, slidey thing I know he wants? And the cleanup will be a bitch."

"So why do you do it?"

"He pays extra. It will run him twenty-five hundred dollars, but it's worth it to him. I think he's one of those dot-com millionaire types and the money means nothing." She grinned. "It does to me."

"Can I help?"

"Definitely, if you don't mind. It will make a good story for your book, too, if you're looking for a bit of humor. I've got to go over to Manny's tomorrow afternoon to pick up a few other things. If you'd like to go with me, you'll get to meet him. He's such a sweetie and his place is an integral part of what we do."

"Who's Manny?"

"Manny's Props and Costumes in Queens. He sees all, knows most and tells nothing."

"Does he know what you do?"

"I think he suspects but we maintain the illusion that I put on amateur theatricals. It's sort of a wink-wink thing. Thank God he's totally discreet."

The following afternoon, Jenna and Marcy opened the door to the giant warehouse that was Manny's Props and Costumes. The front room was filled with smaller items from plastic edelweiss for *The Sound of Music* to a skull for Hamlet. "Hi, Jenna. I'll be with you in a few minutes. Go in the back and help yourself if you know what you're looking for." The man behind the counter was in his fifties, with fleshy lips and a large nose. His hair had probably been brown but was now gray and combed over the top, trying unsuccessfully to cover a large, bald area.

As she followed Jenna into the cavernous warehouse at the rear, Marcy asked, "What are we here for? Not that mud wrestling thing?"

Jenna chuckled. "Nope. We're doing the sheik thing tonight for the sixth time for the same guy. He just loves it. Says it's the only way he can get it up any more."

"Sheik thing? Of course. In the harem room, the one with all the sand."

"That's it. I dress as a visiting princess, kidnapped from my caravan and brought to his tent. You can guess the rest." Jenna strode over to a long iron-pipe rack filled with hangars holding colorful costumes of every variety in various sizes. While Jenna found the items she wanted, Marcy saw one section devoted to period outfits, neatly divided and labeled by century, and an entire rack filled with uniforms from every war from the American Revolution to Korea and Vietnam. There were buckskins for Native Americans, ball gowns for wealthy socialites, oriental black jackets and pants and brightly colored Hawaiian sarongs.

Jenna returned, carrying a set of flowing robes and a skimpy Arabian harem costume for herself. Marcy was surprised to find that she wasn't as shocked by the idea of her sister playing the victim as she would have been just a week earlier. Maybe she was getting used to it all. Was that good? She was trying to get Jenna out of the business, not embrace it, wasn't she?

Outfits in hand, Jenna walked back to the business area with Marcy right behind. The proprietor was now alone behind a long counter. "Manny Grossman, this is my sister, Marcy."

Manny looked her over, then smiled. That look, never meant to insult, but clearly saying, "You certainly don't look like your gorgeous sister."

"We should do an act," Manny said. "Manny and Marcy, songs, dances and snappy patter." He extended his hand. "Nice to meet you."

"And you," Marcy said, shaking the proffered hand.

Jenna laid the items she'd selected on the counter. "Write me up, Manny."

"You're such a pleasure," Manny replied. "I never have to find anything for you. I think by now you know my stock better than I do." He took the two costumes and covered them with plastic sleeves. "Doing that Arabian thing again?"

"Yup. It's in demand." As Manny turned to get his sales ledger, Jenna winked and Marcy grinned back.

Manny wrote up an invoice and Jenna presented her credit card and signed the receipt. "Anything I can put away for you for the weekend?"

"Actually, yes. Thanks for reminding me. I need the English gentleman outfit, size thirty-four, and the maid's uniform, size ten, for Saturday evening. I'll be in for them Saturday afternoon." Maid. English gentleman. Marcy used her growing imagination to quickly create a scene and it made her nipples tighten.

"Fine. I'll set them aside for you." As they left, Manny called, "Nice to meet you Marcy. Consider doing that act with me. Maybe Jenna could put us in one of her entertainments."

Marcy almost choked on her laughter.

* * *

The sisters returned to the apartment and Jenna spent several hours pounding away on her computer. Marcy watched over her shoulder and slowly assimilated the multiple systems that tracked clients, employees and the myriad of other things needed to keep the business running. She listened as Jenna returned phone call after phone call, setting up afternoon meetings with potential clients. Finally, she settled down on the sofa with a book. After one particularly contentious call, Jenna leaned back and sighed.

Marcy looked up. "I gathered from this end of the conversation that you turned him down. Didn't he come recommended?"

"That wasn't the problem. He wanted a type of fantasy we don't do." When Marcy raised an eyebrow, she shook her head and continued. "This guy wanted a young teenager. I told him that we don't do anything underage. For that matter, we won't have anything to do with drugs or anything else illegal. If this guy had been able to get along with someone like Chloe pretending to be a kid, we could have done business, but he was adamant. And pissed. Oh, well. We've got our rules."

Jenna glanced at her watch and quickly downloaded information from the computer to her PDA, then shut the computer down. "We're running very late," she said, and the two women rushed from the apartment.

With the costumes from Manny's hanging on the hook over the cab window, Jenna and Marcy took a taxi across town to the brownstone where Marcy helped turn the room they'd worked on back into a generic motel room. Then, with Jenna instructing, she and her sister set up cameras and lights to video that evening's activities. "The guy who's using this room tonight with Chloe will pay five hundred dollars extra for the tape," Jenna explained.

"Doesn't Chloe mind being in a video?"

"Chloe? Not in the slightest. She's the one who began this

photography thing, and I think she gets an added kick out of thinking the guy will watch it later and get off. Her kind of fame, I guess."

"Hi, honey, I'm home!" Zack's voice carried up the stairs and the sound of it was enough to get Marcy aroused. She'd been doing a lot of thinking about his offer to "fix her up" and was seriously considering it. She hadn't discussed it with Jenna because she knew what her sister would say. Her twin had been after her to do something like this for years.

Jenna leaned out the door and yelled, "Glad to hear that. Can you come up here and move something for me?" He'd called the evening before and assured Jenna that he'd be in residence any time they had clients.

"Sure."

"Okay, Sis," Marcy said, realizing that it was almost six o'clock. "I'll get out of your way."

Marcy encountered Zack in the hall. He looked sexy as hell, dressed in a tight-fitting, cocoa brown shirt and beige, linen slacks. *Actually*, Marcy thought, *he'd look sexy as hell in a burlap sack*. "Have you given any thought to what we talked about on Monday?" he asked.

"I'm thinking about it. I feel like you've taken me on as some kind of cause."

His wink made her tingle as it always did. "I have."

"Why?"

"I already answered that. I think there's a lot inside of you that I'd really enjoy letting loose." He winked again. "In so many ways."

Suddenly getting an inspiration, Marcy's eyes narrowed. "Do you have a thing for Jenna? Is that why you've come on to me?"

"That's a nasty thing to say, Marcy," he said, his expression suddenly angry. "I wouldn't ever get involved with someone as a substitute for someone else."

She deliberately released the tension she felt in the back of her neck. "Sorry. It's happened to me before."

"We'll have to talk about that sometime, but right now I've got work to do."

As he turned, she said, "You're playing at being my shrink and I don't think I like it."

"I'm sorry," he said, his voice softening as he turned back and gently held her shoulders. "I guess I am coming on pretty strong, but you really do remind me of my sister."

"I'm far from suicidal so back off."

"Okay. I stand corrected. But if you change your mind . . ."

Looking into his gorgeous blue-gray eyes she weakened. "I'm sorry I got so bent out of shape." His prodding pushed her to ask herself why she'd resisted so vehemently.

He leaned forward and placed a quick, but quite thorough kiss on her lips. "Friends?"

Her pussy twitched, but she was beginning to get used to her visceral reaction to him. "That wasn't a purely friendly kiss, but yes. Friends."

He turned and disappeared up the stairs.

As she left the brownstone, she realized that she was getting a bit hungry and wondered whether to stop in at the restaurant where she'd met Steve the previous Saturday evening. He had said he was usually there around six and if she stopped in for dinner, what would be the harm? It might help her discover things about herself, things that were now puzzling and confusing her.

She'd come to New York City to try to get Jenna out of the brothel business. Now she wondered how much of her visit was entangled with her feelings about the competition between herself and her sister.

She found herself opening the door to George's Bistro and looking around for Steve's comfortable face. He wouldn't challenge her long-standing perception of herself.

She spotted him, dressed in a gray business suit with a light blue shirt and paisley tie, sitting at a corner table, reading his newspaper. He'd obviously come straight from work. Heart pounding, she made her way over.

"Well, hello," Steve said, a smile quickly converting his expression as she arrived at his table. He quickly put his newspaper aside and rose slightly. "I'm so glad you decided to join me once again. I thought I'd probably never see you again."

"My sister had to work and I was going to eat alone anyway. I thought of you and here I am." Phew. Did that sound insulting? "Sorry. I don't think that came out right."

"Don't worry about it," he said with a dismissive wave. "I'm delighted to have the company. How has your visit been so far?"

"Wonderful. I've seen quite a bit of the city and eaten food from all over the world."

"Like?" Steve asked.

"Let's see. Monday we had real Chinese. Dim sum. I've never had it before. Tuesday it was kielbasa for lunch and Indonesian for dinner. I may need an atlas to keep track."

"You've only just begun. I know a great German restaurant in Yorkville." He paused. "Maybe you'd like to go there with me one evening. Real sauerbraten and the best red cabbage in the city. They make it with caraway seeds and just a hint of dill."

A date. That would be a real date. Jenna was working every evening so what the hell. "I'd like that. Maybe Friday evening?" Had she really said that?

Steve looked startled that she'd suggested a specific evening. She panicked. Maybe he hadn't really meant it to be that specific but he said quickly, "That would be wonderful." Now he looked genuinely pleased, and Marcy exhaled. "When are you leaving?"

"Sunday. Back to work on Monday." They chatted about

her work and the latest political scandal. A date. She had a date.

When they'd finished their meal, he said, "I'm looking forward to Friday so much. I really enjoy spending time with you. You're such a bright lady, and a good listener as well."

"Thanks. I enjoyed this evening, too. Shall I meet you at the restaurant? Say seven o'clock?"

"I can pick you up."

"I know, but I'm staying way across town so it will be easier if I meet you."

"I understand." He wrote the name of the restaurant down on a corner of the newspaper, then tore it off and gave it to her. "I've also written down my home and cell phone numbers in case there's a problem." He kept his pen poised. "I know nothing about you. Maybe you could give me your phone number in case I need to reach you."

It was totally logical. He might need to call things off. "Sure. Let me give you my cell number," she said, rattling it off as he wrote. "It's based upstate so it will be a long-distance call for you."

"I think I can handle it. By the way, you've never told me your last name."

She hadn't, had she. It was time to stop being so timid. "Bryant. Marcy Bryant."

"Well, Marcy Bryant," he said as the waiter put the check on the table. As Marcy reached for her purse, Steve put his hand over hers. "Let me."

"I'd prefer to split the check," Marcy said.

He sighed. "If you insist. But Friday's dinner is on me. It's our first real date and it's my restaurant. Anyway, just in case you don't like it, if I pay, I won't feel so responsible."

She relaxed. "Okay. It's a deal."

Later that evening, back at Jenna's, Marcy thought about her date for Friday evening. She'd have to tell Jenna, of course, so she wouldn't worry, but this was something really personal. She had a date.

She found that she wanted to look nice for it. She hadn't brought anything but sweats and tee shirts, so what would she wear? Certainly not anything of Jenna's. Her sister's size ten would never cover her size sixteen. She realized that she needed to buy something. She wondered when the last time was that she'd cared about her looks. She was ashamed when she realized that it was too long ago to remember.

Marcy walked into the bathroom and took a long look at herself in the mirror over the sink. *Maybe a little makeup would help*, she thought. Eye shadow? Mascara? Blush? She looked at Jenna's basket of products of every sort that sat on the back of the toilet and decided to experiment. An hour and lots of makeup remover later, she realized that she knew nothing about how to apply any of the stuff and she didn't have time to figure it all out herself. After all, it was already Wednesday.

Would someone in a beauty parlor be able to help her? Maybe one of the big department stores had a cosmetics counter where she could get her makeup done. That might just work. Which one? She could ask Jenna, but she was embarrassed to admit that she wanted to fix herself up for a date. It sounded so unlike her, and she was reluctant to discuss any of it with her sophisticated, perfectly dressed and made up sister.

Zack. Could he make a suggestion? It was already Wednesday evening. She wanted to do this privately, and she wondered how she would get time away from Jenna. She didn't want someone to try to make her look like her twin or make odious comparisons. And she needed a new outfit.

The following morning she got her opportunity. "Marcy," Jenna said. "I've got two interviews this afternoon, one at two and one at three-thirty. I'm really sorry. I don't want to keep deserting you and I put a few off till next week, but these two were recommended by two very good customers—"

Marcy cut her off. "Don't think a thing about it, Sis. Not a problem. I've got a few things I want to do, too, so the time will be quite useful."

"Are you sure?"

"I'm positive."

"What kind of things do you have to do?"

"Just some shopping. Gifts for a few folks back home and stuff." She was lying to her sister, but with any luck the finished product would be a pleasant surprise. And if it didn't work out, she could always change back into her regular clothes and wash off the makeup with Jenna none the wiser.

She slipped into the bedroom and called Zack. Although it was almost eleven-thirty he sounded sleepy and sexy as hell. "I'm sorry if I woke you."

"You didn't. I'm just too lazy to climb out of bed."

She pictured him in bed, that body stretched out, then stopped herself. He does that sexy act on purpose, Marcy thought, then said, "You said you might be able to help me. I want to get something different to wear and maybe find someone to give me some help with makeup."

She heard Zack's voice brighten. "Fabulous. Got a date?"

"Of course not." More lies? No. Steve wasn't a date. Well, actually he was. "It's just that you got me thinking." That was true enough.

"Have you and Jenna got time this afternoon?"

"I don't want Jenna to know just yet. In case it doesn't work out."

"Doesn't work out?" He paused. "Okay, whatever you want. What time? I've got to be at the Club by five-thirty."

"You don't have to go with me or even meet me. Just give me the name of a good department store where I can get some makeup and look for clothes."

"I'm going with you so get used to it. What time can I pick you up?"

She let out a long breath. This wasn't going to be as easy or as private as she'd hoped. She really didn't want Zack to become this involved. She could muddle through by herself. Couldn't she? Well, Zack wasn't giving her any choice, so she'd better just roll with the punches. "I could meet you somewhere about one. Will that give you enough time?"

He sounded much more awake. "Sure. Meet me on the southeast corner of Fifty-fourth and Third. One-thirty sharp. That work for you?"

"Okay. What's there?"

"You'll see. Bye." He hung up.

The sky was leaden, the air warm and humid. The weather forecaster on TV had mentioned the possibility of a few scattered rain showers but taxis were still plentiful. The driver let Marcy out on the corner and she saw Zack waiting for her. He was his usual virile self, in low-slung jeans, a red tee shirt and Western-style boots. The picture of him on a motorcycle flashed through her brain.

"Okay," he said, all business, "hair and face first."

"Hair? No. I just want makeup and maybe one outfit."

"Hair! It's a must. You could have such lovely hair," he said, pulling off her barrette and combing his fingers through the long, brown strands, "if you gave it half a chance. It's got great texture, but the cut is all wrong for your face and the color could use a little brightening."

"I don't want anything that drastic."

"You don't want anything you can't just wash off so you can pull back into your shell."

"God, you're such a pest," she said, but without rancor. He was right of course.

"I know," he said, his infectious grin back. "I'm a real pain in the ass, but now that I've got you thinking about improvements, I can't resist pushing you a little bit to make it happen. Really happen." He put on a little boy pout. "Please?"

Irresistible. "You're a pain, but a delightful one. Okay, I'll let someone look at my hair and make suggestions. But I won't agree to anything unless I want to."

"Of course not. But you want to."

She did want to.

Chapter
8

"When's your date?" Zack asked as they headed south on Third Avenue.

The question was so sudden that without thinking she said, "Tomorrow night for dinner."

"Gotcha," he said with his characteristic grin, and she realized that she'd said more than she'd intended.

She should be upset, but he was so—adorable. Okay, she was being a sucker for a pretty face, but what the hell. "Okay. I met a nice guy at a local restaurant and he asked me to go to dinner with him tomorrow evening."

Zack stopped in the middle of the sidewalk and whirled so he was facing her. "You got picked up? Are you sure he's on the up and up?"

"Stop acting like an enraged father," she said, torn between being annoyed and flattered. "He's a nice man. I've met him twice. And yes. I'm sure he's on the up and up."

"Okay. It's just that I care about you." He grinned and gave her a large wet kiss on her cheek. "Way to go, girl. For a while I thought you didn't date, but that's wonderful." He turned and continued walking along Third Avenue. Lightly, he continued. "Now you have no excuse for not going to dinner with me too."

Dinner? With Zack? Nah. It wouldn't work. "We can't. You'll be working Saturday and I'm leaving on Sunday."

He put his hands on his temples and made a loud humming sound. "I see your future. You'll be back. Sooner rather than later."

She couldn't help but laugh. He was impossible. So very impossible. So very possible. Almost trotting to keep up, Marcy followed him until he reached a narrow storefront and opened the door, causing a tinkling sound from inside. The window beside her contained several styrofoam heads with wigs of varying lengths. Wigs? Just inside the door, Zack stopped so suddenly that she almost bumped into him. The wig store looked like a small but ordinary beauty parlor, with operator stations, sinks, dryers and several men and women in black smocks tending to patrons with hair in varied stages of completion.

A very tall, broad-shouldered woman with long, blond hair that curled down her back hustled over. Her makeup was well done, subtly playing up her deep brown eyes and playing down her unfortunately pore-covered skin. "Zack. Great to see you." She threw her arms around his neck and gave him a smacking kiss on the lips. "Long time . . ."

"Long time, Bev. How the hell are you?"

"I'm great and business is booming." Her attention turned to Marcy. "Hi. As you gathered I'm Bev." She unwrapped her arms from around Zack's neck and extended her hand.

"Marcy." When she shook Bev's hand, she felt an unusually strong grip and a small tug of jealousy.

Bev turned back to Zack. "What's up, lover?"

"Marcy here's looking to improve her image and I know you can help. She needs a few pointers on makeup and maybe some advice on her hair."

"Love to Zack, darling." She grabbed Marcy's hand, almost dragged her to a station and pushed her into the seat in front of a wall of mirrors. Bev pulled the barrette from her hair, fluffed it around her face, then pulled it onto the top of her head, studying Marcy's face from several angles. "You must be Jenna's sister. You have the same great bones and those wonderful eyes."

"We're twins."

"Of course you are," Bev said after a moment's hesitation. "But the extra weight softens some of the lines." She turned her face again. "Is this for one of Jenna's theatricals?"

"No, it's just a new look for the world at large," Zack said.

"Okay," Bev said, turning, fluffing and staring. Marcy felt like a particularly interesting insect under Bev's microscope. "Not the same style as Jenna, of course," she mumbled, "and . . . Well, let me show you a few possibilities." She hustled toward the back of the salon and disappeared through a pink curtain.

Zack leaned down and whispered, "Bev has a great eye, but you don't have to agree with anything she says if you don't like it. Just keep an open mind. Okay?"

"Okay."

"Oh, and don't be too shocked," he whispered. "Bev's a guy. This store caters not only to the theater trade, but to transsexuals, transvestites and like that."

Marcy was shocked, but only for a moment. After all, she'd had to get used to a tremendous amount in the past few months, so she decided to look on this as just another step.

Bev returned with several wigs in her hands. His hands. *Oh, hell*, Marcy thought. *Just go with it.* "Jenna and Chloe use this place often," Zack said. "Bev's a genius at creating different personas."

Bev's blush was clearly visible even through her heavy makeup. As she got near, Marcy took a closer look and could see the trace of five o'clock shadow on her—his—cheeks.

Bev dropped the wigs on the counter and took a rubber skullcap from a cabinet. She put it on Marcy's head and tucked all her hair beneath it. Then she carefully arranged an auburn wig with shoulder-length, stick-straight strands on Marcy's head. She combed the bangs with her fingers, and pulled the hair so it curved beneath her chin. "My first choice," Bev said.

Marcy gazed at herself. The color was gorgeous, bringing out the gray in her eyes and the style played down her pudgy cheeks. She just stared.

"Nice?" Zack said.

"It's lovely, but it doesn't look like me."

"Do you want to look like 'you'?" Zack asked. "Isn't it time to be someone else for a change?"

She studied her face so intently that she could barely get words out of her mouth. "Someone else?"

Zack pointed to the woman in the mirror. "That's a woman who's got a date tomorrow evening."

Bev yanked the wig from her head and replaced it with a dark brown one with short, ear-length waves. "I like the color of the first one," Bev said, "but I'm not sure about the style."

For almost half an hour Bev arranged and rearranged wigs on Marcy's head, until her brain was whirling. Zack had settled into a chair just behind her right shoulder, and he and Bev kept up a running commentary while peering at her in the mirror. "I still like this first one," Bev said, putting the auburn wig back on Marcy's head.

"Me too," Zack agreed. "What about you, Marcy?"

She considered. "I guess this is the one I like best, too," she mumbled, "but I'm not looking for a wig."

"Of course not," Bev said. "I'm sorry. I guess I just got so carried away that I forgot that you didn't necessarily know how we work here. We sell wigs, and rent them to folks like Jenna for theatricals and masquerades." She winked at Zack. "But we also specialize in makeovers. I've had lots of training and practice, first on friends, then through lots of courses."

"I can imagine," Marcy said, a dry note in her voice.

Bev laughed. "Of course you can." She winked at Marcy in

the mirror. "I didn't intend to sell you a wig. This is the way I try on lots of different looks so you can see how you'd look. Now that we all agree, I can do a quick cut and color for you and have you out of here by dinnertime."

New cut and color? "I don't know whether I want to do something this drastic and this permanent," she said, gazing at herself in the mirror. She did like what she saw. She was no longer little Marcy from Seneca Falls. She was seeing Marcy, city girl, dating, sipping wine. It was tempting, but so scary. "I mean different color and all. I was just thinking about a new style, something not too, you know, noticeable."

"I can use a great coloring product that will wash out in a few weeks if you're really not sure." She cocked her head to one side and they caught each other's eye in the mirror. "It will really change your look."

"Well . . ." Could she really do this? She did like the wig and she loved what it did to her face.

"I'll also show you how to do your makeup to compliment this new style and recommend some specific products. We don't sell anything like that here, but I can give you the names of several beauty supply houses right in the area."

"Well . . ."

Zack stood. "I'll leave you two together. You're going to do it, aren't you?"

Was she? Of course she was. "Well . . . I guess."

Zack leaned over and kissed Marcy on the forehead. "Good girl. Keep this in mind: It's not how you look, but how you feel about yourself, and I can see the change in you immediately." He headed for the door. "I've got to run, but I'm leaving you in good hands."

"Isn't he just the nicest guy?" She sighed as Zack closed the door behind him. "What a waste."

"Waste?"

"He's into girls." She winked again, then touched her crotch. "Wrong plumbing."

Marcy had almost forgotten that Bev was a guy. She burst out laughing. What the hell did it all matter? She was going to get a new look.

It took several hours for Bev to cut and color her hair, then she spent another hour showing Marcy how to properly apply light foundation, shadow, liner and mascara to enlarge her eyes and bring out their color, blush to highlight her cheekbones and slenderize her cheeks and lipstick to create a well-shaped mouth. Then she subtly altered the look with a few stronger colors. "For evening wear," she explained. Marcy made lists of which products to buy, and, with Bev's help, sketched an outline of her face and arrowed and shaded so she'd remember which colors went where.

She'd been so caught up in the whirlwind that was Bev that she hadn't really taken time to look at the whole effect. Finally, when Bev finished brushing her new auburn hair, Marcy stared in the mirror, trying to see herself as others might see her. She was still fat. Well, heavy. But when she looked in the mirror she saw an attractive woman, not a blob. Zack was right. It was the new look, but it was also the confidence she saw in the mirror. Confidence? Was that her? Maybe right now, but what about later, tomorrow, whenever? Could she keep the attitude that was as much a part of the attractiveness as the makeup and hair? Well, she thought, she could try.

She looked at her watch. Five-thirty. She could certainly catch Jenna before her seven o'clock client. And Zack. Was she ready? She settled the charges with Bev, then stood and hugged her—or him. "You're fabulous and I can't thank you enough."

"Sweetie, the look on your face is reward enough." She held up the charge receipt Marcy had signed. "And this, of course. Say hello to Jenna and Chloe for me. They're good customers, whatever it is they do."

"I will, and thanks again."

She walked down Third Avenue and found the beauty supply store Bev had suggested. Almost a hundred dollars later she continued south toward Fifty-fifth.

She didn't have a key to the brownstone and the door was always carefully locked and alarmed, so she rang the doorbell when she arrived. Zack opened the door and stared for a moment, then beamed. "I knew Bev could do it, and I knew you were something pretty special for her to work with. You look wonderful. Congratulations."

She couldn't keep her knees from weakening at the look in his bedroom eyes. It was more than appreciative. There was a spark of interest. No, couldn't be. This is a man who loves women and that's all. "Thanks. She's just fabulous."

"If she can do what she does for herself and all her friends, I knew she'd be perfect for you. Let's see what Jenna thinks." He called, "Jenna!"

She came down the stairs, looked curiously, then stopped and stared. "Marcy? You look . . . Well, wow." She ran up and hugged her sister.

"It's all right?" Marcy said, her voice barely audible, tears threatening to ruin all her new makeup. She blinked hard several times as she hugged Jenna.

"It's amazing," Jenna said. "You look twenty pounds slimmer and . . . well, and everything. Great. A whole new you." She pushed her sister away, her eyes wandering down her body. "Now you need a wardrobe. Tomorrow. You, me, the island of Manhattan and a fat credit card." Her grin almost split her face. "So many stores and so little time."

"I know you're leaving Sunday, and tomorrow's shopping for you and your sister," Zack said, hesitating and lowering his voice a notch. "Can we have lunch on Saturday? Just the two of us?"

Just the two of us? What did he want? Whatever it was she was eager to see him again. "Sure. I'd like that. If only to say thanks for everything you did for me today."

Several minutes later Chloe arrived and was just as surprised and delighted as Jenna had been. "Chloe," Jenna said, "lunch tomorrow, then shopping for the new Marcy. Yes?"

"I wouldn't miss it." Chloe hugged her almost as hard as Jenna had. "You look sensational. Can't you stay a little longer? I've really enjoyed having you here and I know Jenna is going to be so sorry to see you go."

"I wish I could stay," Marcy said, genuinely saddened at her impending departure. "Work calls Monday morning, however."

"Fuck work," Chloe said.

"I wish I could," Marcy lamented.

"Okay. Let's not get into a downer. We'll take all day tomorrow to play," Jenna said.

The following afternoon, Jenna, Chloe and Marcy visited three department stores, a few boutiques and several hole-in-the-wall discount shops. Although both of the other women tried to convince her to buy a completely new wardrobe, Marcy decided to limit herself to only two outfits, one for Steve that evening, and one for Zack on Saturday. She found what she wanted quickly, but the other two women kept searching. Every time she was talked into trying on another outfit, although it might be becoming and was priced within her range, she resisted. After all, what would happen when Cinderella went back to Seneca Falls and turned back into a scullery maid. "Not yet," she kept saying. "What I've got is fine for now."

Almost breathless from their jaunt around the city, the three women got ready to go their separate ways late in the afternoon. Jenna and Chloe were going to the brownstone and Marcy—now dressed in a pair of full, beige cotton slacks and a flowing, floral top in shades of rose and moss with beige mid-height pumps that matched her new beige leather purse—was heading to Jenna's apartment to get ready to meet Steve. As she held out her hand to flag down a cab, Jenna said, "Have a great time tonight."

"Tonight?"

"Your date."

Marcy was flabbergasted. "How did you know that I had a date?"

"Come on, Marce," Jenna said, looking at her sister indulgently. "I'm your sister. Anyway, women don't go through what you've been through these last two days just for the hell of it. It has to be a date and I understand your desire to keep it private, at least for now. I hope you'll tell me all about it when I get home, or in the morning. But I'll understand if you don't want to."

Relieved and a bit disappointed that her secret was out, Marcy nodded. "It's not really private any more. I just didn't want you to worry or anything. I love you, Sis, and I can't wait to tell you about everything."

She had arranged to meet Steve at Heidi's Brauhouse, the German restaurant he'd raved about in the East Sixties. As she walked in just after seven she saw that he'd already gotten a table off to one side of the crowded room. The restaurant was decorated to resemble the courtyard of a small German town, with flower boxes in the windows painted on the walls and a well-executed image of a man in lederhosen playing an accordion on the door to the kitchen. Lilting German music filled the room. She inhaled, taking in the smell of the place, rich with the aroma of German spices and beer. As she maneuvered between tables, she saw Steve glance at her, then return his gaze to the door. He didn't recognize her, she realized. It was both scary and delicious.

Marcy slipped into the chair opposite Steve, and, as he turned toward her, his expression was priceless. "Holy . . ." he said, his eyes widening. "You look terrific." They'd never actually spoken about her looks and she had the feeling that he accepted her as ordinary looking. Well, she'd changed all that and the look on Steve's face was worth ten times what it had cost her. A hundred times.

When asked what she'd like to drink, Steve suggested a wine called a Gewürztraminer, she agreed to try it. Since she realized the name meant spice dream, she wasn't surprised when the wine had a strange tangy flavor.

"You might not know it," Steve said, "but Germany makes virtually no red wine. To accompany big, strong-tasting, red meat dishes they needed to create something bigger than an ordinary white wine, and voilà, the gewürz was born."

When the waiter asked for their dinner selections, Marcy told Steve she liked almost everything and asked him to order for her. He selected something called a rouladen, a thin beef steak wrapped around a filling of bacon, bread crumbs and onion, which came served with spaetzle and red cabbage for her. He ordered the restaurant's famous sauerbraten for himself, and, as they ate, they talked about nothing specific. When she was halfway through her rouladen, Steve suggested they switch plates so she could taste his meal. She had thought her dish was superb, but his was even better. The food was fabulous.

Later, as they sat over coffee and apple strudel, Steve reached across the table and laid his hand on hers. "I'm really sorry that you're leaving on Sunday and doubly sad that I can't see you tomorrow evening." He'd already told her that he had a prior commitment that he couldn't change. "I think we have something that might go somewhere."

"I'm sorry too," she said, knowing it was true. Steve was a truly nice man and the first one she'd felt this close to in many years. Except Zack, of course, but that was totally different. "I'll be back," she said, "and I promise that I'll call you. I'm planning on being here quite a bit more often than I have in the past. Maybe every few months. And we can talk on the phone from time to time."

She watched his shoulders lift in a long sigh. "That will have to do, but I don't believe that long-distance relationships fare well in the long run."

"Let's not dwell on the future. This strudel is too good to waste with regrets."

His smile seemed a bit forced. "It certainly is."

They left the restaurant an hour later, both a bit sad. He kissed her lightly on the cheek, then he helped her into a cab. As the taxi pulled away she wondered what it might have been like if they'd really kissed. She thought about Zack's kiss the day before and sighed. She and Zack were having lunch the following afternoon, "just the two of them," and she found she was looking forward to it immensely.

The following morning Jenna arrived in the kitchen just after ten. Pouring coffee into her Garfield mug, she said, "Okay, so give."

"You mean about last evening?"

With an exaggerated exasperation in her voice, Jenna said, "Yes, about last evening." She paused. "That is if you want to talk about it."

Marcy couldn't suppress a grin. "Of course I do. It all began when I met a guy last weekend at that little place on Fifth, George's Bistro. Remember?"

"I remember. Stop stalling."

Marcy laughed. She loved watching Jenna pry information out of her. "I stopped in for dinner and when the waiter asked what I wanted to drink he suggested a wine. We ended up eating together."

"And . . ."

"Steve, that's his name, Steve eats there almost every night, so on Wednesday I went there again and we had another nice dinner together."

"And . . ."

"He asked me to meet him at Heidi's Brauhaus in Yorkville and I did, last evening. We had great German food. I had something called—"

Jenna interrupted. "I don't want to hear about the food. Tell me about the guy."

Jenna kept silent as Marcy told her sister what she knew about Steve. "He's really nice."

"Sounds like it," Jenna said. "Are you seeing him again?"

"Sadly, no. He's got something tonight and I'm off tomorrow so this is probably it." Although she'd told him she'd be back.

"Something tonight? Another woman? He's probably got someone else and you're just a quick fling. How was the sex?"

"Sex? There was no sex. Jenna, stop it. Now," Marcy said, her voice rising. "I'm not a quick fling or anything else to him and whether he's got another woman, or a string of them for that matter, I don't really care. We had a few really enjoyable dinners together and that's that. Maybe we'll talk on the phone occasionally when I'm back home, maybe not. He's good company and he made me feel good about myself."

Jenna took her sister's hands. "I'm so sorry, Sis. Truce. You're right. I guess I get a bit protective. After all, I'm the city girl now and there are a lot of guys who just want a quick roll in the hay."

"You've got a bit of a jaundiced eye, Sis," Marcy said, trying to take what Jenna had said at face value.

"Maybe, but you're a bit out of your league here. I think you should start slowly."

"I'm not some little hick from Hicksville," Marcy said, a bit annoyed at her sister's attitude. "After all, I am older, and I'd hope wiser. I don't go to bed with every man I meet, even after our third dinner together. But, if I want to, I will." Here she was defending her right to have sex with any man she met.

"You're older by ninety-five seconds, and I certainly don't

advocate going to bed with every Tom, Dick and Steve you meet. Part of me was being overly protective while another part was just hoping."

"Hoping what?"

"Hoping you'd find some nice guy to play with. You're still a bit tight-assed about sex."

She felt her anger rising. "Tight-assed? You make me sound like some kind of prude and I'm not. I just don't believe in having sex with any and every guy who comes along." Now she was defending her right not to have sex. This was getting much too convoluted.

"I'm sorry. This is getting a bit heated and that's not what I intended at all." Jenna moved behind her sister and hugged her shoulders. "I just wish you the joys of a good, intimate relationship. You don't have to do it with everyone, but sex is fun. It's a blast, and I hate to see you not enjoying what I enjoy. You look so fabulous now and I want you to make the most of the new you. I want you to spread your new wings and indulge yourself in whatever's out there. Life's so short; we only go around once. I'm just afraid you'll regret things you didn't do." She held her hand up to keep her sister from interrupting. "I know. You're you and I'm me and that's fine. Please. Truce. I don't want to fight with you."

Marcy took a deep breath and released her stomach muscles. "I don't want to fight with you either. Truce." Jenna would make her crazy if she wasn't careful. But she did have a point. Marcy realized that she hadn't had sex in over a year, and even then it hadn't been very good, nor did the guy make another date with her. She didn't care about that though. Sex wasn't important to her. She was content the way she was. Wasn't she?

"Okay," Jenna said. "What do you want to do this afternoon? It's your last one here, after all."

Oops. "Zack asked me to have lunch with him."

"Great. Where are we meeting?"

Marcy was sure her blush told the tale. "Actually, he mentioned just the two of us."

Jenna looked startled, then her expression warmed. "That's wonderful. Zack's the greatest and he's been a lifesaver this week."

"You're not mad?"

"Listen, Marce. We're not joined at the hip. I've had my personal stuff to do this week and I'm glad you've got your own things, too. Have a blast. Just remember, he's a professional just like I am so don't get your hopes up." She winked.

"It's not like that," Marcy said, totally frustrated by her sister's attitude. First she was a babe in the woods, then she was going to succumb to Zack's sexual wiles. "I don't know what he wants, but I'm sure it's completely innocent."

"Well, I, for one, hope it isn't."

What did Zack want? What did she want?

They had arranged to meet at a nearby delicatessen and when Marcy arrived she saw Zack already seated in a corner. He was wearing a pair of khaki jeans with a white polo shirt with a small logo on the pocket. When Zack saw her, his face lit up. She knew he loved women, but was she something a bit more special? As always, the sight of him left her heart beating just a bit faster. "Hi," she said as she walked to the table.

"I can't get over how fabulous you look." As she started to sit, he said, "Wait. Just stand there for a moment. I want to get a good look at the new you." He stared for a full minute, taking in everything from her new makeup and hair to her new outfit, a pair of soft, navy slacks with a loose navy-and-white-patterned top with handkerchief points. As his face showed his appreciation she was glad she taken care with herself. Now she wondered whether she should have gotten the third blouse she'd seen, pale blue cotton with long sleeves and a mandarin collar. The person she saw in Zack's eyes was attractive and she loved the feeling it gave her. Finally he nodded and she took a seat across from him.

"I just can't get over the change in you. Not that you didn't look good before . . ."

"Stop stumbling over words," Marcy said. "I know what you mean and thanks for the compliments."

His face relaxed. "I'm glad you came. I was afraid Jenna would talk you out of it."

"Talk me out of it? Why would she do that?"

He sighed. "I am what I am and it's probably not what she wants for her sister. She's very protective where you're concerned."

"Zack, this is getting awfully complicated. Maybe we need to clear the air here." She giggled. "I feel like some old-fashioned father asking what your intentions are, but that's sort of what I need to know."

"I'm not usually blunt, but you asked. I like you a lot. I also think there's a hot, sexy woman inside of you, and I find myself wanting to teach you all the wonderful things that good sex can be." His eyes never left hers. "I don't want to embarrass you, but I think I know what's there, even if you don't, and I want to be the one who opens up the shell and finds the pearl inside."

Marcy was speechless, her heart pounding. She'd fantasized something like this, but never in a million years expected it to happen. He was propositioning her, and more. Impossible. Yet here he was, saying it right out. Zack, the professional lover and Marcy, who wasn't sure she'd ever had an orgasm. Ridiculous. She looked down, suddenly wondering whether it was still her, the same person she'd been yesterday, but she knew she was. She was just slightly better wrapped.

Zack continued. "I see you today, more open to the world than you've been in a very long time. You look wonderful and I take some credit for that change. Now I want to take you further." He leaned back. "Phew, I really didn't expect to say that much, but you asked me to be honest."

"This is so silly," Marcy said, trying to gather her roiling thoughts and emotions. "You can't mean all that. Why would you want someone like me?"

"Someone like you?"

Pain almost closed her throat until she could barely get the words out. "Let's be honest here. I'm a small-town, unsophisticated girl with little experience with lovers, especially with a professional like you. You want to open me up and find a pearl. I'm afraid there's no pearl inside. Just me." She touched the front of her blouse. "This is all window dressing. You can put new clothes on a cow, but she's still a cow." She was crying now. "All I can think of is that you want Jenna, but you'll settle for me."

"Ouch," Zack said, sounding genuinely angry. "You must really think I'm some kind of louse, like the other guy who did that to you. I want Jenna but I'm asking to make love to you. That's makes me a liar, a cheat and several more things I can't even focus on right now. If that's what you believe I am, then you're right. This is silly."

"That's not what I said," Marcy said, taking a tissue from her purse and wiping her eyes.

"Yes," Zack said, his voice tight, "it is. Maybe I'm a bit fixated on sex, but it's the most fun and the best way to learn our own strengths." He huffed out a breath. "I'm offering you something I know you'll enjoy. You can decide to do whatever you want but don't ever think that I'd lie about that or anything else for that matter." He paused, then continued. "I usually read women pretty well. I think you're curious about what we could do together as well, but you're terrified to find out."

Marcy was saved from having to answer by the arrival of the waiter. "Give us some time," Zack said, and the waiter left. Zack took her hand across the table. "Be as honest with me as I've been with you. Tell me what you're thinking. Feeling."

She took a deep breath. "I can't help thinking that this can't be real. You, who could probably have any woman you want, are asking me. I feel like I'm the wallflower at the party, asked to dance by the best-looking guy there. I look around and wonder whether a bunch of guys got together and dared him to do it."

"You do have quite an imagination." His sexy wink rocked her again. "Maybe you should be a writer." She managed a weak smile. "All I'm asking is that you spend an hour at my place. Let me show you what's possible. Then we can figure things out from there. After all, you're leaving tomorrow and there won't be another chance. Take the plunge. With me."

Again Marcy was speechless. Then she said what leaped to the front of her mind. "Professionally attractive and sexual Zack wants to show the little girl from the sticks what good sex is like. She's leaving town so let's leave her with good memories. Or maybe it's just a conquest to you. Repressed and eager, she'll accept anything." By the time she was finished talking she felt her eyes fill again.

"Phew. Where did you get such a low opinion of me? Or of yourself? Your sister is my friend so I wouldn't and couldn't do anything like what you said. If I've hurt your feelings it was never my intention." He stood up. "Obviously I've made a mess of this so I'll just disappear into the sunset. I'm truly sorry. I think we're both missing out on something that could be really good."

She couldn't let him leave, yet she didn't have a clue how to handle what was happening. "Don't go," she said, and, after a moment's hesitation, he sat back down. "I just don't know what to do now. You're right when you say I'm not experienced. I've had my share of relationships, all pretty short. Last evening with Steve was the first real date I've had in . . . Well, let's not get into how long." She felt tears trickling from the corners of her eyes. "I don't know what to do and I'm scared stiff."

His voice softened and he gazed into her eyes. "I know you are, but real heroes forge onward despite their fears. What's the worst that can happen?"

Marcy didn't want to verbalize it, but then she blurted out, "You'll make love to me and it will be a disaster. You'll think I'm fat and ugly. I'll see it in your face and I'll know it will never be any different with any other man. I want to make a life with a husband and kids and stuff. Maybe not right now, but sometime. This feels like some kind of a test and if I fail, it's the end."

"Shit, Marcy." He sighed, then said, "Okay, let's think about the worst case. You'll take your clothes off and I'll see that you're fat. Will that bother me? I know it won't because looks don't make much of a difference to me, but it will matter to you. What can we do? It's the middle of the day and the sun's shining so that lets out doing it in the dark. How about if I wear a blindfold and we make love that way?"

Through tears, Marcy giggled. "Don't be silly."

"Silly? You're the one who's been asked to spend an afternoon romping in the sack and is putting up all kinds of barriers. Who's silly? Okay, no blindfold. Maybe you can keep your clothes on. I've done it that way and it can be decadent."

"You're being stupid."

"First I'm silly, now stupid." He grinned that irresistible little boy grin. "My ego's taking quite a beating here."

"I didn't mean it like that."

Zack put his index finger under Marcy's chin so she was forced to look into his eyes. "I want you. I know what you looked like yesterday and I wanted you then. I'm not proclaiming undying love, just a little lust around the edges. I'm asking for one afternoon of trust from you. No more. Can I have that?"

The moment of decision. She wanted it so much. Risk? Enormous. Reward? Likewise enormous if everything went well. She took a deep breath. "Yes," she said, softly.

Chapter
9

His grin was like a light going on. Zack quickly grabbed her hand, dropped several bills on the table even though they'd eaten nothing, and almost dragged her out of the restaurant. "Before you change your mind," he said as they emerged into the ninety-degree heat of New York in July.

Barely aware of her surroundings, Marcy followed Zack for three blocks to his apartment building. It was an older, multistory, red brick building and, wordless, he led her into the elevator and up to the seventeenth floor. Still silent, he unlocked the front door and with a palm at her lower back, ushered her inside. With only a thin layer of silk between his hand and her skin, his heat was like a brand.

She swallowed hard trying to control her emotions, and looked around. His apartment was as much a surprise as the rest of him. The living room was done in pale shades of blue and gold, with a deeply cushioned sofa, several overstuffed side chairs and a chess table against one wall. The large windows looked out over the city, but when she saw his eyes as he smiled at her, she barely noticed the view.

Her heart was pounding and her fingers tangled in the fabric of her slacks, folding and unfolding a bit of the cloth. She'd been almost incapable of thought since they left the restaurant and now she found she was rapidly losing her nerve. Standing just inside of Zack's living room, beside a small player piano, she started to turn back toward the door. Why was she doing this? It could only lead to pain. So much pain. He'd be totally turned off by her lack of experience and artistry and, what would be worse, he'd be unable to hide it. She'd see that disappointed look in his eyes. She'd seen it before.

Maybe she was incapable of good sex. There were women who just didn't have it in them and she might be one of those. Had she ever had a real, earth shattering orgasm? Not that she remembered. She thought about the first story she'd written and took a small step backward, eyes on the floor. She started to tell him she was leaving, and suddenly he was standing in front of her. He lifted her chin with his finger, making her entire body stiffen. Then he kissed her.

Without touching her in any other way, his lips found hers. It wasn't a deep, sensual kiss, just a light meeting of flesh, a teasing, a tempting. His tongue tickled the joining of her lips, so she tentatively let them part. He didn't invade her mouth as she'd expected, but lightly flicked his tongue over her.

"Don't be frightened," he whispered, moving his mouth to her ear. "I won't do anything you won't like. And if anything makes you uncomfortable and you want to stop, just hold up your hand. You don't even have to say anything. Just touch me on the shoulder with your palm like this." He placed her hand on his shoulder, then lightly nipped at her earlobe. Then he moved away, leaving her hand where it was. "See? If you'd touched me like that I'd have pulled away. Do you want me to stop?"

Slowly, she pulled her hand from his shoulder. God, she didn't want him to stop. When he lifted her fingers and kissed the back of each one she trembled, almost unable to keep on her feet. He took her hand and placed it on his shirtfront. "I'll stop any time, I promise."

"Why?" Through her sensual haze it still plagued her. "Why?"

"Why do I want you? Because I just do. I want to spend some time having fun with you, making love with you. That's it, that's all the reason I need. I don't spend hours investigating my motives; sometimes I just do what I know will feel good. And I know this will feel good." Zack's voice got firmer as he stared into her eyes. "Maybe it's time you stopped looking for reasons to say no, when you and I both know you want to say yes. You made the decision when you said yes in the restaurant and now you're second-guessing yourself yet again." He took a deep breath. "It's time to fish or cut bait, Marcy. Right now." His arms dropped to his sides. "What do you want?"

Could she have sex the way he did, just for fun? She wanted it and finally admitted to herself that she was being silly. There was risk but with any luck the reward would be worth it. Slowly, she smiled. "You. I want you. I'm just scared you'll be disappointed. You seem to feel that I'm capable of becoming a great lover. What if I'm not?"

"Let me worry about that. I think I know you, maybe better than you know yourself." He cupped her face with his palms. "Let me do this." When his lips found hers again, and his hand slid up her back to press her chest lightly against his, she finally just let go.

When she allowed herself to relax, she opened her senses. His scent was masculine, with a hint of a light, spicy aftershave. Beneath her hands his body was hard, the muscles of his shoulders and upper arms well defined. She found her hands gliding over his shirt to experience the cords and hollows of his chest and back, then her fingers found the back of his neck and tangled in his long, soft hair.

When she became aware that he was just standing, letting her touch him, she became embarrassed. "Don't stop," he purred. "I love the feel of your hands on me." He grasped his shirt and yanked it off over his head. His body was gorgeous, smooth, tanned, six-pack abs, the kind you see in the commercials for workout equipment on TV.

"You must work very hard at being this beautiful." She blushed at her use of the word beautiful. This was all so like her fantasy but, of course, he was used to fulfilling fantasies. It was just that he didn't know it was hers.

"I have a weight bench and a treadmill in my second bedroom and I use them frequently. I love it when a sexy women looks at me the way you are doing right now."

She laughed. "Egotist."

"Guilty." He combed his fingers through her hair. "I love this color. It brightens you, brings your face to life." He kissed her again, a deep, penetrating kiss that pulsed through her and turned her blood to lava. She had never before felt this depth of desire. Ever.

Barely allowing their mouths to separate his hands found the buttons on the front of her blouse and, one by one, they opened for him. Soon he was drawing the warm fabric down over her arms. Momentarily she resisted, then let him remove it. She couldn't very well make love with her clothes on, nor could she ask him to wear a blindfold. As he stepped back and gazed at her she watched his eyes for the telltale loss of interest. She didn't find it.

"I'm not . . ."

"I know. You're not a Playboy centerfold." He slid his hands over her skin the way she had explored his just a moment before. "You feel satiny smooth." He pushed the straps of her white, cotton bra from her shoulders and lightly kissed the indentations on her shoulders that were such a part of her. *I wish I had bought some sexy undies*, she thought fleetingly. But somehow it didn't matter now.

Then her bra was on the floor and he was holding her oversized breasts. She let her head fall back, tired of analyzing his every move. "Yes, like that," he purred again. "Just let yourself feel." He pulled at her nipples and she felt them contract.

"You like it when I do that." Not a question. He bent and kissed the hollow of her throat, his hands still filled with her. His tongue licked a slow path down her breastbone, then into the valley between her breasts. He rolled her nipples between his thumbs and forefingers. She gasped at the heat knifing through her.

"You like it when I play with your nipples," he purred. "I want to know exactly what else you like."

She remained silent, unable to gather her thoughts, not knowing what she was supposed to say.

"Not sure what you like? Then we'll make it easier. Which do you prefer, this?" He pinched her nipple. "Or this." He pulled on the other. When she remained silent, he said, "You have to tell me or I'll do neither." Again he pinched and pulled.

It was difficult to catch her breath. "Both," she moaned. So like her fantasy, but so real.

"Not the best answer, but it will do for the moment. Okay, next question." He leaned down and took one nipple in his mouth and suckled lightly. "This?" He lightly bit the other. "Or this?"

"Oh, God," she whispered, barely able to stand.

"Which?"

He nipped her again. "That," she moaned. Fantasy and reality were one, here and now.

"Good." As she felt her knees about to buckle, he swept her up and carried her toward the back of the apartment. *How can he do that?* she wondered with the small part of her brain still functioning. She was certainly no lightweight though he carried her to the bedroom as if she weighed nothing, then stood her in the middle of the deep pile carpet and dragged the thick, red-and-gold-striped quilt onto the floor, revealing matching sheets and a flame red blanket. Incapable of movement, she watched him throw back the covers and lift her onto the bed where he quickly removed her slacks and panties. As she tried to pull the covers over her, he stilled her hand. "Don't," he whispered. "Trust me."

She had little choice but to trust him. She watched as he stood beside her and unbuckled his belt and pulled it from its loops. Then he removed his jeans and shorts. As he straightened, she saw that he was fully aroused. "I can't fake that," he said with a grin.

He was beautiful, masculine. She'd read the term "looking like a Greek god" many times in books, never quite believing it. Now she'd seen it. And he was definitely all man. "No," she had to admit breathlessly, "you certainly can't."

He burst out laughing. Right there in the bedroom, at this critical moment, he laughed. "I hope you're feeling a bit stronger now, knowing what you do about my level of interest. You want this, too, don't you?"

She couldn't help but join his exuberance. "Yes. Yes, I guess I do."

"Guess?" He leaned over and pinched her nipple again. "Guess?" He knelt beside the bed and took one nipple in his mouth while he rolled the other between his fingers. "Say it. You want this." When she didn't answer, he said, "Say it or I'll stop."

She didn't want him to stop. "I want this," she murmured.

"Now mean it."

God, she did. "I want this," she said, her voice as strong as she could make it through her haze. "I want you."

"Good girl. Now, how about this?" He stroked her belly, then slipped his fingers into her pubic hair. "Want me to stop?"

"No," she whispered as his fingers found her, wet and hungry.

"You're going to have to keep admitting it," he said. "I want you. You know that. But you have to know that you want it, too, so you'll have to keep saying it."

His fingers were expert, seeming to know exactly where to

stroke, probing her most intimate folds. She felt her hips move on their own, reaching for more of his touch as she struggled for breath. "Here?" he asked as he rubbed the side of her clit. "Or here?" He tapped the tip of her swollen clitoris.

"Oh, God," she moaned. "Everywhere?"

He laughed again. "Okay. I'll take that as a 'both of the above.' "

How could he be so calm, so lightly detached when she was going crazy? She wanted to find a crack in his seemingly invincible armor so she reached down and ran her index finger over his cock. He jerked and stared at her. Had she done the wrong thing? "If you do that, lady, I won't be able to wait and I want to show you how good it can be." He lifted her hand and placed it beside her on the bed. "Let me show you."

Then he climbed onto the bed and knelt between her calves. He rubbed the spot she loved and she groaned. "That," he said, "or this?" His mouth found her. He flicked his tongue over the tip of her clit, then sucked gently until the pressure caused almost unendurable pleasure. He leaned back with a self-satisfied grin. "Or both?"

"God," she moaned, unable to keep her hips still. "Whatever you want. It's all so good." She was panting like she'd run a mile and she could hear her pulse thumping in her ears. His mouth found her again and sucked while his finger probed, exploring her opening and sliding inside. One, two, three fingers filled her and she reached for something she'd never felt before—and found it.

Her climax broke her into tiny pieces. Then reassembled and exploded again. "Oh, God, God, God," she cried. "Yes. Do it. Do it. Do it."

He left her and she tried to collect the shattered pieces of her psyche. She heard him open a foil packet, then, moments later, he was straddling her, his erect penis probing for her opening, finding it and sliding inside. It happened again as he thrust. Colors swirled and she grabbed for him to hold on for dear life lest she be lost in the maelstrom. She wrapped her arms around his shoulders and her legs around his waist and showed him with her body how deep she wanted him. And he was there, deeper, harder, sweeter. Her movements complimented his as he pounded, then arched his back and roared his orgasm.

"I must be crushing you," he said moments later. He rolled over and pulled the sheet over their sweat-drenched bodies and lay beside her as they both tried to catch their breath. For several minutes there was only the sound of their combined heavy breathing, then he said, "Damn, you're good."

"Me?" she said, totally shocked. "I didn't do anything. You did it all."

"You were perfect. Receptive, responsive, and at the end you were a tiger, taking what you wanted."

Marcy curled against him. He was right to a point. At the end she just wanted, and reacted to that desire. Was that unusual? Of course not. He was just making her feel good. She giggled quietly. He'd made her feel more than good. She thought about the first story she'd written about the woman who wanted to be guaranteed an orgasm. *All you need*, she said to the heroine of the story, *is this man*. He works miracles.

Zack held her close against him. "At this moment, the guy usually asks, 'Was it good for you?' but I guess I don't have to. Your scream said it all."

Scream? "My what?"

"You screamed. Almost destroyed my hearing."

"I didn't."

"You did," he said, laughing. "You must have a bit of a sore throat."

For the first time since their lovemaking she became aware of a tickle in her throat. She had screamed and hadn't even been aware of it. This orgasm stuff was amazing. Amazing. She started to laugh. The joy of it. She sat up and soon was doubled over, and Zack was laughing with her.

"Sex is great, isn't it?" he said when he caught his breath.

"I guess I found out what all the shouting is about."

"It'll make you a better writer." He laughed again. "That's a hell of a reason for making love. Call it research."

She was consumed with laughter again. She'd never realized that sex was such fun. God, it was terrific.

"Marcy," Zack said, suddenly serious. "I wish you'd consider staying in the city for a few more weeks. You could get together with some of the people you couldn't arrange to see this week, and we could see each other often for more"—he waggled his eyebrows—"*research.*"

She couldn't help but ask, "Why?"

"You're impossible. I'm going to answer you for the last time, then I'm never going to do it again. Because I enjoyed it. We enjoyed it. I want to play more with you, show you things. I want you to touch me." Touch him? She didn't know how. He paused. "Don't get that panicked expression. If you don't know where and how to touch, I want to teach you—you're such a quick learner. Every man is different and if you learn from me, you'll be an expert on how to please me. What man could want more than that?"

That grin was almost irresistible, but she had to get back to Seneca Falls. She could take some of her vacation time . . . Maybe later in the summer. She'd be opening herself up to lots of hurt making love with this man, but after what she'd experienced over the last hour . . . What if she fell in love with him? What if her heart got so involved that she couldn't find her way out? On the other hand, what if she never experienced this joy again? "I'll think about it, Zack."

"Try to make sure that's the only thing you think about."

"What do you mean?" she asked, cuddling against him again.

Zack turned on his side and propped himself up on his elbow. He gazed down at her, then threaded his fingers through her hair. "Don't let regrets take you over." He stroked her face. "I can predict what's going to happen. Sometime in the next day or so you're going to think better of this afternoon. What did I do? you'll think. What did I let him do? Then you'll want to hide under a rock back in Seneca Falls and deny all the wonderful feelings we shared today." He leaned down and kissed her. "Don't do that. Please. Wherever you go from here, whatever you do, don't regret what we did. It was wonderful, and something we both wanted. Just remember that."

She kissed him lightly on the lips. "I will. I promise."

She saw him glance at the clock and frown. "Shit," he spat. "I was afraid of that so I almost didn't look. It's almost five and I'm due at the Club at five-thirty."

They'd met at lunchtime Where had the afternoon gone? "Is it that late? I've got to call Jenna. She's probably worried sick."

"I'm sure she knows you're a big girl and can take care of yourself."

Chagrined, Marcy said, "You're right, of course."

"I'm sorry that we can't continue this delightful interlude, but I just don't have the time. Forgive me?" He kissed her again and she could almost taste his regret. Then he pulled away, taking her silence as assent. "Good." He climbed out of bed, gloriously naked. He was so beautiful and without modesty. "I'm going to grab a quick shower and then run out of here. Why don't you call Jenna if you want, then take a leisurely bath and do whatever you had planned for this evening?"

He disappeared through a door to what Marcy assumed was the bathroom. She considered what Zack had said. Regret what they did? No, not a chance. It had been wonderful. But would she hide out in Seneca Falls? That remained to be seen.

She heard the shower start and stretched out on the bed, pulling the sheet back over herself. She was determined not to regret a thing and if little threads of doubt crept into her mind she'd squash them. She had wanted this and it had lived up to, actually surpassed, her expectations. All the encounters she'd had in her dating years couldn't hold a candle to any of this. Was it Zack's talent as a lover? Probably. Was it her readiness to open up and experience? Maybe. Whatever made this afternoon so wonderful, she thought with a grin, it was fun.

Love? No. Nothing that had happened could or would be confused with love in any form. But caring and giving? Of course. It was obvious that Zack cared about giving her pleasure, helping her to enjoy sex to the fullest. She almost giggled. This was what good sex was all about.

Several minutes later, the shower stopped and Zack emerged, still naked, his hair wet and slicked against his head. God, he was so gorgeous that she wanted to jump him and ravish every inch of his amazingly sexy body. With a beautiful economy of movement, he pulled on a forest green polo shirt, briefs and a pair of taupe slacks, then slipped his feet into socks and loafers. "I'm sorry this afternoon has to end like this," he said, leaning down to kiss her lightly.

He smelled of soap and she knew she smelled of sex. "I'm sorry, too." She took a deep breath, then admitted, "It was wonderful."

"It was, wasn't it," he said with that quirky smile that heated her blood. "I'd love to do this again."

"Me too." A lot. A real lot.

"I hope we will. I keep trying not to think about how far away you'll be. Please stay in touch. Leave me your phone number back upstate so I can call sometimes?" It sounded like a question. Was he having doubts about her?

"Of course. And if I forget, you can always get my number from Jenna."

"Great," he said, sounding relieved. "I've gotta dash now." And he was gone.

Marcy replayed the last few moments. It seemed to her as if

Zack was truly sad she was leaving. Well, maybe she'd be back. Maybe sooner than he expected.

Wasn't there a risk, however, that she would magnify what she and Zack had? She'd have to be really careful not to decide this was some kind of predestined love. Nonsense. Good sex and a possible friendship. That was enough.

At home later that evening she booted up Jenna's computer and opened a new document in the word processor. She was still aroused, mentally as well as physically. Her mind was filled with erotic images and this was a great time to put some of them down on paper. She'd been thinking about the elaborate video equipment Jenna had showed her and how they'd fit into a story. As she started to type she laughed at how she seemed to pick names for her characters that all began with the letter *M*.

THE MOVIE

Melinda's husband Hal had found out about the Eros Hotel through a friend and had broached the idea to her several weeks before. "I want to make a porno flick with us as the stars," he said. "Remember I told you about the Eros Hotel? That place Don told me about? Well, they'll do it for us. They'll have someone take the pictures and, when we're done, give us the only copy of the tape to watch over and over." Melinda noticed that his voice trembled with expectation. "It's a bit pricey, but I would really love to do it." He got his patented little boy gleam in his eyes. "Would you do it with me?"

Melinda thought about it. Hal always fancied himself a great lover and he'd been that once. Sadly, in recent months he'd become predictable, but Melinda had learned to be content with it. She'd read books about how to spice up a relationship and nothing she'd read had done much good. Maybe this would be a way to put the spark back into their love life.

"How much?"

She watched Hal take a deep breath. "I talked them down to fifteen hundred, including the tape."

He'd already talked to them. He really did want this, and it might just do the trick. Fifteen hundred dollars, a lot of money; it would be a small price to pay for help in the bedroom. "Not as bad as it might be, and we do have your bonus."

"It was two thousand originally but I told them how much you wanted it." That little boy grin again. God, he handled her, but in this case she wanted to be handled. "I told them it was for your birthday."

"My birthday isn't until April."

"I know that, and you know that, but the lady at the Eros Hotel doesn't know that. Would you do it?"

She sighed and grinned. She loved Hal completely, and she knew he loved her, too. "Sure. I'll give it a try."

Hal beamed. "That's great. I'll set it up."

One evening two weeks later Hal and Melinda arrived at the simple brownstone that housed the Eros Hotel and were admitted by a large man in a plaid shirt and jeans. He checked their names on a list, then guided them to the third floor and into a simple room with a bed, dresser and several chairs. As the man closed the door, a woman stepped out of an alcove on the far side of the room. "Hi. My name's Joyce and I'll be helping you two with the film this evening. I'll do as much or as little as you like."

"What does that mean?" Hal asked.

"Some people want me to just take the pictures and remain totally silent. Others want me to tell them how to arrange for the best shots and still others want me to direct all the action."

"I don't think we need direction," Hal said quickly.

"It might be fun to have someone make things more interesting. You know, do some different stuff," Melinda said.

"You think so?" Hal said.

"Sure."

"Okay, if you want," Hal agreed, reluctantly.

Joyce nodded. "Do you want to play out a little setup? Like you, Melinda, are a hooker who arrives for an hour with a john? Or you're a couple reunited after a long separation? Or would you just to be a couple heading for bed in the evening? Sometimes it's a little awkward figuring out how to begin."

"Get the camera," Hal said. "I'm so turned on now that it's not difficult to begin at all."

Joyce laughed. "Great."

"Why don't we try to slow things down a bit?" Melinda said, looking at Joyce who caught her glance. "Let's make it good for the movie. After all, we don't want only five minutes of film."

Joyce nodded at Melinda. "She's right. Why don't you two begin standing up? Some holding and kissing to begin with."

"You've got the camera?" Hal asked.

"Don't worry about the pictures." Joyce raised her hand and revealed a small, handheld video camera. "There are also several cameras mounted around the room, as well as mikes and such. I control everything from a small remote in my pocket. I'll edit the shots and make you a film you'll really like. I promise." She raised the camera and nodded.

Melinda was a bit daunted by the idea of making love while someone else watched, but if Joyce could get Hal to understand that he needed to do more to excite her before intercourse, it would be worth the embarrassment. Hal put his arms around her and passionately kissed her. Hal had always been a great kisser so Melinda closed her eyes and let herself enjoy the feel of his mouth on hers. Somehow the thought that someone was watching seemed to enhance the pleasure.

Soon they parted and Hal urged her to lie down on the bed. "Why not wait a bit?" Joyce said. "There's no hurry. How about a little dancing?"

"Come on," Hal said. "I didn't sign up for dancing, just for hot sex and a movie."

"Don't be like that, Hal," Melinda said. "I want the movie to be really good, hot and sexy. Why not do things slowly? It will be like in those sexy novels I like to read."

"That stuff isn't real. Lords and stuff. Everyone's really good-looking and all. Real people do real stuff."

"Why don't we just do like Joyce suggests and see what happens?"

Hal didn't look convinced, but he went along. Joyce put some easy-listening music on the radio and Hal wrapped his arms around Melinda and shuffled his feet while Joyce unobtrusively pointed the video camera at them. Melinda was enjoying herself thoroughly and slowly she became aware that Hal wasn't looking as uncomfortable any more. She rested her cheek against his chest and felt the warmth of his skin through his shirt.

"Why don't we unbutton this?" she said, fingering his buttons. Slowly, she slipped the top button from its hole, then several more until she could part the front of his shirt and rest her face against his bare skin. "I love your skin," she said, and she felt him kiss the top of her head. He was still a little stiff, but he was putting up with these preliminaries.

"How about unbuttoning Melinda's blouse, Hal?" Joyce said. "Then you can be skin to skin."

Quickly, Hal opened his wife's blouse and she pulled it off while he removed his shirt. Now only her bra came between her chest and his. "Do you want to play with her breasts while you dance?" Joyce asked.

Wordlessly, Hal cupped her breast and teased her nipple. "I can see it getting larger," Joyce said. "You do that very well."

Melinda felt him relax still more. She raised her face and slid her hand to the back of his neck. Still shuffling their feet, their lips met. The kiss was deep and full, just the way they both liked it.

"I'd like to have some shots of you taking Melinda to bed, Hal," Joyce said.

Slowly they parted, and Hal guided her to the bed and stretched her out on it. Then he pulled his belt from his pants. "Don't rush," Joyce said. "Why don't we get some pictures of your mouth on her breast?"

Hal reached behind Melinda and unhooked her bra, then locked his mouth onto her nipple. "That's not an orange you're sucking," Joyce said. "Be gentle. Take your time. Bite a little, nibble. Let me get some good shots."

For a moment Melinda thought Hal would balk at being given instructions, but she moaned and writhed beneath his hands, trying to encourage him. "Ooh, that looks really good," Joyce said.

Melinda didn't know what was making her hotter, her husband's mouth or Joyce's suggestions. It was so erotic to realize that someone else was directing the action. She watched Hal, but out of the corner of her eye she could see Joyce moving around to get good video of their foreplay. "This is really hot," Hal said. "I never realized making a video would be this sexy."

His hand stroked her breast, then moved lower to brush over her belly. It partly tickled and partly aroused. The tickling kept her from getting too hot too fast. She wanted this slow. Really slow.

Hal took his time. In contrast to his usual style, Hal licked and suckled while stroking her ribs and shoulders. She smoothed her palms over his back, then used her nails to scratch light furrows. She could hear his breath catch, then speed up.

His hand found the crotch of her jeans and he rubbed. She felt Joyce move his hand. "Right there," Joyce purred. "Just like that. The camera loves this. Good. Find her clit through her clothes and make her really hot."

Hal kept rubbing and Melinda found herself growing impatient. What a role reversal, she thought. She took his hand and moved it so he could slide it under the waistband of her jeans. He unsnapped her, then quickly found her wetness and rubbed. "That's really good," Joyce said, continuing to photograph them from every angle. "Maybe you two should be naked now."

It didn't take long for them both to remove the rest of their clothing. Then his fingers continued working their magic between Melinda's legs. "I'm going to use a spotlight," Joyce said. "It will feel a bit warm but just disregard it."

Melinda heard a snap then heat on her wet flesh. "Now lick her pussy," Joyce said. Hal leaned over and his tongue replaced his fingers. "Lean back so I can see your tongue," Joyce said. "Oh, yes, great picture." The tip of his tongue was pushing her closer and closer to climax. Did she want to come this way or with Hal's big cock inside of her? Hell, she didn't care.

"I'm going to come," she yelled, and Hal stopped his licking and moved so the tip of his cock pressed against her opening. "Move this way," Joyce said, obviously positioning Hal's body for a good picture. "Yes, like that. You've got such a great-looking dick. Let me see it slide in and out. Great. Her juices are really flowing."

This woman was making comments about the state of their excitement, and, instead of finding it a turn-off, Melinda was in heaven. This was the kind of sex she'd always wanted. And Hal seemed to be enjoying it, too. He thrust and withdrew, in and out until she was just at the edge of coming. "Now touch her clit. Right there," Joyce said. She must have showed Hal where to touch because his fingers found the exact right spot.

And she came. Hard. "Shit, baby," Hal said. "I can feel you come."

"Now for the come shot. Do you want to come on her belly or breasts?"

"I want to come right where I am," Hal said, barely able to get the words out. "Right. Where. I. Am." With each word a hard thrust, then, with a growl, he came deep inside of her and collapsed on top of her.

Minutes later, Joyce said, "I'll leave you two, do a bit of

video magic, then get the cassette. You can pick it up in the lobby when you're ready."

"That was wonderful," Hal said. "It's never been any better."

"I know."

"We'll have the film. Maybe I can remember what made it so good."

"I'll be sure to remind you," Melinda said, and they both laughed.

———◦———

Chapter
10

"What in the world happened yesterday afternoon?" Jenna asked the following morning over coffee.

"Oh, Jen, I'm so sorry. I should have called you. I hope you didn't worry too much." Marcy popped a lime jelly bean into her mouth.

"Not that, silly. You're a big girl now and I don't worry about you like that. I mean hot sex."

Marcy almost choked on her jelly bean. "Hot sex?"

"You know those ridiculous feelings we sometimes get about each other. Like the night you thought I was being assaulted and you dashed down here all worried. Well, yesterday afternoon I had a vision of you and a really intense orgasm. I've never felt anything like it before."

Marcy felt herself blush to the roots of her hair. "Orgasm?" she squeaked.

"Sorry. I didn't mean to intrude. I just hope the reality was as good as what I felt."

It was silly to play innocent with Jenna. Marcy could only grin. "It was."

"Zack?" She paused. "Sorry. None of my business."

"True," Marcy said. "I'll tell you only this. I might find the time to come back for a while to *research* my book more thoroughly."

"Ahh. Now we're calling it research. Well, I'm all for it. You're welcome anytime you can arrange it, for as long as you'd like to stay. And, purely for research, if you come back, I'll arrange for you to meet some of the other players at Club Fantasy."

"That's exactly what I'll need. I've gotten a handle on some of the inner workings, but I need experiences to flesh out the stories." She giggled. "Flesh out. I can't seem to say anything, or even think anything this morning without it being a double entendre."

Jenna joined her laughter. "Been there, done that." When she calmed, Jenna said, "So when do you think you might come back? Not that I'm pushing you to do that, of course, but I'd love to have you."

"I don't know. Soon, I think."

Jenna leaned forward and took her sister's hand across the kitchen table. "I can't help hoping that this means you've got a bit more understanding of what I do. And maybe a bit more tolerance."

"Hey, Jen," Marcy said, shaking her head. "I haven't judged you. I do understand it." She paused. "I'll admit to being shocked and angry at first at what you'd become, but the more I live with it, the more I do understand. Really." And she did.

"I'm glad, Sis. I was really worried last winter. I thought what had gone wrong between us couldn't be fixed."

"I'll admit that I worried, too. Let me be completely honest. When I thought about writing the book, I was doing it so I could make lots of money and get you out of the business."

With a nod, Jenna said, "I suspected as much."

"That's not where I am now, however. I'm still going to write the book, but I'm doing it for a lot of reasons, not the least of which is to learn. About you, about the Club and about sex. But also, maybe I want to teach in the book, too. Maybe, as a society, we need to be more open about sex and more tolerant about having sex with people just for fun." She couldn't keep the image of Zack from her mind. Sex for fun.

"Bravo, babe. I couldn't agree with you more. I'm really sorry you're leaving today, just when your attitude's been adjusted."

Marcy found she was genuinely sorry she was going home, too. In Seneca Falls she wouldn't see Zack, or Steve, or be a part, even a small part of Club Fantasy. And what about her book? Maybe it had been a ruse, for herself as well as for Jenna, but that didn't mean it hadn't become important. "Maybe I'll come back for a little more time."

Jenna hugged her. "I'd really like that, Marce. I love having you around, even though we can't spend evenings together."

"Yeah," Marcy said, a hint of sarcasm in her voice. "Making you sleep on the sofa, having me poke into your business and get under your feet. I'm sure it's been grand for you."

Jenna took her twin by the shoulders and held her gaze. "I've loved every minute of it. And with your new attitude, if you came back, I wouldn't have to be careful of everything I say for fear of embarrassing you or making you think less of me."

"Think less of you? Don't be silly. I think you're terrific."

"Even if I am a hooker?"

"High-class fulfiller of fantasies."

"Right."

Marcy's brunch with Jenna and Chloe was light and cheerful, but when it came time for her to catch a cab to the airport all three women became morose. "Think about coming back," Chloe said. "We'll miss you." Marcy knew Chloe didn't like good-byes so she wasn't surprised when she bussed both her cheeks and hustled out of the restaurant.

"Okay, let's get a cab to LaGuardia."

"Don't come with me, Jen. I know you probably have things to do to get ready for tonight and I'm fine."

"I do have things, but they can wait."

"I said I'm fine." She tried to blink away the tears. "Really. I hate the airport thing. Just let's say that I'll be back. Sooner rather than later."

Tears filled Jenna's eyes, too. "Promise?"

"Promise."

"Hug Glen for me." She grinned. "I can't wait until our vacation. Two whole weeks, just him and me. Sun, sand and a big old hotel on the Jersey shore."

Marcy knew how much Jenna was looking forward to spending the second half of July alone with Glen away from the business. "You know," she said, when her mind returned to the present, "maybe you shouldn't hug Glen. I might get jealous of the new you. He might not recognize you and forget about me."

"Fat chance." Marcy was wearing the outfit she'd worn for dinner with Steve Friday evening. "He'll be in for a shock, though, that's for sure. Now let me get out of here." She picked up the suitcase she'd bought to bring her new clothes home and rushed out of the restaurant, leaving her sister sitting at the table.

As she entered their favorite local restaurant several evenings later, wearing what she now thought of as her Steve outfit, Marcy saw Glen in their usual booth. His gaze flashed across her as she entered, then returned to the door. Then, looking totally nonplussed, his head snapped back to look at her. She saw him silently say, "Holy Shit" as she crossed the crowded room. He took her by the upper arms and kissed her soundly. "You look amazing. When . . . ? How . . . ?

"I can't get over the change in you, Marcy. You look great."

"Still fat," she said, self-deprecatingly.

"Stop that," Glen said, a hint of annoyance in his voice. "Can't you just feel good about it?"

She sighed. "I guess I've been fat for so long that it's difficult for me to come to terms with looking okay."

"You look more than okay. You look alive, attractive, sexy even. And this is from the man who's engaged to your sister."

"Thanks, Glen. Sadly, feeling good on the inside is a lot more difficult than changing the outside. But I'm working on it."

He kept shaking his head and gazing at her. "It's amazing. Sorry, I guess I'm staring. How was your trip and what finally got you to do all this?"

They spent the next half hour talking about Jenna, the Club and life in New York. When she tried to gloss over her makeover, Glen pressed her for details. She told him about Bev and all the fun she'd had shopping. She didn't mention Zack. "I'm thinking of spending more time there," Marcy said.

"In the city? With Jenna? I think that would be a fine idea. When?"

Marcy had done a lot of thinking about that. She knew that Jenna and Glen would be gone for the last two weeks in July. Chloe had reluctantly agreed to handle the business during Jenna's absence and, fortunately, Rock would be back as well. "I was thinking of giving her a week to get back in harness, so to speak, after your vacation, then going down for a few weeks in August."

"Sounds great." He got serious. "How's she doing, really?"

"She's great, but missing you. She's really looking forward to your trip. She sighs and looks dreamy every time she talks about it. 'Sun, fun and games' she calls it."

"Games." He leaned back in his chair. "I look forward to that, too. I love her so much, but it all scares me."

Marcy stared at him, puzzled. "Scares you?"

"Yeah. I guess it always has. She's a pro, you know, and I'm just a guy. What the hell do I know about pleasing someone who's done everything?"

Marcy was shocked. She'd always thought that Glen had accepted everything about Jenna and was taking it all in stride. "You're not serious, are you?"

"Yeah," he said, softly. "I am. She does more in a week than I've done in my lifetime. How can I keep her happy?" He rested his elbows on the table. "I'm scared to death, Marcy."

Marcy thought about her reaction to making love with Zack. He was a pro, too, and she'd been having the same feelings. He said he wanted to teach her and, lord knows, she wanted to learn. But what about when he got tired of being a tutor. *Stop*, she told herself. *You've just begun to look at sex as fun. He's like a toy for me as I am to him.* But what about going further, as Glen and Jenna had? Love complicated everything. Could Jenna be happy with a smaller life? Could Zack? "Love is a whole new adventure," she said. "Sex can be fun for sex's sake, but Jenna loves you and that makes it totally different. She's not looking for adventures in bed with you. She's just looking forward to being with you, both in bed and between times."

He scrubbed his face with his hands. "I hope so. I really hope so. God, Marce, I love her so much. I'm willing to let her be what she is and where she is now, but what about the long run? Is she ever going to be willing to settle down here and have kids?"

"Of course she will."

"I wish I were that sure. We've talked about it endlessly. I love being a lawyer and I've got a practice here. I can't move to New York and be the husband of a woman who runs a bordello. I've weighed that against my love for her and I just can't. And I don't know whether she'd ever be totally happy living back here in Smallville."

"Be patient, Glen. Give her some time and I'm sure she'll do the right thing."

"What if the right thing isn't me?"

Marcy sipped her water. She didn't know the answer to Glen's question, any more than he did. *What if the person you love is in a totally different place from you, mentally? What about Zack? Stop it. You've known the guy for less than a week. Stop carving your entwined initials on trees.*

Tuesday of the following week Marcy sat across the desk from Ms. Henshaw, the human resources director for AAJ. "I'll never understand you Bryant girls," she said. The word *girls* set Marcy's teeth on edge, but she kept her face impassive. "First your sister, now you."

"I'm not asking for a long leave, just a few weeks. I've got the vacation days saved up and I want to take the last three weeks of August off." She could always return early but she wanted to take some serious time to get to know Jenna, Zack and herself. Exploration. And, she smiled as she thought the word, *research.*

"That's a difficult time," Ms. Henshaw said. "Lots of people are on vacation then."

Why was she guarding AAJ like this? Marcy wondered. She's just doing her job and trying to increase productivity. Ugh. "Actually, it's a good time, for just that reason. Business will be slow and my services won't be missed as much. I'm sure Paula Galloway can handle anything while I'm away, and if, in an emergency, you need documents translated, you can e-mail or fax me and I'll be happy to do what I can." Paula had replaced Jenna and was a delightful woman with a great ear for languages. She usually did the running translations for meetings and phone conversations while Marcy worked with the intricacies of document translations.

"Well," Ms. Henshaw said, "as long as you're going to return I'll try to make it happen. Not like your sister, of course. We were very disappointed when she didn't come back to work when her leave of absence was up."

Marcy remained silent. How could AAJ hire someone with

so little understanding of people to do Ms. Henshaw's job? *Lady,* she thought, *you can't hope to win my undying loyalty by criticizing my sister.* But she needed this vacation and she couldn't risk alienating the powers that be. "I'm certainly planning to return, Ms. Henshaw, and Jenna's quite happy where she is. Actually, she's earning quite a bit more than she ever did here." She couldn't resist the jab and could almost see Ms. Henshaw harumph.

"Well, I'm happy for her." The words came out between gritted teeth. Jenna's loss had been difficult for the company and it had taken almost nine months to find Paula. Ms. Henshaw's smile was wooden. "I think it will be all right. Just give me a few days to get the paperwork in order and check with Paula. And next time you speak to her, say hello to your sister for us all."

She really wanted to tell this woman to take the job and shove it, but fortunately she usually didn't have any dealings with her. Marcy stood and smoothed her full, calf-length, black skirt and straightened her black blouse. As she left Ms. Henshaw's office, she caught a glimpse of herself in a hallway mirror and straightened her spine. She'd slipped backwards. She was wearing her usual outfit and no makeup. Her posture had regressed and she saw that she was slouching. The only trace of her visit to Manhattan was her hair, but she'd pulled the fading auburn strands back into her usual barrette at the back of her neck. Why? She stood and studied herself. *Am I the same person I was before I left? Or the same one who came back from New York City?*

That evening after work she prowled the mall and finally entered a small boutique called "The Full Figured Woman." She'd always shied away from this particular store because she felt, if she tried something on, she'd look like someone had tried to gift wrap a piano. Now, since she'd been shopping with Jenna and Chloe she found herself more willing to take a few chances. She wandered between the racks dreading the usual "Can I help you?" from the *de rigeur,* seventeen-year-old, anorexic sales girl.

"Can I help you?" She turned, expecting some high-school fluff trying to earn extra money over the summer. She was surprised to see a very large woman wearing a neat, navy blue, tailored skirt with a bright red, man-tailored, silk shirt and a navy-and-red patterned scarf tied around her large hips.

"I'm just looking," Marcy said, trying not to stare. The sales lady probably weighed fifty pounds more than she did, but she looked trim and professional. She didn't hide her weight, but neither did she allow it to rule her wardrobe.

"Take your time and call me if you need anything. My name's Jo. The try-on room is in the back, in case you find something." She pointed to a door behind a rack of panties and bras. "The more professional outfits are on this side, the casual over there."

Marcy wandered for quite a while. She usually shopped in one of the big anchor department stores and pretty much bought the same things over and over but now she was ready to experiment. Here were racks of pastel blouses, tailored slacks, dresses with waistlines and even bathing suits. For fat ladies.

She selected a few summery blouses and two pair of loosely fitted slacks and walked to the back of the store. The try-on room surprised her. The stalls were bigger than those she was used to, with lots of hooks to hang her choices on. She had expected the rooms to be a bit darker, with a minimum number of mirrors. After all, what fat lady wanted to see herself reflected seven times? This one, however, was brightly lit, with walls now covered with her reflection, dressed in her usual black.

She thought about her two New York City outfits, now hanging in her closet. She had liked the way she had looked in them and tried to fix that in her mind. Since her dinner with Glen she'd been backsliding and she didn't want that. It was time to change her image for good. She put on a pink shirt with a slender row of ruffles down the front. Ruffles? With her oversized bosom? She slipped on a pair of coffee, linen slacks and walked out to where she could move around and see herself.

"You can tuck that in, you know," Jo said.

"I don't think so." Both the outfits she'd bought had big, blousey tops made to be worn over the waistline of the slacks.

"Of course you can. Not indiscriminately, of course, but this top is meant to be tucked in." She walked up behind Marcy and said, "May I?"

When Marcy didn't respond, Jo reached around and tucked the blouse into the slacks. Actually, it didn't look half bad.

"You can break up the line if you like with a jacket or vest, but plus-sized ladies are allowed to have waistlines. You're well-proportioned with a nice shape. You should show it off."

Well-proportioned? Nice shape? She looked. She certainly didn't have an hourglass figure but her waist was narrower than her hips and bustline.

"I can show you some bigger jewelry," Jo suggested. "Larger earrings and something chunky around your neck will create a whole new look for you. And you need shoes. A higher heel will lengthen your body and create a narrower aspect."

Marcy glanced at Jo's three-inch heels. "I'm always afraid of falling."

"Yeah," Jo said, smiling ruefully, "I used to be too." She leaned against the wall and lifted her foot, showing off the heel of her shoe. "These are different and we're lucky they're in style right now. They not ankle busters. The heels look narrow from the side, but are wide enough so you won't feel you're walking on spikes. I have a few styles you might like. May I show you?"

Marcy was hooked. By the time she left the store she'd put a considerable dent in her credit card, but she had two dresses, two new pairs of slacks, several new tops—a few that tucked in—and three new pairs of shoes. She had even let Jo help her select several new bras that fit a better than her old ones and six new pairs of sexy, large-sized panties. She also had several new pieces of large, but lightweight, summery costume jewelry. When Jo had asked whether she needed help with makeup, Marcy had laughed. "I know what to do," she'd said, "I just don't do it."

"Well, you should," Jo had said. "You are, in part, what you project. Be proud of yourself and others will see you in a different light." She'd sounded just like Zack.

The following morning Marcy showed up at work in a crisp, butter yellow blouse and white, summer slacks. She had used blush on her cheeks, eye makeup and a deep coral lipstick. She'd added a heavy-looking, white necklace with matching earrings. The white heels that Jo had selected for her would take a bit of practice to walk comfortably in, but so far her feet didn't hurt. "Wow, Marcy," Helen in sales had said when they met in the parking lot. "You look terrific."

Helen's sentiments were repeated several times as she made her way to her office. She was still the same overweight Marcy she'd been two weeks earlier but she felt a hundred times better. She settled herself behind her desk, grabbed a handful of jelly beans from the jar on her desk and got down to work.

She missed her sister for the two weeks that Jenna was away but was delighted that she didn't hear from her. Jenna was obviously having a great time. Marcy had dinner with Glen after their return and he seemed happier and, if possible, more in love. "I think we're closer to setting a date," Glen told her. "Maybe this winter."

"Will she continue to commute after you're married?" Marcy didn't know whether to hope he'd say she'd give up the business or not. A month before she'd have been relieved and delighted if Jenna decided to move back to Seneca Falls, but now that she'd seen how much her sister enjoyed the goings on at Club Fantasy she wasn't so sure. *Oh, well*, she thought, *it's not my decision.*

"I think she's closer to leaving the city. We both want kids and it isn't going to happen while she's in the business. In addition to using condoms for health reasons, she's on the pill. Neither of us want surprises. You're both in your thirties and I think her biological clock is starting to tweak her a little bit."

"Sure," Marcy said, "but women have kids in their forties these days."

"We know, but it's much riskier and it's more difficult to chase down a toddler while learning about kids for the first time when you're not a kid yourself."

Marcy had been trying not to think about her future, husband, kids, like that. She wanted to have a family but she didn't have any candidates for a lifelong partner. A picture of Zack flashed through her mind. Not a chance. She'd want someone who'd be willing to settle down, and Zack didn't seem like the settling down type. *Stop it*, she thought and returned her attention to Glen. "Give Jen a little more time and I think she'll be ready to come back here."

Glen's face lit up. "You really think so?"

Did she? "Yeah. I really think so."

The following Saturday she flew down to LaGuardia and took a taxi to Jenna's building. Looking around Jenna's comfortable apartment she wasn't so sure about her sister's settling down. What if she never wanted to leave the city? What would happen to Glen? Marcy loved him like a brother and knew that he was doing everything he could to deal with Club Fantasy. How difficult it must be to know that someone he loved and wanted to spend the rest of his life with was having sex, night after night, with other men? She was finding herself wondering about Zack and what he was doing each night. Jealous? Don't be ridiculous.

Jenna had apologized for not being able to pick her up at the airport. She'd had an interview with a potential customer for Club Fantasy that she couldn't change. The interviews often took over an hour so Marcy had just made herself at home. Jenna had told her she'd bought a small dresser just for Marcy's things so she unpacked, waiting for her sister to get home.

As she finished organizing her toiletries, Jenna opened the front door and shouted, "Get in here and let me look at you."

As Marcy walked into the living room she watched the expression on her sister's face. "Babe," Jenna said, "you look terrific. I was really worried that you'd go back to the way you were. I see I needn't have been concerned."

Grinning, Marcy pirouetted, showing off her new white slacks and black-and-white-printed blouse. She was even wearing a wide, white, leather belt. She'd looked at herself when she'd tried the outfit on and marveled at how inaccurate all the things she'd believed about style had been. "It's not half bad, is it?" she asked.

"Not half bad at all. Have you lost weight?"

"Not a pound," Marcy said. She didn't want to work at dieting, and now that she'd discovered that she didn't have to look dowdy, she was much more comfortable with her shape.

"Well, you look fabulous." Jenna embraced her sister, then, holding her shoulders, pushed her away. "I can't get over it. It's like the aliens have replaced my sister with this fashionable, well-dressed clone."

"I'm still the same me." To change the subject, she asked, "How's Rock's dad?"

"He's been home from the hospital for several weeks and is getting physical therapy. Rock flies out each Sunday and comes back on Wednesday. Zack is around for the Sunday evenings."

"I know. He told me."

"You've talked to him?"

She'd talked to him. Often. She hadn't told her sister because somehow it was too personal. But what about Zack? Why hadn't he told Jenna? Was it also very personal for him? She hoped it was.

Chapter
11

He'd called her the day after she returned to Seneca Falls. He said he was checking that she'd arrived safely but he must have known that from Jenna. She'd been flattered and they'd talked for about half an hour. When she hung up, she didn't remember much of what they talked about, just that it had been easy and friendly. That didn't mean she didn't tingle from the sound of his voice and his warm laughter, but she made an effort to keep it all in proportion.

He'd called again a few evenings later and again they'd just talked. For over an hour. They'd ended the conversation because they both wanted to watch the same CNN special. Marcy had been amazed at how much they had in common. Jock versus shy, fat girl. Who would have thought it?

Another evening she told him all about her college and grad-school years and her relationship with Jenna. He explained that he had a BS in psychology and was most of the way to a masters degree. "Makes me really good at what I do."

"How did you get into—well—doing what you do?"

He chuckled. "Rock actually. We met at the gym and got to talking, like guys do. Eventually, he told me what he did and it seemed like an easy way to make quick money. I wasn't making diddly as a teaching assistant, so I asked him whether I could take some of his overflow."

"Teaching assistant?" She hadn't known much about his past and this part surprised the heck out of her. Not that she didn't think he was intelligent, but she was still stuck with lots of stereotypes.

"Yeah. I thought I wanted to teach college so I was using the TA money to try to finance an advanced degree. I was really tired of mooching from the family. Once I began to entertain, I could afford my own apartment. Then I realized that I hated teaching psychology so here I am."

"What are you going to do when you . . ." She almost said "when you grow up" but instead she said, "don't do this any more?"

"Darned if I know. I've got lots of money in the bank and I'm happy. I guess I'll let the future take care of itself."

Marcy wished she could let go that easily. She'd planned ever since she'd opened her first 401K. The conversation moved on to safer topics.

"I miss you," he said a few days later.

She giggled. "I miss you, too. Actually, Ms. Henshaw in Personnel called me today and gave me the final okay for three weeks off starting after Jenna gets back from vacation. I'm going to be spending the last three weeks in August in the city." She'd been almost afraid to tell him, fearing that he'd back off when he realized that this wasn't just going to be a long-distance friendship. Friendship? That's what it was, of course. She grabbed a handful of jelly beans from the jar on her bedside table. A friendship. Right. She popped one and chewed. A friendship.

"Fantastic. That's wonderful. I can't wait to see you again." He sounded like he really meant it.

"Me too," she said, softly. *Don't get your hopes up*, she told herself. *He's a man who loves women, and he demonstrates it every night with a different female. He's just being nice to you because he likes you and your sister. That's all.*

"I want to be with you again," he purred. "Up close and personal, as they say."

Marcy felt her body tingle, remembering. "More research?"

"Call it what you will. I want to be with you, hold you, make long, slow love to you. I want to learn about all the things you enjoy and teach you all the things I enjoy. Would you like that?"

She felt her nipples respond to the pictures he was putting into her head. "Yes," she whispered.

"What should we do first?" he asked.

"Are we having phone sex?" she said, trying to lighten the atmosphere.

"Of course. Why not? I haven't wanted to tease you before, but now that I know I'll be able to touch you again, we can have some fun. Do you have a problem with that?"

"With phone sex? I don't know. I've never done it."

"It certainly doesn't replace the real thing, but since we can't be together for a couple of weeks, this will have to do." When she hesitated, he said, teasingly, "Having doubts again?"

She managed to laugh at herself. "Of course."

"Just chalk it all up to learning about sex for your book."

"Right. The book. Okay," she continued, her body wanting what he could give. Keep it light, though. "I've no idea where to start."

"What are you wearing?"

"Wearing?"

"Sure. I need to be able to picture you. Let's start with me. I'm in the bedroom, lying on my bed. You remember my bed, don't you?"

How could she forget? Those red sheets had played a part in several middle-of-the-night-memory parties during the past few evenings.

"I'm wearing black drawstring shorts and an old, light blue sweatshirt with the sleeves cut off at the shoulders. What about you? Where are you?"

"I'm in my bedroom, on my bed."

"Great." She could hear the grin in his voice. "We're in bed together. Sort of. What color are the sheets?"

"Light blue."

"Now we're getting somewhere. What are you wearing?"

"I hate to admit it but I'm wearing a pair of old, baggy, tie-at-the-waist, cotton pants and a tee shirt."

"Baggy? Not like the new you at all but I'll have to settle. What color are they?"

"This is silly."

"It isn't at all. Are you able to picture me?"

"Yes," she said, seeing him in her mind on his bed, his sexy hands holding the phone beside his ear.

"Well, I need to be able to see you, too. What color?"

She giggled. "If you insist. My pants are blue-jeans color and my tee shirt . . . It's white, sort of a sleep shirt, with a picture of Winnie the Pooh across the front."

"Winnie the Pooh? Nah. That won't work. Take it off."

"What?"

"You heard me, take it off. Tell me what color bra you're wearing." When she didn't move, he said, "Come on. This is important."

Reluctant, but deliciously excited, too, she pulled the old tee shirt off over her head and looked down. She'd recently bought herself a few new pieces of lingerie. She'd realized at the time that no one would see them except herself but it made her feel better. "It's pink."

"Just pink? I need to be able to see your beautiful breasts in it. Does it have any flowers or bows?"

Beautiful breasts. She clung to every compliment. "It's got some lace on the sides and there's a little string bow in the center of the front."

"That's perfect. I can see you now, and so can my cock. It's getting a little hard just thinking about you. Tell me about your body. Are you hot? Just a little, maybe?" When she sighed, he said, "I heard that. You are. I'm glad. Are your nipples hard? Can you see them through the bra?"

"Yes." Her voice was breathy.

"Touch them. Rub the palms of your hands over them. Rest the phone on the pillow beside your head so you can hear me and use both hands to touch your breasts."

She did. She'd masturbated almost every evening thinking about Zack but this was much more exciting. Hearing him guide her was almost as good as having his hands on her. "Slowly circle your palms with your nipples. Both your breasts and your hands are enjoying the touching. While you're doing that I'm lightly running the palm of one hand over my cock. It's getting harder, knowing what you're doing."

She could clearly picture his hand on his shorts. "How does it feel?"

"It feels very good. Not as good as your hands would feel but hearing your voice makes you more a part of it. While I'm doing this, take your bra off so you can touch your naked breasts." He paused. "Are you doing it?"

She sat up, unhooked her bra and dropped it on the bed beside her. Then she settled back with the phone beside her ear. "I did it."

"I can see your wonderful, full breasts. Touch them. Do what you were doing. Rub your palms over your naked nipples. God, this is making me hot."

Her hands seemed to have a life of their own, following Zack's instructions. "It's making me hot, too." Until she heard her own voice she didn't realize she'd said it aloud.

"I'm glad," he said with genuine warmth. "I'm going to take off my shirt and shorts so I'll be down to my briefs. Why don't you take off your pants, too?"

Without thinking about what she was doing she did as he'd asked. "I did," she whispered.

"Good." She could hear his raspy breathing. "Now touch your beautiful pussy with your fingers, through your panties. Are they pink, too?"

"Yes," she said, "they're pink, too. Nylon, slippery. I'm touching my panties now."

His long sigh made her smile. "Find your clit through the fabric and stroke it. See how different it feels when there's something between your fingers and your skin. Is your clit hard? Can you feel it?"

How could she not feel it? Rubbing herself was pushing her toward orgasm. "Yes."

"You know just where to touch yourself and I'm rubbing myself at the same time. I'm going to slide my hand under my briefs and hold my cock. Do you want to touch yourself naked or does it feel too good the way you're doing it now?"

"This way," she said, her voice not her own, hoarse and thick. She was panting, her heartbeat roaring in her ears.

"Keep doing it. I'm holding my cock, stroking from the base to the head, then back down. My balls are tightening and I want to come, but I'm going to slow down now and wait for you."

"Don't wait," she said. "I don't know whether I can do this with you listening."

"You can. I know it. I can hear your breathing and I know how hot you've gotten. Keep stroking. Find all the places your fingers know so well, the ones that can make you come. I know how wet you must be, how slippery your pussy has become. Do you want to put your fingers inside?"

"No," she said. "Just. This. Way." She did know just how to do it and suddenly she lost control and felt the spasms rocket through her body. "Yesssss," she hissed.

"I won't be far behind you," he said, his breath now harsh and fast, "not far. Not far . . . Now," he said, and she heard his long, drawn-out groan. "I can't wait until you're here with me, in my bed. When are you getting here?"

"A week from Saturday."

The previous evening he'd called. "I happen to know that Jenna's busy most of the day tomorrow."

"How do you know that?"

"I asked."

So he'd been asking Jenna about her. She wondered what her sister thought of all that. She'd said nothing on the phone. "I've no plans for tomorrow night," Zack said, "so call me when you get in and I'll pick you up. We'll have dinner first, if you're not in too much of a hurry. I probably won't be able to eat a thing but I want to savor everything. Is that okay with you?"

She couldn't wait to see him but she had to guard herself. He was a professional lover after all. He said so himself. "Sure," she said, deliberately keeping her voice light. "I'll call you when I get in."

Now she was in Jenna's apartment, unpacking her new clothing and putting things in the small dresser, hesitant to call. What if . . . ?

About a week before her arrival, she'd also called Steve. He'd sounded happy she was coming back to the city. She'd made dinner plans with him for Sunday evening. After all, Zack will be working at the Club anyway. She berated herself for making plans with Steve just because Zack would be busy, but she needed some sanity and balance in her life and Steve was a nice man who wouldn't get the wrong idea. Company for dinner and that was all. Period.

Zack found himself looking forward to their evening more than he cared to admit. He'd been thrilled to learn that she was coming back to spend a decent amount of time. Marcy was a wonderful woman and he found himself thinking of her more than he'd thought about any other woman. He'd actually turned down several paying customers for Saturday evening just to join Marcy for dinner and, of course, great sex. It was interesting and a bit puzzling. He was looking forward to her company just as much as he was anxious to enjoy her in bed. They'd had great phone sex, but their ordinary conversations were wonderful as well, filling parts of him he hadn't realized were empty. They shared so many things in common, from books and movies to travel, and their differences were complimentary and seemed to fit.

He'd actually enjoyed their arguments about politics, she a Democrat, he a Republican. They agreed on Mideast policy and the various wars and skirmishes around the world, but disagreed on the handling of the economy. Their arguments were heated since both were well-read but they never carried over into their personal lives. He'd never met a woman like her. And it scared the hell out of him.

He had told her that he loved women and it was true, to a point. So far his relationships with women had all been superficial. He had never let anyone get beneath his skin the way Marcy did. But how could she feel anything serious for him when he was, well, what he was?

He'd keep it light and hope that he could keep Marcy from burrowing too deep.

Marcy called Zack just before dinnertime. She'd been in the apartment for several hours but had been deliberately putting off the call. Half of her was astonishingly excited, her body tingling, the crotch of her panties wet. The other half was almost reluctant to see Zack. She was treading water in very dangerous seas, worried about drowning, unable to sort out her feelings. Was it Zack or just good sex? He was a great guy but being a great guy was his job. She felt like she was looking at a terrific used car with a used car salesman.

What to do? Damn the torpedoes, full speed ahead. "Hi,

Zack, it's Marcy," she said when he answered his phone on the first ring. "I'm at Jenna's."

"I'm glad to hear your voice. Can I come over and pick you up?"

"I can meet you somewhere?" If he came to the apartment they wouldn't get dinner until midnight, if then. And she didn't know whether she could make love comfortably in Jenna's apartment.

She heard Zack's warm laugh. "Probably a good idea." They arranged to meet on a corner in midtown, with Zack unwilling to reveal where they were going.

At six-thirty she stood on the sidewalk almost melting in the unrelieved heat and humidity. Having lived upstate all her life she wasn't quite adjusted to the heaviness of the air and the sights and smells of New York City in the summer. She watched the passersby wend their way through Manhattan, the bicycles and Rollerbladers with whistles in their mouths warning pedestrians away, cars, trucks and taxis honking with impatience, pedestrians moving more slowly in the heat, sucking down sodas and iced lattes, slurping ice cream and eating fruit from plastic glasses. And the smell, a combination of hot asphalt, exhaust fumes, hot dogs and sauerkraut from a Sabrett's vendor on the corner and a particularly heavy perfume from a woman walking past. Manhattan in August.

She saw Zack as he turned the corner and watched his face light up as he spotted her. Her heart lifted but she pushed the feelings down. Great sex from a nice guy. Don't get carried away. God, he looks good. His jeans low, his shirt tight, hugging his chest.

He closed the distance between them until they were breast to chest and he wrapped his arms around her. His kiss was deep and sensual, promising things to come. When they finally separated, he said, "I'm glad to see you." He pressed his groin gently against hers. "Very glad."

She felt his erection and cupped his buttocks to press it more firmly to her. "Me too." Then she realized where they were and backed up.

He grinned. "Wicked, isn't it?"

"Yeah," she grinned back. "Sure is."

"You look fabulous," he said, admiring her outfit, her white slacks and a new attar of roses blouse. "I see you've tucked your shirttails in. The changes in you are wonderful." He picked up her hand. "You've done your nails."

One evening after work Marcy had gone into Pearl's Nails and had tips and wraps. She had also allowed herself to be talked into a pedicure. Now her fingernails were a deep mauve and her toes, which poked out from her white sandals, were bright red. "Yummy," Zack said. "Painted toes, too."

Embarrassed by the attention, Marcy said, "Enough of that. Where are you taking me for dinner?"

He took a deep breath and draped his arm over her shoulders. "Have you ever had Korean barbecue?"

"I've had Texas barbecue. Anything like that?"

"Nothing at all, but I know you'll love it. Come on."

They entered a small restaurant in the middle of a side street and were led to a strange-looking table, extra wide with a metal center. As she settled into her chair opposite Zack, the waiter handed them each a menu.

Zack gently took hers. "If it's okay with you, since you've never had this before, I'll order." When she nodded he ordered marinated steak. "I only got one main course. I didn't think we could finish two, and we don't want to, uh, linger." His wink was erotic and mischievous. "Wine?"

"I don't really need a stimulant," she said, then blushed.

"Just water and barley tea," Zack said, and the waiter disappeared. "You'll really like the tea. It tastes midway between tea and cereal." He sighed. "I'm blathering. I think I'm nervous and that's a totally new experience for me."

He was nervous? She was a wreck. "Me, too." Marcy noticed that they'd been given napkins, chopsticks and a metal soupspoon.

Zack reached over and took her hands. "I've been looking forward to your visit. Last time you were here I had almost no free time because of Rock's problems. Now that I've got time and I know you better, there's so much of the city I'd like to show you." He winked. "And there's all that research."

Marcy blushed again and slowly blinked. "I have to be honest with you, Zack. I'm trying not to get carried away by that. The sex was wonderful but I have to go slowly."

"Why?"

She paused, then grinned. "I don't know. I don't know what makes sense any more, what's right."

Zack looked totally puzzled. "Right? Is there a right and wrong to this? You're single and so am I. We're consenting adults and what we're doing isn't hurting anyone. Even the government allows as how this is okay. So why not?" He lowered his voice until it was just a whisper. "If you don't want to continue our sexual relationship, that's fine. I'll be really disappointed, of course, but I'll manage. I have so looked forward to, well, everything, but if you'd rather not, we can just keep it friendly."

She knew he was manipulating her, but he was pushing her into something she truly desired. She also realized that he'd do without if it was what she really wanted. "No," she said, quickly. "I don't want that."

She watched Zack's shoulders relax. "That's good. Let's just let it be whatever it is."

Marcy needed to say something more. "Zack, I just don't want us to get things confused. We've become friends and I'm glad of that. And we've been lovers and that's terrific, too. But those two don't necessarily add up to anything. I don't want either of us deluded into thinking there's more than there is."

"Marcy, I'm not asking you to marry me. I want us to be together when we want to, and do whatever we want to. That's all. No strings. No declarations of undying love."

Marcy let out a long breath. They would keep this where it belonged. She was kept from having to say anything more by three waiters: one bringing bowls of clear soup, a second a tray containing half a dozen small dishes of what looked like vegetables in light dressing and a third who removed the panel at the center of the table and dropped a heavy, metal griddle into the opening. He lifted the corner and ignited the burner beneath. The three then left.

"I see that Korean barbecue has nothing to do with Texas," Marcy said, glad of the change of subject.

"Obviously not," Zack said. He pointed to the small plates. "These are side dishes. Bean sprouts, bamboo shoots and a little salad with lettuce and sesame oil." He pointed to another. "This is kale, I think, and this over here is kimchee. It's very hot so try a little and see what you think." When she reached for her chopsticks, he asked whether she needed a fork.

"No. I'm pretty good with these." She demonstrated by lifting a small leaf of the hot, Korean, pickled cabbage. She tasted it and almost choked. Zack suggested that she cool her mouth with bits of the other vegetables, and after a moment she could speak again. "Phew. You're right about that stuff. It's crunchy fire."

"Some folks love it, but it's usually too hot for me, too."

She looked around and saw a few of the other diners, mostly Asians, munching on the kimchee with obvious relish. "I guess it's just what you're used to."

"It's amazing what you can get used to," he said with a leer, and Marcy had to grin.

The waiter arrived with a plate of thinly sliced beef, two bowls of sauce, one thick and one thin, and a plate of large leaves of lettuce. "I'll cook it," Zack said to the waiter, who nodded and walked away. Zack deftly used the tongs provided to spread some of the meat on the now-hot grill. She watched his fingers, unable to push the image of his hands on her body out of her mind. He must have felt her thoughts because he looked up and their eyes met and held.

He smiled, then returned to the meat. When the beef was sizzling, he said, "Take a lettuce leaf and put some meat on it. Then spread on the bean paste and roll the whole thing up." He demonstrated and she followed. "You learn quickly," he crooned as he munched on the lettuce and sensuously licked his lips. *Everything at this dinner is going to be a double entendre*, she thought, and her body reacted predictably to each one. She bit down on the cold, crisp lettuce with the warm beef inside and smiled. "It's wonderful."

"It is, isn't it."

When she'd finished her first lettuce roll Zack took her hand, put her index finger into his mouth and sucked off all the drippings. Then he followed with each of her other fingers. "Didn't want to waste any."

The heat at the table had little to do with the grill and she loved it. They ate, mostly in silence, with long, meaningful looks and erotic licking of lips and sucking of fingers. Zack showed her in many ways that he was as aware of her as she was of him. When the waiter finally cleared the plates, Zack asked, "Dessert?"

She laughed. "Not a chance."

Zack paid the check, and as they walked toward his apartment he held her hand. The light breeze did little to cool her. The silence as they walked was filled with erotic images.

They arrived in his apartment and, rather than strip off their clothes and run to the bedroom, as part of her wanted to do, Zack poured them each a glass of white wine and they settled on the sofa. "God, I've missed you," he said. "The phone's just not enough."

"For me either," she admitted. "I think about you a lot."

He pulled her around until her feet were in his lap and pulled off her shoes. "These toes have been intriguing me ever since we met earlier." He sensuously stroked her big toe. "I love a woman with a pedicure."

Marcy couldn't decide whether what he was doing felt good or tickled. Should she tell him how ticklish she was? When she instinctively pulled back, Zack asked, "Are you very ticklish?"

"Yeah," she admitted.

"Then you have to tell me. I want to know everything. If I ever do anything that isn't completely pleasurable, you mustn't be polite. The things I do are for your pleasure as well as mine. Promise you'll say something?"

She paused, then said, "Okay. I promise."

He pressed harder into the arch of her foot and rubbed with his thumb. "Nice?"

"I can't imagine anything you could do that wouldn't be," she purred.

He tickled the sole of her foot and she pulled away, laughing. "I can," he said. "I want us to try everything, but I can't do that if you won't keep your promise."

"Okay. Sorry. That didn't feel nice." She put her feet back into his lap.

"There are people who find tickling very erotic." He slipped a finger between her first two toes and pulled it back out again, imitating the motions of intercourse.

"What you're doing now is very sexy," she said, "but tickling's not my thing."

"We're learning." He took her foot and pressed it against the hard ridge in his slacks. "That feels good."

While she rubbed his crotch with the sole of her foot she watched the obvious pleasure shine on his face. There was so much more to this then inserting tab A into slot B as she'd once put it.

After a few minutes of mutual stroking, Zack said, "I've

been determined to wait, let this last, but I'm crazy hot for you."

Marcy stood. "Last one to the bedroom is a rotten egg."

They stripped off each other's clothing and dove onto the bed. He was inside her almost immediately and she reveled in the hardness of his cock. He pulled himself onto his knees and lifted her hips so he could thrust into her more deeply. Holding her buttocks, he came. Unwilling to let her go, he propped her on his thighs and explored her vaginal folds until she was screaming, begging him to let her come. Several strokes on her clit and she climaxed.

They lay side by side talking, then made love for a second time. She didn't arrive home until after three, by which time Jenna was sound asleep on the sofa. Marcy tiptoed into the bedroom and hugged herself. She'd been afraid that her memories of Zack had deified him, but he was as wonderful as she remembered.

Sanity was in short supply.

Chapter
12

Dinner with Steve on Sunday evening was wonderful and in many ways the complete opposite of her evening with Zack. They ate at a sidewalk restaurant in Greenwich Village and talked easily about anything that interested them. He enjoyed baseball and spent quite a while relating anecdotes, making the sport interesting for her. She told him about several books she'd read that she thought he'd like. It was comfortable with none of the intense heat she felt with Zack.

As she sat across from him, she realized that, until recently, this was the kind of man she'd pictured building a permanent relationship with—so much more suitable. Now, there was Zack. As they parted, Steve asked whether he could take her home.

"Not tonight," she said. "I'm still a little tired from traveling." When he leaned forward to kiss her cheek she pulled away.

"I sense you're making excuses. There's no need. If you don't want to see me again, I'll certainly understand."

She wanted to see Steve again, but she didn't want to give him false expectations. Right now her thoughts were filled with hot visions of romping with Zack. "Steve, I like you. Very much. I just don't want you to get the wrong idea about where this is going."

"Okay, what's the wrong idea?"

What to tell him? "I enjoy spending time with you as a friend and I'd like to continue. However, I don't want you to think there's more here than I feel right now."

His sigh was long and drawn out. "I'm disappointed, but I would like to continue to get together with you from time to time. As friends. I enjoy your company and would miss that."

Marcy kissed his cheek. "I'd like that, too." She quickly flagged down a taxi and climbed in. "Call me?"

Steve's smile was a little sad. "You know I will. And maybe over time you'll change your mind."

Marcy and Zack met at odd hours during the following week. They toured the city, Zack showing her everything from the Statue of Liberty to the Cloisters, from the Bronx Botanical Gardens to the Coney Island Aquarium. They made love often, and every time it was exciting and new. Marcy was amazed at how much freer she felt about her own sexuality. She found she didn't mind it when Zack looked at her naked body. She still weighed over one hundred and seventy, but it didn't seem to matter as much. Maybe, as Zack often said, she'd shed some of the baggage she always carried about her weight.

She found she was a bit uneasy about the time that Zack spent "working." She knew that he was entertaining other women and tried not to be jealous. It tweaked her from time to time, but when she saw him she forgot about everything else.

Marcy spent lots of time with Jenna and considerable time writing. Her novel had become a mixture of plot and short stories about encounters at Club Fantasy. She wasn't sure the hot sex at the Eros Hotel, as the Club was called in her book, had the right tone, but she kept turning out pages.

One afternoon when she'd been in the city for just over a week she sat down to write and realized that Jenna had left the computer program she used to keep track of the Club's activities open. Before using the machine, Marcy wanted to save her sister's data for her. *How does Jen back this up?* she wondered and looked through the computer stand to try to find backup disks. When she found none, she looked for blank diskettes or CDs and still came up empty. Reluctant to close the program without adequate controls, she went to the stationary store around the corner and bought a ten-pack of CDs. Then, when she returned to the apartment, she backed up all the data.

Later, when Jenna came back from Manny's, Marcy said, "You left your data program open and it worried me to work with it there. I wanted to shut it down but I couldn't find your backup stuff, so I created a CD for storage." She showed Jenna where she'd put it.

"Yeah, I know I should backup more often than I do but . . ."

"Should? How often do you back up your stuff?"

"Well . . ."

"I should have known," Marcy said, shaking her head. "Okay, I've just done it. Do you know how?"

"I guess. I really hate this computer stuff so I put it off as long as I can, then just do it as quickly as I can before closing the machine down."

So like her sister. "While I'm here, do you want me to do some of the entry work for you? You know I enjoy that sort of thing." From the time they started school, Marcy had always been the organized one while Jenna did everything by the seat of her pants.

"Would you?" Jenna asked, eagerly.

"I'd love to. You'll have to show me how it all works."

For the next hour, Jenna showed Marcy a little of the computer programs and spread sheets she used to track both employees and customers, much of which, she said, she'd adapted from the system used at Courtesans, Inc. Marcy asked pertinent questions, and realized that there might be ways to streamline the system to keep from having to enter data more than once. "You don't handle payroll here, right?" Marcy asked. She knew Jenna had a service handle much of the payment details.

"I use a service who takes care of all that, and does health insurance, taxes and everything."

"Health insurance, too? Well, that's good," Marcy said. At least she was sure that her sister wouldn't go to jail for nonpayment of quarterly taxes and her employees were protected, too. Even if she didn't do it herself, Jenna obviously provided for everyone. "If it's pricey, I could handle much of that for you," she said. It would give her a way to be useful.

Jenna giggled. "I'd pay anything to anyone not to have to do more computer stuff, but the company that does it all does a good job and I can handle the expense. Anyway, you're not going to always be here."

Ruefully, Marcy said, "I guess that's so."

"However," Jenna said with a gleam in her eye, "if you did the fantasy fulfillment part of the data entry—the client's wishes, what we've already done, with whom and like that— even just for the time you're here, it would be a gigantic load off my mind."

She could be helpful and get to know more of the inner workings of Club Fantasy. "Sure, I'd love to."

Jenna reached into a desk drawer and pulled out a stack of papers. With her "I'm looking charming" look, she held out the sheets. "I'm a little behind."

With a laugh, Marcy took the thirty or so sheets and, when Jenna left for the club, began to plow through the entries. After spending several hours to get all Jenna's records up to date, Marcy understood the well-thought-through but awkward programs. *I guess you can't get something off-the-shelf to track the activities of prostitutes and their johns.*

After she finished Marcy wandered through a huge computer software store near Jenna's apartment and found a few programs that would track employee and consultant earnings and complete periodic federal and state tax forms, handle payroll and even track medical insurance payments and benefits. She didn't buy any, but it was interesting to learn how much existed. Just in case.

Marcy was delighted that Jenna had set up a meeting for the following afternoon with a woman named Shelly who worked for Club Fantasy. Marcy looked forward to getting a different perspective on the activities at the Club.

They met at the same Soho restaurant that she'd first met Zack in several weeks before. Shelly Miller turned out to be closer to Marcy's idea of the perfect high-priced call girl. In her mid-twenties, she was about five foot nine, with long, blond hair that looked like it came from a shampoo commercial. Her eyes were hazel, almost green with long lashes and perfectly wing-shaped brows. Her makeup was applied with a trained hand to bring out her perfect cheekbones and play down her slightly receding chin. Her figure was of model quality, with slender hips and uplifted breasts that looked totally natural. She was dressed in tight jeans and a tank top that left little to the imagination. She slid into the booth beside Jenna, facing Marcy.

"It's so great to finally meet you, Marcy," she said. "Jenna talks about you a lot, especially in the past few weeks since you've been visiting."

"It's nice to meet you, too, Shelly."

The three exchanged small talk until the waiter arrived with salads for Jenna and Shelly and a hamburger and fries for Marcy. Shelly gazed at the plate and almost drooled. "God, I wish I could do that. I eat salad until it's coming out my ears. Dieting sucks, but I've got to do it."

"You're so gorgeous that I can't imagine a pound or two would matter," Marcy said, creating a pool of ketchup beside her fries.

"It wouldn't be a pound or two. It would be ten or fifteen and then where would I be?"

So much emphasis on weight, Marcy thought. *I'm happy just the way I am. I don't have to compete with anyone. What a change. Thank you, Zack.* "Tell me about yourself," Marcy suggested between bites.

Shelly put down her fork, appearing finished. Marcy noticed that she'd only eaten a small piece of tomato and several bites of lettuce, all without dressing. "Will you use me as a character in your book?"

"I might pattern someone after you but only in generalities. No one will be recognizable."

She let out a quick breath. "That's good. My folks still don't know what I really do. They wouldn't get it."

"What do they think you do?"

"I came here from Iowa five years ago to become a model. I was homecoming queen, Miss Iowa Corn and Miss Bremer County. I missed out on Miss Iowa but lots of people in my hometown thought I was great model material. Typical story I guess. Anyway, I got quite a few modeling jobs almost immediately and made nice money. I did catalogs and stuff and sent lots of pictures home to my parents. That lasted for about two years but then I began to get old."

"Old?"

"Sure," she said. "In the modeling business twenty-two is ancient unless you're one of the lucky ones. I was never really first tier, or even second. No commercials, no runway stuff. I'm not tall enough for that. Three years ago I met Erika through a friend and we talked. She's such a wonderful person, a real lady. She told me about Courtesans, Inc. and wondered whether I'd be interested in some part-time work. At first I was horrified, but over time the idea grew on me. Three months later I called her up and the rest is history."

"Do you like the work?"

"I love it." Her smile showed perfect, white teeth. "I have

fun with people. I get to go places I never would have if I'd stayed in modeling and I make lots more money. I've got enough put away to practically retire."

Retire. Marcy wondered how much money Jenna had put away. Snapping back to the present, Marcy asked, "Have you ever regretted it? You know, leaving modeling and—" How could she put this delicately? "—doing what you do."

"Don't be embarrassed to say it. I'm a very high-priced call girl. Regret it? Not for a moment. Well, that's not totally true. I have to lie to my parents, and that really hurts. I'm not ashamed of what I do, but I know they just wouldn't be able to deal with it. I still do the occasional modeling job and I send examples of my work to them. They still think that's all I do here and everyone's happy."

"Tell me about your clients. What type of person do you usually entertain? What fantasies do you prefer?"

"Oh, all types. I don't do just fantasies. I still keep up with what I used to do for Erika: parties, visiting business men, like that. But at Club Fantasy I've been lots of different people: a Nazi spy, a cheerleader, a lingerie model, a visiting porn star, lots of things. I've done bondage, threesomes, lesbian stuff, just about everything."

Jenna had remained silent, but now suggested, "Tell Marcy about the cheerleader one."

Shelly chuckled. "This guy, Bruce, had told Chloe that he'd always wanted to make it with one of the cheerleaders for his high school football team. He'd been a bench warmer and had never gotten into a real game, and he'd always envied the quarterback. He wanted to be that quarterback and 'get the girl' in every way.

"As you might imagine I was a cheerleader in high school and I did date one of the lettermen, a fullback actually." She got a faraway look in her eyes. "I remember the cheers as though it were yesterday and so Jenna arranged for me to play the scene with this guy. We researched his high school colors, green and white, and Chloe got me a uniform just like the ones from when he was there. We got him a football uniform, too."

Jenna picked up the story. "We cleared out one of the rooms and put down one of those astroturf carpets. We found a wooden bench in the storage room and, this was pretty clever if I do say so myself, videotaped a football game and used the sound, including the commentators voices, on low for background noise. We scattered helmets and water buckets around and added a stack of towels. It looked pretty authentic. I'm not sure whether the realism matters that much since most of the people we entertain are so overwhelmed with the fantasy that their mind fills in the gaps, if there are any."

As Shelly continued the story, Marcy pictured the scene. Shelly, in a tight sweater and very short skirt, white socks and sneakers, pom-poms shaking, doing cheers as the client walked in.

Bruce sat down on the bench and put his helmet on the "grass." Shelly continued her routines for several minutes while Bruce watched in silence. Finally, she finished a cheer and dropped to her knees in front of him. "Hi, Bruce. I just can't wait for the game to start."

"Really?" Bruce said, totally overwhelmed.

"Sure. I love to see you run down the field. That touchdown you scored last Saturday just blew me away."

"It did?" He looked totally nonplussed.

"Sure. Don't you know that I watch you every weekend?" She smiled at him, looking up through her long lashes. "I watch every play you make. I guess you're sort of my hero."

"I am?"

Shelly moved closer so she was crouched between his knees. "You are. I think you're just wonderful."

The look of adoration in her eyes must have given him courage. He reached down and took a lock of her hair in his fingers. "I watch you, too. I think you're the best cheerer of all the girls. And the prettiest, too."

"Thanks," she said, eyes downcast.

"I love your hair." He leaned over and buried his face in a handful of her long, blond mane. "It looks so beautiful and smells so good." He tangled his fingers in the long strands. "I picture you sometimes, with nothing on, just that wonderful hair."

Shelly giggled. "You're a nasty boy, you know, thinking about me with no clothes on."

"I know."

Shelly tipped her head back until he could kiss her. At first his lips were tentative, but over time the kiss deepened until he was almost devouring her. She pulled back. "Would you like me to do a cheer just for you?"

He looked disappointed, but said, "Sure."

"I would be more comfortable if I took off this sweater. Would that be okay with you?"

His grin was priceless, and Shelly quickly pulled her sweater off. She wore nothing underneath. Bruce couldn't take his eyes off her breasts as she bounced through another round of cheers. Eventually, unable to restrain himself, he grabbed her and buried his face between her breasts. He rubbed his hands all over her body, seeming to love the slippery feel of her slightly sweaty skin.

Quickly, she removed his football jersey and pants until he stood naked in front of her. "Want this off, too?" she asked, indicating her tiny skirt. He nodded, so she removed the skirt and panties beneath. She was now as naked as he was, except for her sneakers and socks. "Leave them on," he said, his voice hoarse and his breathing ragged.

Shelly looked down at his rock-hard erection, then dropped to her knees. "Rah, rah, rah," she said, and with each syllable she licked the head of his cock. Her hot breath bathed it in erotic warmth. "Rah, rah, rah." Over and over she licked.

Finally, Bruce grabbed her hair and pulled her mouth toward him, thrusting his cock between her bright red lipsticked lips. Holding on for dear life, he fucked her mouth until he came.

"That was the first time we did it," Shelly said as she sipped her ice water, bringing Marcy out of her fantasy. "Since then he's gotten better at holding himself back and last time we actually fucked for the first time. On the astroturf." She playfully rubbed her behind and chuckled. "I had ass burns for a week. Next time we'll use the towels."

"You've obviously done this one often with him," Marcy said, joining in her laughter.

"I think it's about a dozen times. He keeps calling for another cheerleading session, as he calls it. At fifteen hundred bucks a throw, I'm only too happy to oblige."

"Seven-fifty for Shelly," Jenna said, "and the same for Club Fantasy. Not bad for an hour's work."

"Sometimes I can arrange it so I have two clients in one night. If I bring my own guy I get more, too." There was a glint in her eyes. "Not a bad way to make a very, very good living."

As the summer waned Marcy was less and less willing to return to Seneca Falls. To Jenna's delight, Marcy had taken over all the computer input and had streamlined the process enormously. She'd also spent many wonderful evenings with Zack and had seen Steve several times, but keeping their relationship on a purely friendly basis had become increasingly difficult.

She'd also fallen in love with Manhattan. While Jenna was busy or off with Glen many Mondays and Tuesdays, Marcy explored. She visited dozens of museums, large and small, from the Metropolitan Museum of Art to Chauncy's Tavern. She took a tour of the stock exchange and the UN building. She saw several Broadway plays and became as enchanted with that fantasy life as she was with the Club. She wasn't unaware of the troubling side of New York: drugs, crime, noise, terror alerts but none of that diminished her feeling of having come home. How could she go back? She'd been seduced by the city, and, of course, by Zack. One afternoon, she and Jenna sat in the living room.

"Jen, if it weren't for my salary, I'd stay here indefinitely."

"So why don't you. I can support us both."

"Not a chance. I couldn't live like that. I need to earn a living." She grabbed a jelly bean.

"Isn't the book going to make lots of money? And AAJ is sending you documents often. Wouldn't that combination make you independent enough to stay here?"

She'd told Ms. Henshaw that she'd do a little work if AAJ got in a jam, particularly while Paula was on vacation. This week they'd sent her three proposals to go over. She'd spoken to the document's author several times and made sensible suggestions. When they'd all agreed, she'd faxed the document back.

"Yeah, I might eventually have enough but not for a while yet. I've done the document work for nothing, since I'm on salary and the book is coming along. I've written lots of stories and the plot's taking shape, but I've got quite a ways to go yet."

"Tell Ms. Henshaw to shove it all, and stay here with me," Jenna said, looking genuinely enthusiastic.

"I've really thought about it, but I can't. If I were to stay here I'd need my own place and even with my savings I just couldn't swing it."

Looking surprised, Jenna said, "Couldn't you continue to stay here?"

"Not really. I would need my own space. I'd want to have people over every now and then, and this is your apartment."

"People? Like Zack and Steve?"

Looking slightly embarrassed, Marcy nodded. "Like that. And anyone else I might meet."

"So you need to earn a buck. I could pay you for the data entry you're doing." When Marcy shook her head, Jenna thought a moment, then said, "You know I pay quite a bit to the company who does my payroll and like that. Could you take that over? I could pay you what I'm paying them. Then it wouldn't be like I was paying you for something extra."

Marcy would love to do just that, but she'd have to quit her job, and she didn't know whether she could take the risk. Could she? Maybe even, like Jenna, she could begin with a leave of absence if they wouldn't agree to more vacation time. "I did look into it and there are computer programs that do all that, if you've got the time and savvy to set it up right."

"You could work with Barry, my accountant. He deals mostly with the payroll company now, but I'm sure he could help you with whatever you need."

Marcy was sorely tempted. "I could ask for another month off to see whether we could get it working." Hope was a dangerous thing, but she wanted to do this so badly.

She'd thought about what she had back in Seneca Falls. A job she didn't particularly like, few friends except for Glen. She contrasted that with what her life had become in Manhattan. In a short time Zack and Steve had become important to her in different ways. She considered Steve a friend and Zack a fantastic lover. And she had other friends: Rock, Chloe and, of course, Jenna.

She had an odd thought. If she were to have a party for some big occasion in Seneca Falls, who would she invite? Besides Glen, who was Jenna's fiancé after all, there was no one. A few acquaintances, but no real friends. Here, she'd have quite a guest list.

On her last Thursday evening, she had a date with Zack. They had dinner at a small, outdoor restaurant, holding hands over dessert and trying to prepare themselves for her return to Seneca Falls the following Monday, Labor Day.

"Just a year ago this weekend," Marcy said, "I came here

for the first time. I had a terrific visit, but I had no idea what went on on the upper floors of the brownstone." She huffed out a breath. "I was so incredibly naive."

"Who would have suspected anything? Even a much more sophisticated woman couldn't have imagined the reality of Club Fantasy."

"I guess. I just feel like I was such a country mouse back then."

"And now?" His wolfish grin warmed her heart.

"Now, I'm such a different person. New wardrobe, new makeup."

Zack squeezed her hands. "New inside, and that's the most important part."

She grinned. "Yeah. And a new you."

"I wish you weren't going back."

She hesitated, then said, "I was actually thinking of not going back."

His face lit up at about a million candle power. "Oh, God, that would be so great. Would you really stay?"

"At least for a few more weeks."

"Will that Henshaw woman give you the time off?"

"Frankly I don't know and I don't care. I know they need me and might be willing to give me a bit more slack. And I have the vacation time. I thought I'd ask for two more weeks." Hedging. Always hedging.

"And if they say no?"

How brave was she feeling? Looking into Zack's eyes she felt she could do anything. "Fuck 'em."

Zack grabbed her hand and pulled her up. "Fuck me instead." He dropped some bills on the table and hustled her back to his apartment.

Chapter
13

In Zack's apartment, they kissed, then Zack asked, "Are you interested in playing a more adventurous game this evening?"

"Adventurous?" She and Zack had done so much already.

Zack rummaged in his closet and pulled out a black, canvas tote bag. "I keep a few goodies in here for more creative sex play."

She suddenly wondered whether he'd ever had any of his clients here in his apartment. In his bedroom. "I've had women up here professionally," he said, again reading her mind. "Not since we first made love here, however. Once that happened, it didn't seem right to bring anyone else here."

Relieved somehow, she said simply, "I'm glad." Having a relationship, whatever that meant, with a professional male prostitute changed so many rules. Strangely, she found she wasn't jealous of the women he entertained, just protective of her place in his life, whatever that was. *Damn*, she thought, *I don't have a clue what our relationship really is.*

"Anyway, we've enjoyed so many delightful times here"— he winked that sexy, knee-buckling, soul-warming wink— "that I thought you might like to try something a little off-center." He reached into the bag and pulled out several lengths of soft, white rope. "If you're willing, we could play with these."

He didn't have to explain what that meant. He wanted to tie her up. The mere thought made her knees shake. Without realizing it, she licked her lips.

He leered at her. "You know, Marcy, I have learned to read you like a book, and I love what that book's saying right now." His voice lowered. "Come here."

His voice was commanding, and suddenly she felt timid. "I don't know," she said, meekly.

"Yes, you do," he snapped, "and you'll do as I say."

His orders made her pussy twitch. She had never dreamed that something as simple as a change of his voice could make her so hot. Slowly, she walked toward him.

"Good girl." He took her in his arms and kissed her. Then his voice softened and he held her gaze. "You know I would never hurt you, Marce, and I think you would have fun with some more aggressive play. But first you have to agree to something." He draped the ropes over his arm, than cradled her chin in his palms. "It's really important."

Puzzled, she said, "Okay. What?"

"I have to be totally sure you'll say stop if something doesn't feel right. I don't care if it's only a foot cramp or something that really turns you off. For whatever reason you have to stop me. If you won't agree with that, I can't do anything—let's just say more creative."

"No problem," she said.

He took a deep breath, still looking at her intently. "Not good enough. You just gave me a lightweight, off-the-cuff answer and I need something much more serious from you. I've done lots of things in my sexual career and enjoyed most. However, once in a while a woman wants something I'm not comfortable with. When I started in this business I thought I needed to be willing to do anything, and I did a few things that I really didn't like. No more. If a woman suggests something that I don't want to do, I tell her how I feel and, if neces-sary, give her money back.

"With us, it's not that simple. I need your assurance that you'll stop me if anything I suggest isn't your taste. Anything. And I promise the same to you, without question."

Marcy thought, then said, "I understand."

"You know I'll stop, don't you?"

"Of course."

He looped a length of rope around her waist and used it to pull her close. "Maybe we need a safe word. You might enjoy telling me to stop when you know I won't."

"If I tell you to stop, you will, right?" Stop seemed like a good enough word. Why was he making such a fuss?

"Maybe you want to say, 'Stop. Oh, please stop,' and not mean it. Let's use the word tulip. If you say stop I won't, but if you say tulip, then I'll stop everything. Immediately. And the same goes the other way around. Agreed?"

"Sure," she said, unsure of what he was suggesting. "Tulip." He pulled the rope tighter until it was almost cutting her in half. "Okay," she laughed, a bit nervous and unsteady. "I get it. Tulip."

He immediately let the rope drop to the floor and a slow smile softened his face. "I'm sure you do." He voice dropped again. "Strip!"

Marcy still didn't feel totally comfortable disrobing before she was warmed up, and, although most of the time she was content with her body, now she hesitated.

"I told you to do something!" Zack barked like a top sergeant.

This is a test of some kind, she thought. He had told her to do something, as part of sex play, and she had to make a decision. He'd given her a "safe" word and she could use it now. But should she? Maybe, if she did, he wouldn't continue, he wouldn't want to play anymore, he'd walk away from whatever it was that they had. She swallowed and started to unbutton the oversized, lavender shirt she was wearing. Then she couldn't continue. "Tulip," she said, almost weeping. It was over. It had been so wonderful, but it was over.

He enfolded her in his arms. "You're perfect," he said, holding her close. "I need to assure you of two things. First, if you want to stop things, it will always be okay with me. It might be a bit frustrating, but there are so many ways to make love that eliminating one hardly makes a dent.

"Second, and more important, I love the sight of your body. I know how you look. I've loved every inch, every pound. I love you the way you are. When I look at you I see *you*, not the way you look."

I love you the way you are. He'd used the *L* word. No! He hadn't meant it that way, and, right now, she realized that she didn't want to hear it. Not now. Not yet. Not until they both understood more.

"I care about you, too," she said. Then she unbuttoned the remaining buttons on her shirt and let it fall to the floor. She smiled up at him, then slowly, very slowly, removed the rest of her clothes. She watched his eyes and believed what he'd said about her looks.

"Enough dawdling," he said. "It's time. Get on the bed, on your back." When she didn't move quickly enough, he added, sharply, "Do it now!"

It was all she could do not to grin. She was so happy. The Marcy of three months ago was merely a not-so-fond memory. She felt like she owned the world. This sexy stuff was such fun, and now appeared as if it would be more fun. She was wet, and hungry already, even though he hadn't touched her yet. She quickly stretched out on the bed.

"Hands up over your head. Do it!"

She raised her arms and let her hands rest on the pillows, then watched with fascination as he tied first one wrist then the other to the headboard. The ropes weren't uncomfortable but when she pulled, she realized that she was securely fastened.

"How does that make you feel?" he asked her, now quite serious.

She wanted to give him a serious answer so she thought a moment. "I feel helpless. It's scary, but exciting, too."

"I had hoped you'd feel that way," he said with his irrepressible grin. "I love to play power games." He looked her over, his eyes taking in everything from her manicured fingers to her pedicured toes. "It excites me to see you like this, at my mercy."

She remained silent, waiting as Zack stood silently, gazing at her. The waiting, she quickly realized, was an integral part of the game. She was so vulnerable. Her body and, she suddenly realized, her feelings.

Finally, Zack took one ankle and slowly pulled it so he could tie it to the lower leg of the bed, then duplicated the procedure with the other. She was helpless, immobile, spread wide and open to anything he wanted to do. Had he been anyone else, she might have been reluctant to be so powerless, but she trusted him without question. And it excited her until she could feel her juices trickle between her cheeks.

Zack stripped to his briefs, tiny black ones, then rubbed his palm up and down the obvious bulge. "See how hot you make me?" He leered wolfishly. "But I'm in no hurry." He pulled a small, brown bag from the bottom of his closet. "I went shopping yesterday." He pulled a gift-wrapped package from the bag and held it out for her. Then, with a silly grin, he said, "Oops. I guess you can't open your present, can you? I'll just have to do it for you."

He perched on the edge of the bed beside her hip, then slowly pulled the tape from one end of the box. "I love opening presents," he said, "and, although I bought it for you, it's really a gift for me." Seemingly unhurried, he peeled piece after piece of tape from the shiny silver paper.

"You're making me crazy," Marcy said.

"Yeah. Ain't I terrible?" He carefully removed the paper

and folded it in half, then in half again, finally putting it aside. "Now let's see what's in this innocent-looking box."

He dragged the lid off and pulled out a black, velour bag. Opening the zipper, he pulled out a long, thick dildo. "This is model 45A, guaranteed to give milady pleasure."

Marcy had seen an artificial penis like this on a website once and she'd been curious. Not curious enough, however, to buy one. How inexperienced she'd been then. And she'd thought she could write a book about a sex club. What a joke. She was a different person now, however, and as she watched his long fingers stroke the phallus, then lick the tip she was eager to see how the instrument felt. "I'll bet you're puzzled right about now. I'm sure you're thinking that something so large and thick will never fit inside of you."

She had been thinking just that. The penis was about ten inches long and probably three inches in girth. Never happen. It would be sad to disappoint him but, she had to admit to herself, there was no way.

"Oh, yes, it will. You'll be amazed. I'll show you." He moved between her legs. "Usually I'd play with you first to get you really wet and hungry, but I can see you're already soaked and open for me, and for my friend here. Let's just see how this will work." He teased the tip around her folds, then pressed it against her opening, gradually sinking it deeper and deeper, filling her as no erection had before. She felt stretched to her limit. Good? She wasn't sure. He pushed it into her body as far as it would go, then left it lodged within her. "Tell me how that feels."

What could she say? "I don't really know. Nice, I guess."

"Oh, please," he said, sounding exasperated. "Nice. What a measly little word." He tapped the end several times, causing the dildo to move within her.

The dildo's movements aroused her, increasing her heat. He wiggled the phallus and waited, watching as it became deliciously, excruciatingly difficult for her to keep her hips still. She wanted it to fuck her. She wanted him to fuck her, but talking about it was still difficult for her. "It makes me hungry."

He grinned. "That's better. I like you hungry." He tapped the end of the phallus again. "Hungrier and hungrier. What are you going to do about it?"

She knew she was panting, her breath rough in her ears. "There's nothing I can do about it," she said, allowing her hips to move so she could feel it more.

"Right. Nothing." He tapped. "You're flying, yet unable to climax. You're getting pretty desperate." Tap, tap. "You'll do pretty much anything I want, just so I'll let you come. Right?"

Damn it, he was right. Someone who, not too long ago, was embarrassed by a picture of a dildo was now so aroused that she'd do lots of things she'd not even dreamed of back then, just so he'd let her come.

"Right?" Tap, tap.

She let out a long, shuddering breath. "Yes."

"You've come a long way, Marcy, and you've loved the trip." He pulled the dildo out, then pushed it back in. Then he twisted the base and the dildo began to hum inside of her. She started to come right then but he must have sensed it so, with a laugh, he pulled the dildo out. The small spasms slowly receded. "Not so fast. Let's just see what else is in my little bag."

Another gift-wrapped box and another agonizing wait. Eventually, as her body cooled, he pulled a pair of nipple clamps from the package and dangled them in front of her. "These will hurt just a bit and you must say *tulip* if you really want me to stop. You know," he continued, "it can add to the game if you beg me to stop."

"You're really going to use those?" she asked. Pain as pleasure. She wasn't sure about this.

"Of course. You need to experience all sensual things. For the book, of course."

She was cool enough now to laugh. "For the book." How would it feel to ask him not to do that, knowing he would? "I don't think I'd like that."

"I disagree." He knelt beside the bed and took one of her nipples in his mouth, sucking and pulling until it was swollen and hard. "I think you'll like it just fine."

"Please don't," she said, quickly discovering that it did add something to the experience to beg him to stop. Nipple clamps. She wondered whether the sensation would excite her the way his mouth did. He twisted her nipple, then clipped the black clothespin onto her flesh. It hurt at first, but the slight pain shot directly to her vaginal tissues and made them twitch and swell still more. How high could she get without orgasm?

He moved around the bed and repeated his delicious torture on her other breast. By the time her nipples were connected via the clips and a chain between, she was so hungry she was going crazy. She needed to come. Not wanted, needed. Is this Marcy Bryant from Seneca Falls, New York? Who cares?

She closed her eyes and felt him thrust the dildo deep inside of her, the rhythm exactly right. "Yes, baby," he purred. She came quickly, hard spasms rocking her entire body. Then, instead of a piece of plastic, he was inside of her, his cock thrusting, his body stretched over her and holding her hands as she screamed.

Later, she felt him untie her, turn out the lights and enfold her in his arms. They slept.

She awoke at about three A.M. and felt him move beside her. "I have to go home," she whispered.

"Why? I'd love it if you'd stay." He wrapped his arms around her and held her close. "We could have coffee in the morning. After we make love in the sunshine, that is."

"I can't. I don't know whether I'm comfortable with Jenna knowing I stayed out all night." It sounded silly, but it was true.

She heard his chuckle in the dark. "You're over twenty-one."

She joined his laughter. "I know and I'm really sorry. I just have to build up to staying out all night."

He turned, and she felt him prop himself on his elbow. "Staying with me?"

"No, no, it's not that. I can't think of anyone I'd even consider it with but you. It's that being out until the next day is a big step for me." Not only did she feel strange about being out all night, but staying felt like some kind of escalation in their relationship, at least to her.

He flipped on the light. "Do you think Jenna doesn't know about us?"

Marcy sighed. He understood only part of her reluctance and she'd deal with that for now. "I'm sure she does. It's just . . . Be patient. I'm adjusting to everything."

"Okay. But tell her. Soon. I want you here, with me, all night."

At ten o'clock the following morning, Marcy was sitting in the kitchen with a cup of coffee and an empty Dunkin' Donuts bag when Jenna came in. "I was surprised to hear you get up this morning," she said. "And a little pleased."

"Why surprised and why pleased?" she said, genuinely puzzled.

"I was surprised because I sort of thought, since it was almost the end of your vacation, that you'd stay over at Zack's."

Marcy couldn't control her blush. "You knew? About us and all?"

"Please," Jenna said, obviously trying not to laugh. "I'm pretty perceptive, but you're still a little naive too, Sis. You can't have thought that I believed you two were platonic friends." Jenna poured her coffee and settled at the table. "I love Zack. You know I do." She sipped her coffee. "I can't help it if I worry, too." She placed her hand over here sister's. "Marcy, please don't get too serious about him. He's a flirt, a

lover and, although I don't think he'd ever hurt you deliberately, he's . . . Well, he's Zack."

"Is that why you're pleased that I didn't spend the night?"

"Frankly, yes." When Marcy's eyes narrowed, Jenna continued. "Hey, don't be angry with me. I love you more than anyone in the world, including Glen, and that's saying a lot.
Zack's a male prostitute. He's freer with women than most
men."

"I think I can take care of myself," she said through gritted
teeth. "Zack would never do anything to hurt me. Ever." Why
was she feeling so angry? she wondered. Just last evening she
had been reluctant to stay over at Zack's and she still wasn't
even sure how she felt about him. It was great sex and all, but
there didn't have to be anything more. Was she leaving herself
open to real pain? Maybe it was worth it, for now.

"Of course he wouldn't. He's the most wonderful guy
going. And he's damn good in bed, too. I have it on good au-
thority from his customers." As Marcy took a breath to ask a
painful question, Jenna held her hand out, palm out. "No, I've
never been to bed with him. I'd have told you if I had." She
made a face. "That would feel almost incestuous with you and
him being, well . . ."

Marcy sighed. Until that moment she'd never considered
the idea of her sister in bed with Zack and she was glad that it
had never happened. "Okay, yes, we're having sex, and good
sex for the first time in my life." She calmed herself down.
She'd probably behave the same way if the situations were re-
versed.

"Of course you are. That's his business."

That one hurt. It *was* his business and he was fantastic at it.
She'd caught herself several times in the past few weeks wondering whether there might be more, a dangerous thought. No
love. No future. Just a hell of a now. Jenna was merely bringing her back to earth as she had to do several times each hour.
"I know," Marcy said, her anger dissipating. "I know. I'm

being very careful not to magnify anything out of proportion. We're just having fun."

Jenna hugged her. "I don't want you to go back home and be miserable."

"Actually," she said, her face brightening, "I'm not going home so fast."

"Really? How come?"

"I called Ms. Henshaw early this morning and arranged for a two month leave of absence, on the condition that I continue to do some work for them via fax. She's going to call later so we can agree on an hourly rate since I won't be on salary any more." God, this was a big step but she had to do it for so many reasons, Zack at the top of the list.

"I also called the woman with the ad in the elevator." A "For Sublease" sign had hung in the building's elevator for almost a week. "We've met a few times on the way in and out and she knows I'm your sister. I'm subletting her place for September and October. Her son's in the service in Germany and her daughter-in-law is going to have her first grandchild any day now. She needs the money for the trip." She remembered the relief on the woman's face. "She wasn't sure she would be able to go at all if she didn't rent out her place. Now she can. So I have an apartment and I did a good deed."

Jenna's spontaneous burst of joy was gratifying. "That's wonderful! I love having you here so much, and you certainly didn't have to move out. We get along just great."

"I know, but we both need space. If you're still willing to have me do you payroll and all, I'd like to meet with your accountant. I'm pretty sure I can do it, but I want to get together with him and tie up all the loose ends. I won't ask you to pay me what you've been paying the service, however." She winked. "I'll give you a good deal, I promise. And I'll continue doing it, even if I move back home." Home. Was it Seneca Falls any more? Manhattan felt like home now.

"Was Henshaw difficult to deal with?"

Marcy chuckled, recalling her long conversation with the woman from Human Resources. "I wonder about you Bryant girls," she said in a voice closely approximating Ms. Henshaw's. "What is it about Manhattan? One whiff of city air and you're reluctant to come back."

Jenna burst out laughing. "She's right, but it's not the air."

"Well," Marcy said, still in Ms. Henshaw's voice. "I guess we can arrange a leave without pay. We really do want you to come back."

"She actually admitted that?"

"She did. After all, it took all that time for them to replace you with Paula and I think that's tapped the local market. If I go, they'll be hurting. Not that I care that much about AAJ right now, but the consultant work is necessary so I can pay the rent."

"I'm sure you've got some money in the bank, too."

Marcy grinned. "Yeah, I have, but I don't want to spend it all at once."

Jenna hugged her again. "You're staying," she cried. "I can't get over it."

"Neither can I. Now I'll have time to do some serious writing."

"The payroll and all that shit will take a lot of hours."

Jenna never cursed, so she must really hate the paperwork. "I know that, but what you've been paying all that money for is actually only about a day's work around the first and the fifteenth."

"And fielding questions about medical insurance and time off and all the rest of the crap I do."

Crap. "And the problem with that is? Jen, I can handle this. I'm the organized one, remember?"

"God, it would be so good to have it all in the family."

That afternoon, while Jenna was out on an interview, Marcy thought about her adventures of the previous evening and sat down at the word processor. Her stories seemed like a mirror of the sexual changes she'd been through in the past three months. She grinned as she typed.

POWERLESSNESS

Why in the world did she want this? Melanie wondered. She'd always had a pretty active sex life with boyfriends both long- and short-term. Now, between boyfriends, she'd heard about the Eros Hotel where everything was possible, and discreet. She'd checked out the plain-looking building and had been unimpressed, but had agreed to meet the woman in charge at a restaurant Melanie had selected. No possibility of discovery. A woman named Coleen had interviewed her, assuring her that activities would be satisfying, creative and discreet. She could have what she wanted, do what she wanted and no one would ever be the wiser.

As CFO of a medium-sized corporation, Melanie couldn't risk any notoriety and somehow she trusted this woman and could afford the outrageous fee she charged. It would be a minimal risk, but a risk well worth taking. She was so hot just thinking about it.

She'd discussed her fears of discovery and Colleen had suggested that she wear a mask or disguise throughout her evening and that all payments could be made in cash, in advance, so she didn't need a purse or credit card. No records, no trail to follow. She was guaranteed both anonymity and satisfaction, or her money back. By the time she was finished, she knew she had to do it.

Now here she was, wearing heavy makeup and a wig. It all seemed silly now, but it made her feel free, somehow. She didn't have to be herself, Melanie Marcus, CFO, power behind the company. She could be Melanie. Just Melanie. And she wouldn't have to make any decisions.

She changed into an inexpensive, off-the-rack dress she found in the changing room and added the ten dollar bra and three dollar panties. She folded the clothing she'd worn neatly and put them in a plastic bag. None of her expensive clothing to identify her. Paranoia? You bet. But now she was free.

She walked into Room 31, which looked like a motel room at any Best Western. As anonymous as she was. She sat on the edge of the bed, unsure what to do next. Well, according to her wishes, she didn't have to do anything. It would all happen. Then a man appeared from behind the drapes. "What the hell are you doing here?" he growled.

"I don't know what you're talking about. I'm here . . ."

"Shut up. I really don't care why you're here but you're in my way. I've got to hide here until the cops are gone. So just shut up and you won't be hurt."

It was just like her dreams, only real. Oh, God. Real. It was all the Eros Hotel, of course, but she decided not to think about that part. This was what she wanted and she'd ride the tide. "Yes, sir," she said. "Just don't hurt me."

She looked at the man sharing her fantasy. He wasn't particularly good-looking, with thick, shaggy brown hair, bushy eyebrows that almost hid his eyes, thick, very sexy lips and a scar that ran from his temple to the corner of his mouth. His clothing was nondescript, jeans, a dark, long-sleeved polo shirt and loafers. His breathing was rapid, like he'd been running.

After a minute or two, she could see his body relax. "It seems that you didn't bring the cops, lady. That's good." He leered at her, staring at her breasts. "So maybe we can have some fun while I wait."

She found she was shaking. She knew it was her fantasy, but she couldn't seem to stop trembling. "I don't think so," she said, deciding to tough it out.

"I think so," he said, then, in an instant he was behind her and she felt a scarf stuffed in her mouth and another tied around her head to keep it in place. Then, before she could react, her arms were bound to the bedposts with soft rope and he had grabbed one ankle and begun to tie it to the bed's footboard. She struggled to no avail. She was completely helpless. When he was done, she quickly surveyed her body and discovered that she wasn't in any pain, just totally immobilized. It was wonderful, yet scary, just like it was in all her dreams.

"That's really good," he said. "For now, I think I'll leave one leg free. The better to play with you."

When she kicked out with her free leg, he dodged and laughed. "I like them feisty so keep it up. Makes me hot." He lewdly rubbed his crotch.

When she quieted, knowing there was nothing she could do, he said, "See? I like it when a woman knows she can't do anything to stop me. Now let's see what you've got under there."

He took a large pair of scissors from his pocket and snapped them a few times. The snicking sound was both terrifying and arousing and she could feel her pussy react. Pussy. Did Melanie, CFO, think in words like that? Not a chance. But Melanie No One could and did. *My pussy's getting wet and my tits are begging for him to touch and bite and hurt me a little.*

It took only a few moments for the man to cut her dress up the center and part the two sides. "Not bad," he said as he reached down to roughly squeeze her breast. "Nice tits. Well, maybe a little small, but anything more than a handful is wasted." His laugh had a nasty edge.

She kicked out with her free foot and felt a whoosh as her kick landed. "That's not nice," he said, and slapped her thigh. Hard. "Not nice at all." He rubbed his arm, then laughed. "But feisty. You're okay, lady." He grabbed her free leg and twisted it until it hurt. "Feisty is nice, but don't get too active. I might just have to hurt you a little more." With his free hand, he pushed the crotch of her panties aside and thrust two fingers into her sopping pussy. She flew. She didn't remember ever being so excited, and he'd hardly touched her. No pleasant foreplay, just taking what he wanted.

"Such a hot, little girl," he crooned. "You like this, don't you?" Still holding her leg he sawed his fingers in and out. "You're really hot for this."

She shook her head, but she knew that he knew better. She was so high. He pulled his fingers out, leaving her hanging on the edge of a massive orgasm. She wanted to use her fingers to get herself off but her arms were totally immobilized. If he'd just let go of her leg she could probably rub her thighs together to get herself off, but, laughing, he tied her ankle to the other side of the footboard. Her hips squirmed but she couldn't push herself over the edge.

"I do love to see you wiggle like that," he said with a smirk. "I know what you want, slut, but you won't get it. Not until I'm damned good and ready." He rubbed his crotch again. "But I'm not ready yet, maybe not for a long time."

How long could she stay like this? she wondered. If she let herself cool would she get hot again? As she'd explained to Colleen she'd always been a bit impatient about sex. *Oh, well*, she thought, *there's nothing I can do about this*. The man leaned over the bed and cut the front of her bra apart. "I knew it. Really nice tits. I prefer ones with reddish nipples but I guess brown will have to do." He tweaked her already swollen nipples with both hands. "Let's see what these will do for you."

He reached into his pocket and pulled out what looked like a chain. Nipple clamps. She hadn't authorized anything like that. She'd have to talk to Colleen about that. She squirmed as he approached, then he clipped one clothespinlike device to each nipple. They didn't actually hurt, she realized. They just made her aware of her breasts. Constantly aware. "Feel those? Make your little titties hot, don't they."

He laughed as he sat on the edge of the bed. Then he gave a little yank on the chain that connected the clips. She'd cooled off a bit, but now the tugging was making her hot all over again. He sat for a long while, letting her come down, then tugging on that chain.

Finally, he stood and reached into his pocket again. She

stared at his hand, wondering what now. His hand appeared empty. He reached between her legs and pressed his palm against her nylon-covered clit, then moved it slightly. She heard a humming and then the vibrations of the device he had cradled in his hand reverberated through her body. As she almost reached orgasm he pulled his hand away.

"You want to come, don't you my little slut?"

Unable to deny anything, she nodded.

His laugh echoed in her ears. "Not yet." He pulled the flat vibrator off his hand and tucked it inside her panties so it pressed intimately against her. Then he again reached into his pocket and pulled out a small, metal box, about the size of a small cell phone. "Wondering what this is?"

She nodded.

"This is your friend," he said, then pushed a button. The dildo began to hum. *Shit*, she thought, *shit, shit, shit*. So good. She closed her eyes. "Open your eyes and watch what I can do." He pushed another button and the humming became a gentle thrusting, a pressing against her until the device was shaped to fit her contours. Another button and the device began to heat, not uncomfortably, just more warmth to add to her own heat. For what seemed like an eternity he pushed buttons, constantly changing what the vibrator was doing against her. Every time his fingers moved she clenched, waiting for his next exquisite torture. She was kept on the edge, and the edge kept getting higher.

"You know," he said, finally putting the remote-control device on the bed, "I think you've had enough."

She couldn't catch her breath and sweat was running down the sides of her face and between her breasts. "I think you're ready." He leaned over and rubbed his finger against her swollen clit, then sucked it through her panties, playing with the vibrator control at the same time.

That was all she needed. She came, a climax stronger and longer lasting than anything she'd ever experienced. It went on and on, and she seemed to come over and over, until she was exhausted.

She must have either passed out or dozed, because when she returned to the real world, the man was gone, her arms and legs were untied and the gag had been removed from her mouth. Her body was deliciously sore, especially between her legs and her nipples. Damn, she thought as she struggled to sit up. That was the best. The absolute best.

She saw her real clothing on a chair beside the bed and slowly dressed. She realized that this had been just the first of many visits to the Eros Hotel. She'd be back.

Chapter
14

By the third week of September, Marcy had met with Club Fantasy's accountant, Barry Greenstein, who'd recommended a computer software package that would dovetail nicely with his accounting records. Marcy had bought the package and customized it according to Barry's directions. Now she'd begun to duplicate the work of the firm that handled the payroll and was pretty sure she'd be able to take over their functions. She decided to run parallel for a month, just to be positive. She gave a lot of thought to whether she'd be able to continue the payroll operations if she returned to Seneca Falls, but she realized that with her ability to tap into Jenna's computer from her own desktop upstate, fax machines and e-mail she'd be able to handle it all long-distance.

She stopped seeing Steve. They'd spent a few evenings together, but she finally told him that she felt like she was cheating on him, since she was seeing someone else on a regular basis. She kept his phone number and agreed to call him if she changed her mind.

Seeing someone on a regular basis was a bit of an understatement. She and Zack spent several nights a week together, sleeping at his place or in her new, sublet apartment. The apartment fit her needs beautifully, a small living room with something called a sleeping alcove, fitted with a sofa that turned into a comfortable double bed and a tiny strip of a kitchen that suited her lack of cooking skills.

Zack's kitchen, on the other hand, was filled with a host of modern appliances. He cooked for her at least once a week and she was learning to help prepare his favorite Indian dishes. Well, if she admitted it, she had learned how to cut up vegetables and fetch ingredients for him. They went to movies and the occasional Broadway play. They'd become so comfortable that they didn't run to the bedroom every time they were together. They frequently cuddled and slept without making love. Her life had settled into a delightful pattern.

Her book was half finished and the writing, at least of the erotic stories that she would sprinkle throughout the pages, was rolling off her fingers. It was all perfect. She had time for Jenna and Zack and time to write.

AAJ had also begun to hire her to do translations long-distance. After a frightening lull through the first two weeks of September she'd gotten a call from her old boss, Robert— never Bob—Genero, a gap-toothed man who'd always been friendly with both sisters, describing an emergency and asking her to do a translation of an involved legal document regarding a takeover in Milan. She and Ms. Henshaw had already negotiated a generous hourly rate so Bob had faxed her fifty pages. It took her several days and a trip to the bookstore for several texts, but she eventually faxed the results back. Bob had been delighted and assured her that her fax would be humming. It comforted her to know that she'd soon be receiving paychecks on a regular basis.

Marcy met with a lot of women who worked for and with Jenna and found them to be genuinely nice and friendly. Several were women she thought she could become friends with. A delightful blonde named Helen, a bisexual with a live-in female lover, told her about the evening she'd spent playing an eighteenth-century whore, with a scandalously low-cut dress that she'd worn with no underwear and red painted nipples. A tall, slender blonde named Tammy, a free spirit like Chloe, who wanted to become a professional ballerina, told her about her evenings, including one in which she danced in the nude for, then with, an older man who spoke very little English.

A tiny woman named Mei explained that there were men who loved Oriental women. "I don't know what it is," she'd said, "but lots of men want Asian ladies, with long, straight hair and Oriental features. I have several long, heavily embroidered dresses with slits up the sides. Guys just go crazy." She winked. "I have a graduate degree from Columbia in international business but some men love to hear me garble the language. I've gotten really good at pidgin English."

A week before she'd met with a man named Mario, a Latin type with a neat moustache, a swarthy complexion and long, black hair. "I've been a matador, a gang member and a tango dancer. Actually, I've taken several courses at a dance studio and can show off with the best of them on the dance floor. Women eat that stuff up." He also demonstrated how sexy he sounded with just a touch of a Spanish accent.

She spent several afternoons with Rock, who told her silly stories that made her laugh, and serious tales of his adventures both with Club Fantasy and with his friend Erika and Courtesans, Inc. "It was a wonderful organization," he said. "Well-educated, high-class women who gave pleasure willingly to businessmen from all over the country."

"I've never met Erika, but I hear she's quite a lady," Marcy said.

"That's a good word for it. She's a lady. She climbed up from a disastrous beginning with a husband who deserted her, leaving her with a daughter in private school in Europe and a pile of debts. The way she rose above all that might make a great book."

"I hope I get to meet her sometime," Marcy said.

"She and Stuart are so happy out on the island that they

don't get into town much any more. And her daughter Rena and her husband have given her a couple of grandchildren to keep her busy."

"Is Club Fantasy so different from Courtesans, Inc.?"

"Fantasy fulfillment, which Jenna and Chloe created, is a whole new concept. People love it. I think they could stay open seven days a week and never have a free room."

"That's the way the Eros Hotel is. Tell me about you."

"There's not much to tell. I met Erika and joined her group. She sort of gave me to Jenna and Chloe to play bouncer and resident bodyguard."

"Have you ever had to do anything? I mean throw someone out or get money?"

Through his laughter, Rock said, "I don't do collections. It's not like you see in *The Sopranos*, and, fortunately, I've never had to bounce anyone. My presence keeps guys from trying anything out of line, and that's my purpose. I make sure that evey new customer sees me and knows I'm at the Club when they are."

"Do you use the rooms sometimes?"

"Sometimes, on Monday or Tuesday, but not when anyone else is entertaining. I wouldn't want to be distracted from either activity. When I'm with a lady she's my only concern. Any one of us who does his or her job well is totally involved in his partner at all times."

Toward the end of October, Jenna arranged a meeting with a young woman named Darlene McGuire. Unlike Shelly and the others, who had their own customers and used the facilities of Club Fantasy for a cut of the fee, Darlene worked primarily with men whom Jenna or Chloe had contacted and interviewed. She had few, if any, outside clients.

While Shelly was the quintessential model-prostitute, Darlene was short, with curly, flaming red hair and freckles. She wasn't exactly overweight, but she was plump and bosomy, and there was a natural sensuality that radiated from her. They met at the Club on a Monday when it was closed, and settled in the kitchen. When Darlene brought out a bag of donuts, Marcy knew she was just the woman she wanted to talk to.

"So I understand you're writing a book," Darlene said, putting four donuts on a plate. "I've always wanted to write, if only to tell some of the stories from my lurid past."

"You know," Marcy admitted, taking a French cruller, "writing's not as easy as I thought it would be. I figure I need about four hundred pages. That's a lot of words and a lot of ideas to generate. Sometimes my brain is just tapped. That's why I wanted to meet with you and some of the other women who entertain here." Funny, she now said the word entertain without hesitation.

"I never thought about it that way," Darlene said, wiping her sugary mouth on a napkin. "I can give you lots of ideas. Just mention me in the dedication at the beginning."

"Sounds like a deal," Marcy said, pulling out a pad and pen. "What name should I use?"

"Mine, of course. I don't use a phony one. Everyone I know knows what I do, and if they're not fine with it, fuck 'em."

Marcy giggled. "I love your attitude. Some of the women I've talked to have to hide things from their family." Like Shelly.

"I don't know how my folks would have reacted. They died several years ago and I'm an only child. No one to get embarrassed by their relative, the hooker."

Over the next hour, Marcy found out that Darlene, a native New Yorker, had gotten into prostitution to pay for her college education. "My folks had no money, not even enough for a state school. I dated a lot and, at that time, gave it away for free. One guy wanted something exotic and I laughingly said that I'd do it for a hundred bucks."

"What did he want?"

"A threesome with one of his friends, a guy I knew slightly. I can't tell you how shocked I was when he told me he'd pay me the money, but I thought it over and agreed. Actually, it was fun, but since he'd offered I took the cash. He told someone who told someone else and from that point on I guess I was a hooker. Funny, it never really bothered me." She sipped her coffee.

"I met Chloe last winter, just when Club Fantasy was looking to hire a few women to fulfill guys fantasies sort of full-time. She was looking for the small, cuddly type and luckily I fit the bill." She took another large bite of her pastry, and, as she licked the sugar from her lips, Marcy saw the sensuality in her movements. "The hours work out great for me. I'm a paralegal during the day, and I'm saving up to go to law school. I figure that by next fall I'll have enough saved to quit my day job and go. I did great on the law boards, so I just have to figure out which school to go to. I'm leaning toward NYU."

A lawyer? She could almost hear the last of her stereotypes crumbling. "Aren't you tired in the mornings? How many evenings do you work?"

"I don't stay out too late and the fact that the Club is closed Mondays and Tuesdays helps. I usually work about three evenings a week, mostly weekends, but it varies."

"Do you specialize in something or do you do lots of different types of fantasies?"

"I do pretty much anything. I love threesomes, both with two guys and with a guy and another girl."

"Threesomes? I've never really explored that kind of thing. What's it like?" She had made her comment ambiguous enough so that Darlene wouldn't know how inexperienced she truly was.

"It's a gas," she said, "and such a common fantasy that I think I could do just threesomes and make a good living. I think the Club does maybe half a dozen a week."

"Wow. I never knew there were so many guys who wanted that sort of thing."

"Guys and a few women, too. Cheryl and I do it a lot with guys. Have you met Cheryl?"

"No. Jenna mentioned her but she's really busy so there's never been time."

"I can imagine. She's got three kids under six, so she's pretty tied up all day." Darlene giggled. "And we sometimes get tied up at night, too."

Marcy was startled. "Three kids? That's quite a handful."

"They're a hoot. Five, three and seven months. I've had dinner at her house lots of times. I'm in love with her husband, but he's disgustingly monogamous."

"Before coming here to be with Jenna I never imagined women in your profession as having families."

"Mike, her husband, is in his first year of internship and doesn't make diddly squat. So she works when he can be home with the kids and sometimes his mother stays over. She thinks Cheryl is a part-time stewardess which accounts for her odd hours. Cheryl makes the most of the nights she can be here."

Marcy remembered when she'd first found out about Club Fantasy. It wouldn't have occurred to her that the women, and men, who worked there would be educated, married, with kids. Stalling for time as she digested this information, Marcy took another bite of her pastry, then cleared her throat. "Tell me about what a threesome is like."

"I guess there are basically three types. In one, a guy wants to get it on with two women at once. He might want to have one woman sucking his cock and the other crouched over his face, want hand jobs or oral sex from two women at once." She paused, gathering her thoughts, then continued. "In the second kind, a guy wants to watch two women get it on, then join. Lots of nipple and clit sucking, licking and like that. I guess I'm pretty much bisexual, so I enjoy doing it with guys or girls. For me, good sex is good sex, no matter the gender of who's giving and who's getting."

Marcy was trying to absorb what Darlene was saying. She knew she was only interested in guys but she had to admit that she'd had a lesbian fantasy from time to time. She'd never consider acting one out, however. "And the third type?"

"Those guys want to watch a woman make it with another man. Personally, I'm not sure what the attraction is. Watching was never my thing, but if someone wants to watch me fuck someone, and pays for it, that's the best of all the worlds. Great, hot sex, and a check at the end of the evening."

"Watch and not participate?"

"Sure. Sometimes they join in, but many of the guys just want to watch and jerk off. Sounds frustrating to me, but what do I know? I just do what the guy with the cash wants."

Mario had mentioned making love to a man's wife while he watched but Marcy had thought this was unusual. "So the other guy, the one you're making love with, is a male prostitute?"

"Sometimes. Or sometimes two guys want to share a fantasy. That's okay, too, but they both pay. If the third is one of Jenna's guys, then the guy watching pays double the fee. Works out great in every way."

A picture flashed through her mind of tiny Darlene making love with Zack while someone else watched. She wanted to ask whether she'd ever done it with Zack, but she couldn't get the words past her lips. She cleared her throat and redirected her brain. "Do woman ask for threesomes, too?"

"Sure. Lots of women want two guys to service them at the same time. There are lots of combinations. Maybe she wants to have her pussy licked while she gives head to another guy, or one sucks her tits while the other fucks her. There are lots of scenarios."

Fascinated, Marcy asked, "Is that kind of fantasy usually pretty straight or does the dress-up stuff enter into it?"

"I've been a Nazi spy shared between two prison guards, a Southern belle forced to service her maid while the new owner of the plantation watches, a captured lady who services a pirate crew. I've been one of two nurses doing it with a patient, a teacher with two pupils, you get the idea."

"I certainly do. Do you enjoy it every time?"

"Not every time. Sometimes it's just a bore, but I like the money. If an evening gets particularly dull or the guy has bad breath or something, I just think about my bank account and plan my law classes for next fall."

Marcy and Darlene talked for another hour, then she and the tiny woman parted. Back in the apartment, Marcy sat down at her word processor and formed a picture of some of what Darlene had described.

THE PIRATE CAPTAIN

How had the folks at the Eros Hotel done it? Marianne didn't care, because this was her fantasy and they'd guaranteed that it would be as good as anything she'd ever dreamed. She'd changed into a short, black, raggedy-bottom skirt, a white, full-sleeved shirt and wonderfully comfortable high, black boots. No underwear, of course. What pirate captain wears panties and a bra. She tied the red bandana around her head, letting her short, blond curls wisp out below, fastened the wide, leather belt she'd found low around her hips and slipped a wicked-looking dagger in the sheath. She'd found a small, cloth bag attached to the hanger which contained a pair of large, gold hoop earrings and several bangle bracelets and she quickly put them on. Then she opened the door from the dressing room and entered the realm of the pirates.

She knew she was still on the third floor of the Eros Hotel, but if she let herself go she'd really believe she was on the beach waiting for her lieutenant. The sand was warm beneath her feet and huge plants surrounded her. She could almost feel the strong sun overhead, although, if she'd really thought about it she'd have realized that it was just a heat lamp. She didn't want to think about it, just feel.

"We've stored all the loot on board, Captain," a rough voice said behind her. She turned and saw a burly, shirtless man in long, black pants and boots with a sword hanging from a leather scabbard around his waist. His hair was long, his beard thick and his massive chest was covered with thick, curly hair. "But look what we found."

He pulled on the rope he'd been holding and a tall, well-built man emerged from the bushes. He was dressed in shredded tan pants and a tattered white shirt. His feet were bare. Her lieutenant used his hand to raise his captive's face. He was whiskered, with long, straggly, sandy hair and the bluest eyes Marianne had ever seen. The man glared at them both and, when he snarled, his white teeth contrasted with his deeply tanned face. "You'll both be hanged for this," the man said. It was only then that Marianne realized that his hands were tied behind his back.

The lieutenant pulled on the rope attached to his captive's belt and the man stumbled and fell at her feet. "What's this?" she asked, trying not to grin. She knew what he was, of course. He was hers for the evening. As was James, her lieutenant.

"He must have been on the ship we sunk and he probably swam ashore when we boarded her. We found him hiding in the jungle."

"My government will hear of it if you mistreat me," the man at her feet snarled.

"Unless you're very good and very lucky your government won't hear from you at all."

"You can't do this," he said, his voice now more tentative.

She merely raised an eyebrow. James said, "Let's make this clear so that even you can understand. You're out in the middle of the ocean, on an island no one's ever heard of. Our ship is just offshore, yours is at the bottom of the lagoon. We could just leave you here. Do you think you could survive? Alone?

Without food or water except what you can scavenge?" When he didn't answer, James said again, "Do you? The right answer is No, Ma'am."

Marianne watched the realization slowly dawn on her captive's face. "I guess not."

"Not the right answer," James said again. "It's Marianne who decides whether you live or die. The right answer is, No, Ma'am."

It was only a few heartbeats until he said, "No, Ma'am."

She smiled. "Right answer. If you're going to board our ship you will have to earn your keep. Maybe we could make you a cabin boy. What do you think, James?"

"He's pretty scrawny."

Actually, he was anything but scrawny, Marianne thought as she looked him over. Even in his crouched position she could tell that he was almost as muscular as her lieutenant. "Stand him up so I can inspect him. I'll decide whether he's worth taking aboard."

James pulled the man to his feet. He was beautiful. The folks at the Eros Hotel certainly knew how to pick them. "What's your name?" she asked.

"Lucas," he said through his teeth.

"Well, Luke," she said, deliberately diminutizing his name, "what do you think you could do to earn your keep?"

"Nothing," he snapped.

"Okay," she said. "Then we'll just leave you here."

"No," he said quickly. "Don't leave me. I don't know what I can do."

Marianne paused, then said, "I do know. You can service me. If you're talented enough."

"Service you? I don't know what you mean."

"Of course you do. You know exactly what I mean."

"But Captain," James said, "you've never before wanted anyone but me."

"Just for a while, James," she said, moving closer and fondling his crotch. "You and Luke can share."

"But Captain . . ." James said with a frown.

"No buts, James. That's the way it will be, if Luke is able to keep my interest, of course. Otherwise, I will be all yours again and we'll just leave him here. Give me the rope."

"Yes, Captain," James said, handing the rope to her.

"Now you can show our new toy what's required, James."

"Yes, Captain." He walked behind her and reached around to cup her breasts through her blouse. As she watched Luke's face, she felt James nuzzle her ear, then nip at the sensitive tendon that connected her shoulder to her neck. While he kissed and licked her, his very talented fingers found her nipples and pinched and pulled them until they were so tight they were almost painful.

She let her head fall back slightly, then motioned to Luke. "Kiss me."

She watched the decision he had to make play across his handsome face, then, as if reluctantly, he approached and lightly touched his lips to hers. "You'll have to do better than that if you're going to remain alive."

Her grin was almost feral as he appeared to resist, then grabbed the back of her neck and gave her a deep kiss. His tongue found its way into her mouth, stroking hers as he changed positions to deepen their contact. James was still behind her playing with her nipples and she was in heaven. She could feel her nether tissues swell and moisten, and part of her wanted to fall on the sand and let the two men pleasure her. The other part wanted to play out the fantasy as far as it would go.

When Luke move back, she smiled. "That was pretty good. Now let's see what I've got. Strip."

Again he glared at her, but slowly unbuttoned his shirt and then removed it and his pants. Like her, he wore nothing beneath so she could admire his beautifully made body. His shoulders were well-developed, his hips narrow. His chest was smooth, with just a scattering of crisp hair that narrowed to a vee that pointed to his crotch. His penis was flaccid, but still long and thick. She wondered how it would look erect. "Turn."

Slowly, he showed her his sculptured back and tight, well-formed buns. Wonderful. Perfect, she thought. "Turn." Again he faced her.

"You look good enough, but to serve me you'll have to follow orders without question. Can you do that?"

"Yes, Ma'am," he said, his eyes hot with resistance. *He knows enough not to cross me*, she thought.

"Good. Then I want to see what I'll be getting. Stroke your cock."

As she said it she felt James's soft laughter behind her. "You're the very devil, aren't you, Captain." He nipped her and pinched her nipples hard.

"You can't ask me to do that," Luke said.

"I can't?" she said with a raised eyebrow.

It took only a minute for Luke's hand to move to his cock. Slowly, he rubbed the length of it. "Make it grow for me," she growled, "or I'll have James do it."

Luke closed his eyes and slowly his cock swelled. It was amazing, thick and long, becoming harder as he stroked. She felt James unbutton her blouse and pull it off. "Open your eyes, Luke," Marianne said. He lashes flicked up and his gaze fastened on her breasts, now full and swollen from James's attention. From behind, her lieutenant held her breasts cupped in his large hands. "Suck while you play with your cock."

With James holding her breasts, Luke bent forward and flicked his tongue over the tips. Then she felt his teeth bite lightly. It was as if he knew just how hard to press to make her pussy twitch and her juices flow. She was glad that James was behind her, supporting her, or she would have collapsed in a heap. This was everything she'd ever dreamed of.

Then Luke's fingers found her nakedness beneath her

skirt. He brushed her pubic hair lightly, teasing her clit as it swelled. Then he was on his knees, his tongue where his fingers had been. *God, his mouth is amazing,* she thought with the small, conscious part of her brain. His tongue delved into her folds, making her juices flow down the inside of her thigh. Then one finger found her opening and slowly, ever so slowly, slid inside.

It wasn't enough. She needed to be filled. Thicker, harder. She was barely able to take a breath and her pulse was pounding in her ears. Quickly, she was stretched out on the sand, Luke's mouth fastened on her pussy, James licking and sucking on her nipples. She was going to come and, although she wanted to hold back, she couldn't.

She screamed but the licking and sucking continued. She'd never been able to climax twice, but soon she was rising again. She saw Luke unroll a condom over his cock, a complete anachronism but necessary, then his hard erection was nudging at her opening. She wanted him to pound into her, but he entered her only about an inch, then stopped.

James's cock was near her mouth so she took it between her lips. The harder she sucked, the deeper Luke drove his cock. The two men were obviously communicating because, if she stopped licking, Luke pulled back. It was a new experience. She could control the way she was being fucked by the way she used her mouth. She loved it. For long minutes she sucked and licked, teasing herself as much as she was teasing James.

Then she could wait no longer. She made a complete vacuum in her mouth and pulled James's cock deep inside. Luke obliged by grabbing her buttocks and pounding into her cunt deep and hard.

James pulled back and ejaculated on her chest while she and Luke came almost simultaneously. Then Luke picked her up and carried her to a small cot just behind one of the bushes. "Rest here, then you can dress when you're ready." Both men left her then.

She knew she only had a little while until her time was up, but she was hooked. The Eros Hotel had immediately become an addiction and she had to have more. Would she relive this fantasy? Probably, but she had so many more to explore. It would take a long time to live out all of her fantasies, but she knew the Eros Hotel could make each one come true. Yes, it would take a very long time.

Chapter
15

Several of the women she'd met had discussed activities that went on in the basement of Club Fantasy and hearing about it from a distance was fine with Marcy. Zack had invited her to play there now that power games had become part of their sex play but somehow the activities in "the dungeon" as it was called, frightened her, for several reasons.

She didn't want to deal with the fact that both Zack and Jenna played with heavy, off-center sex stuff, nor did she want to accept that something like being chained to a wall or being spanked could excite her. There was just enough of the small-town girl in her to pull away from the most serious games and an investigation of the infamous dungeon.

However, after a long conversation with a woman named Tasha who worked at the Club, she realized that it was all for the sake of pleasure and that her fears, although serious, needed to be faced. What was she afraid of? she wondered. Was she worried that she'd enjoy it too much? She was also worried that seeing Zack in those surroundings would only emphasize that he was a professional prostitute. Would that affect her increasingly serious feelings about him? Did she want to take that risk?

Okay, she thought, *it's time*. She could chalk it up to research for the book, but in reality, she now felt that she was ready for the worst Club Fantasy and Zack could do. Worst? Or would she discover she enjoyed this, too.

One evening she mentioned to Zack that she thought she was ready to see what went on in the basement of the brownstone "Would you really like to see it?" he asked with one of his famous leers. "I'd love to show it to you and . . ."

Suddenly, Marcy was both nervous and excited. "I think I'm ready."

Zack called the following Monday afternoon and invited her to meet him at the brownstone. The Club was closed and Rock was visiting his family in California, so when Marcy arrived she let herself in with the key Jenna had had made for her. She punched the alarm code and called, "Zack?"

Zack appeared through a door in the hall, the one she knew led to the basement. She was more nervous than she'd been with him in a long time, but once she saw his warm smile, her fears lessened. He grabbed her and kissed her thoroughly. "Hi."

Catching her breath, Marcy answered, "Hi, yourself."

He nuzzled her nose, then said, "Ready?" When she nodded, he said, "Follow me."

As she hesitantly followed Zack down the stairs to what was once a normal basement, she formed all kinds of images in her mind. Dungeon. Walls that looked like stone, torchlight making shapes dance on the walls, the musty smell of old furniture. She pictured chains and manacles hanging from the walls and she could almost hear screaming.

The reality was nothing like what she'd feared. Two of the walls were paneled in dark wood while the other two were covered with mirrored tiles, as was the ceiling, all reflecting the light from several ceiling fixtures and two crook-neck lamps. Hooks of all sizes and at varying heights protruded from one wall and hung from the ceiling by chains of differing lengths. She pictured submissive women hanging from them, unable to free themselves, available to whatever their master wanted to do to them.

Whips, crops and paddles of all sizes and shapes were hung on the walls, ready for use. As she stared, her eyes widened. She didn't know how far she was ready to go. Granted, she and Zack had played with bondage, but this? Tulip. That was the safe word and she had promised to use it if she felt uncomfortable. She released a long breath.

On one side of the room stood a table unlike anything Marcy had ever seen before, with rings and hooks along the sides and enclosed space beneath containing who knew what. There were several cabinets along another wall, topped with highly polished counters, and a few closets, their closed doors emphasizing their mystery. She wondered what they contained: cock rings and ball spreaders? Hoods and gags? Ropes? Nipple clamps, dildos and vibrators? Chains with large padlocks? Marcy remembered an interview with one of Jenna's employees and they talked about delicious fear. What this mixture of anxiety and excitement she was experiencing what they'd been talking about?

"We can change the ambiance here with just a few adjustments." He approached a recessed panel of switches and flipped one. Suddenly, the room was darker, making it almost hard for Marcy to see him. He must have thrown another switch and the lights flickered, creating the look of torches the way she'd imagined it. He turned the lights back on and she realized she'd been shivering. He turned a dial and she could hear the sound of voices, far away, forceful voices punctuated occasionally with screams. "A bit theatrical," Zack said, "but lots of clients like it."

"I'll bet," Marcy said, barely able to get the words past the lump in her throat.

"I can see your chest rising and falling really quickly," Zack said, crossing the room and putting his arm around her shoulders. "Is that from excitement or from fear? We won't do anything you're not ready for."

"What if I'm never ready for some of this stuff?" Marcy asked, more worried about his answer than she cared to admit.

Zack looked surprised at the question. "Then we won't do it, of course," he said. "Listen, Marce, I love sex in all its forms, but I don't have to do everything with you."

Of course. He had so many others he would play with, she thought with a pang.

"That's not what I mean," he said, reading her mind as he often did. "I'm happy with you and whatever activities you're not interested in, well, that's that. If I never tie you, or anyone, to the bed again, that would be okay with me."

Marcy took in a deep breath and let it out slowly. "Sometimes I get scared," she said. The depth of her feelings for Zack concerned her more and more. She heard Jenna's warning. *He's a male prostitute. Don't get too involved.* She was already in too deep and it terrified her.

Fortunately, Zack had misunderstood. "Don't worry," he said. "Nothing will happen that doesn't give pleasure."

Letting him know how she felt was counterproductive. He'd run like a scared rabbit. If she were being honest with herself, however, she might have to admit that she was in love with him. No. Not now. Not here. She inhaled deeply and let go of her fears. Whatever happened, it would be wonderful or she'd stop. She'd worry about her feelings about Zack another time. "Okay, what's your pleasure?"

Zack held her, letting his caring flow into her. She was such a wonderful addition to his life, and his treasure. He found himself thinking about her at odd hours, wondering what she was doing. He continued his entertaining and still loved making love with wonderful and varied women, but when he thought about pleasure, it was Marcy's face that filled his mind. He was sliding down a slope, thinking more and more about a future with her. But how could he even consider it when he was what he was. Well, he thought, he'd deal with that aspect later.

He looked around the room. So many things he wanted to try with her. Games, toys, so many ideas whirled through his mind. Then he smiled to himself. He knew how much she loved dildos and he had something really new for her to try. He released her and opened a closet, pulling out a strange-looking rocking horse a friend had built for him and his clients. His clients. Could he enjoy things with Marcy that he also had enjoyed with other women? He put that out of his mind. Pleasure was pleasure, no matter how it was conceived.

He pulled the rocking horse to the middle of the room. She would enjoy this. He couldn't wait.

A rocking horse? Marcy thought. It was very realistic look-ing, black, with a white mane and tail and large black rockers that allowed the wooden animal to move back and forth. Several switches filled a small panel on the horse's rump. Marcy didn't understand so she stood quietly. Then Zack reached into a drawer and pulled out several strips of soft leather with what looked like buckles at the end. "Remember the word," he said.

"Tulip," she said. "I won't forget."

First he undressed her, kissing her skin as he worked. The ideas the room put into her head excited her, but his kisses were loving and caring. It felt strange to be naked when he was still fully dressed. Finally, he kissed her mouth, a deep, knee-buckling kiss that warmed her soul.

With a slight smile, Zack buckled the leather around her wrist so that long ends dangled. Then he attached short, leather straps to her ankles. He reached into another drawer and pulled out a slender, black dildo and fastened it to the seat of the horse. "Okay, climb on."

"I don't know about this," she said.

"I do, but you can stop at any time. Will you trust me for a few moments?"

With little hesitation, Marcy said, "Of course."

She lifted her leg and climbed over the rocking horse. He gently settled her so that the slender dildo penetrated her easily, then fastened her ankles together beneath the horse so she couldn't support her weight on them. She had to sit firmly with the dildo deeply imbedded inside her. Strangely, it was so thin that she barely felt it.

"This little guy is pretty ingenious," he said, patting her horse's rump. Then he buckled her wrists together beneath the neck of the horse so she was leaning over its neck. The final step was to attach nipple clamps to her breasts and pull the chain tight around the horse's head. "Now," Zack said, "ride 'em cowboy." He pressed a button on the horse's behind and the animal began to rock of it's own accord. As it rocked her body shifted so the chain pulled at her nipples and the dildo moved slightly in and out of her pussy. Since she was without the use of either her hands or her feet she couldn't control anything, just go with the motions of the animal between her thighs.

"God," she said as her heat began to build. "That's amazing."

"It is, isn't it." He settled into a black, leather lounge chair and watched as she literally fucked herself. Higher and higher she climbed with no control over her body. It was an entirely new sensation, and she loved it. She clenched her vaginal muscles to enhance the sensation, now unaware of Zack, sitting with his eyes fixed on her. "I love watching you taking. Just taking."

She closed her eyes and concentrated on the feelings. Higher and still higher until sweat was trickling down her sides. She wanted to climax but she found, to her surprise, that she couldn't quite reach orgasm. She tried to rise so she could ram the dildo more deeply inside of her or move around to fill herself more completely, but even clenching her thighs against the horse's sides didn't help. She wanted to lean back and change the angle of the slender dildo, but that merely pulled the chain attached to her nipples. The pain pulled her back down.

"Nasty animal, that one," Zack said. "You're finding that you can't quite come, aren't you?"

"I need it," she panted.

"I know." He stood and walked to the horse, then turned a dial, speeding up the rate of the horse's rocking. "How's that?"

It seemed to make things worse. "God," she said. "I need to come."

He chuckled. "I'll help you." Another switch and the dildo seemed to grow thicker, filling her more fully. "And I think I'll make you come. Right. Now!" He slapped her naked thigh several times and, screaming, she came over and over again. He kept slapping and the spasms kept clenching her vaginal muscles around the now-huge dildo.

"Stop," she said, eventually, breathless and exhausted. "No more. Tulip."

Zack quickly unfastened her and lifted her from the horse. He sat in the lounge chair with her curled in his lap. When she could think again, she found that her mind was whirling. She'd climaxed from a slap. Several slaps, actually. Was she a pervert? Pain as pleasure? "I don't understand," she said.

"About what? Good sex?"

She took a deep breath. He'd slapped her. Was that his perversion, too? "You hit me."

"I slapped you during sex. That's quite a different thing. And you got a thrill out of it."

Hiding her face against his shirt, she said, "I guess I did."

"Does that worry you? It shouldn't. Sometimes a little pain at just the right moment can be very exciting. It doesn't mean anything."

Tears trickled down her face. "I'm afraid it does. There must be something wrong with me. Something sick."

Zack used his index finger to tip her face. He kissed her wet cheeks, then said, "Open your eyes and look at me." She looked and saw a softness that she might have mistaken for love. "I wouldn't ever do anything to hurt you, either physically or mentally. If I'd known how unhappy it would make you I never would have done it. Think about it for a moment, though. Sex is a game of sensations. You like it when I scratch you and I love it when you run your nails down my back. Is this so different?"

She nodded slightly. It was completely different.

"Try to be honest for a moment. Did it give you pleasure?"

She started to deny it, but Zack had asked her to be honest. "I guess."

"It stung when I slapped you and that heat flowed to your sweet pussy. You climaxed. Right?"

"I guess."

"Here's my theory. Anything that gives pleasure and doesn't harm anyone is fine between consenting adults. We're certainly consenting adults."

"I guess." She knew she sounded really upset.

"You're getting to sound like a broken record. Okay. Tell me, what harm did my slaps do. To anyone."

She thought about it and she couldn't come up with an answer. Some things were just wrong. Weren't they? "None. But it's wrong."

"Is it? Why? What about the nipple clamps. Those cause pain that ends up being pleasure and there's nothing wrong with any of that."

"Stop being logical. I hate it when you do that," she said with a self-deprecating smile. "I don't know what's wrong with it."

"If you don't like it, I'll never do it again, but I won't ask the same of you. When I'm really hot, sometimes a slap on the ass like that adds just the right amount of spice and I encourage you to do that for me occasionally."

She turned so she could look him in the eye. "Really?"

He smiled indulgently. "Really, and I can't very well ask my clients to do that. They want their own pleasures."

Marcy was warmed inside and flattered. He was asking her to do something he desired and couldn't get from anyone else.

"There's nothing wrong with a little pain if it's also pleasure," he continued. "There's a lot of spanking and such done around here. Try to relax and just roll with it. I don't mean for yourself, but be tolerant. You might want to write stories about it for your book. Maybe a gentleman who wants to spank a naughty maid, or a teacher who takes a ruler to a recalcitrant student. Haven't you read stories like that in books or on the net?"

"Yes, but I kind of dismissed it. I thought that only perverts did stuff like that."

Zack grinned, his cheeks shadowed by his slight five o'clock shadow. "Like me? Like Jenna and Chloe and all the others you've met? We all play with pain and pleasure from time to time, and it can be delicious, as you've seen firsthand, if you'll pardon the pun."

As always, his grin was infectious. "More education for the little, naive girl from the sticks."

"Don't you dare insult my girlfriend."

Girlfriend? When did that happen. "Want to rent a video and go back to my place?" he asked, deftly changing the subject. Did he realize what he'd just said?

"Sure," Marcy said. "Let me take a quick shower upstairs." As she stood, she felt the sting in her buttocks. Maybe it was okay.

After she got back to her apartment, Marcy thought about what Zack had said for quite a while and was amazed at how far she'd come in the past few months. She'd accepted prostitution, threesomes, spanking, all things she'd not have dreamed about a year earlier.

The following day she thought about the previous evening and, as she often did, worked out her feelings at the word processor. She was amused at how her stories had changed. From a woman who couldn't have an orgasm to a story like the one that was forming in her mind.

THE MAID

The Eros Hotel provided everything for its clients, but for the fifteen hundred dollars per hour charge on his credit card, Brad expected this kind of service. He hurriedly changed into the clothes had been given, an outfit appropriate to his role, master of the nineteenth-century estate. He was impatient, but he understood the need for the trappings of his fantasy. He also enjoyed the anticipation. Still, he almost didn't button the front of the vest. Finally, he sighed and fastened the vest, then the jacket, dropping the large, gold watch into the vest pocket, fob linked through the buttonhole.

He glanced in the full-length mirror in the dressing room, then slipped his twenty-first century clothing, wallet and keys into the high-tech safe and set a new combination. Eros thought of even the smallest details. Everything complete, he walked through the door and down the hall to Room 21. Who would he find this time? He'd been to the Eros Hotel almost a dozen times and he'd yet to encounter the same woman twice.

He opened the door to Room 21 and strode inside. *Walk like your character,* he had read in the instructions months earlier, *and you'll become him.* "There's no one here to take my jacket," he called, unfastening the single gold button.

"I'm so sorry, sir," a voice with a slight accent called from beyond another door. "I'm really sorry but I'll just be a moment. Please excuse me, sir."

Brad sighed. "Be quick about it," he called. "You know I don't like to be kept waiting. My servants should be prepared to see to my every need."

"Oh, yes, sir," the voice said. He heard the door open then caught his first glimpse of his lady for the evening. She looked to be about twenty-five, tiny, probably no more than five feet tall, with her brown hair stuffed beneath a cloth cap. She was not really pretty, but desirable somehow, with huge brown eyes and a thoroughly kissable lipstick-reddened mouth. She wore a traditional maid's uniform of white blouse and white apron, but her black skirt was short and fluffy. She also wore long, mesh stockings and ridiculously high heels. Well, maybe it wasn't a traditional uniform but rather the one he'd seen in several porn movies.

"May I take your umbrella and jacket, sir?" she asked, her eyes downcast.

Brad stopped staring and snapped back into character. "You certainly may. What's your name."

"Margaret," the girl said. "I'm new, just hired this week." There was a trace of an Irish lilt in her speech. "I hope you'll forgive my tardiness in welcoming you home."

"I'll consider it. Where's my coffee?"

Apparently flustered, the girl retreated into the other room, to return a few moments later with a cup and saucer balanced on a small tray, a silver coffeepot in her other hand. She placed the pot on the small table beside the "master's chair" and motioned for Brad to sit down. As he settled into the wingback chair she poured him a cup of coffee and said, "I'm told you like it black, sir."

The Eros Hotel knew all his likes and dislikes, down to the tiniest detail. "That's right. Stand beside me and tell me why you were delayed in answering my summons."

Margaret stood beside Brad's chair, her thigh brushing his elbow. "I was fixing my stockings, sir," she said. "I had gotten a tear in one and had to change." She lifted one leg for his inspection. "See? It wouldn't do for me to appear in anything imperfect."

Brad glimpsed the ruffled garter just at the level of the short skirt, then reached out and touched the shapely leg beneath the bumpy mesh. "That's certain," he said, "but how did you manage to damage your first one? They cost money, you know."

Primly, Margaret gazed at the floor, her hands clasped in front of her. "I'm really sorry, sir. I was making up the bed in the next room and I caught my leg on a rough spot on the frame. I'll pay for the stocking of course."

"Of course, but you'll have to pay for your clumsiness, too." He touched the inside of her thigh and, as she stood beside him, slid his hand upwards. As he reached the garter, he felt her tremble, but he slipped his hand further up, over her smooth skin. Expecting to find the crotch of her panties, he was surprised when he touched her naked, wet pussy. He almost lost it right there, but he slowly stroked her hot flesh and cupped her plump buttocks. "I won't dismiss you for your tardiness or your clumsiness, but you'll have to be punished so you'll be sure it won't happen again. Do you understand?"

"Yes, sir," she whispered. Brad could feel her shiver and hear her breathing speed up. The Eros Hotel always fitted the women to their roles, so he knew she'd get off on the same things that he wanted today. That was one of the most delicious things about Eros. The women always seemed to be enjoying things as much as he did. "Over my knee."

Margaret bent over, slowly settling across his lap. He knew she could feel the growing bulge in the front of his trousers, but he was well able to wait, and, of course, it was in the woman's best interest to go as long as she could. The cleverness of making the payment an hourly rate meant that the women wanted him to last, yet be completely satisfied so he'd return often. Margaret wiggled as if getting comfortable across his thighs. Then he raised her skirt.

God, her ass was gorgeous, creamy white skin with a slight brown shadow in the crease between her thighs. And the entire picture was framed by her skirt and black hose. Slowly, he swirled his palm over her skin, relishing the expectation, both hers and his. "You know that I'm doing this just to teach you a lesson, don't you?"

"Of course, sir. I know I must be suitably chastised."

"Right. I think ten ought to suffice. Count them for me."

"One," she whispered as his palm fell onto her asscheek.

"Louder," Brad snapped, slapping her other cheek, harder this time.

"Two!" she cried.

"Better." His hand fell a third time, then a fourth, each slap followed by Margaret's count. A fifth and sixth followed, then Brad stopped to savor the moment. Her cheeks were becoming bright pink, hot beneath his resting palm. "You have four more to go," he said, "but you can make it easy or difficult. Do you want to lessen your punishment, my dear?"

"Oh, yes, sir. What must I do?"

Brad pushed her to the floor between his spread knees and unzipped his fly. He merely pointed to his hard cock, thrusting from his trousers, glad that he never wore underwear during his visits to Eros. Shyly, she gazed up at him from her position between his thighs. She licked her lips and smiled. "Oh, yes, sir." She took his cock in her hand and moved her fingers so that he felt the need to come despite his best efforts. This was the best part, using all his willpower to resist ejaculation. Eros knew that about him, too. "Not so fast," he snapped.

"Sorry, sir," she said, a grin on her face. Then she lowered her reddened lips to the tip of his cock and slowly sucked the tip into her warm, wet mouth. As she sucked, she tightened her grip on the base of his erection so he couldn't come if he wanted to. The pressure was immense, but the pleasure was still better. God, she had a talented mouth, causing just the right amount of suction and swirling her tongue over the tip of his prick. He considered whether he wanted to come in her mouth or her pussy and decided that he wanted her beautiful little snatch around him when came. But that wouldn't be for quite a while.

"Enough," he said, his voice harsh. "You still have four slaps remaining."

"Yes, sir," she said, standing and then stretching out across his lap, her elbow pressing against his naked, wet cock, driving him mad with lust. Her ass cheeks were still pink, but he reddened them considerably with his next two slaps. "You didn't count. That's five additional for your disobedience."

Genuine tears flowed down her face as she looked at him. "Please, sir, no more."

"Unfortunately, it's your own fault, and I'll need the paddle to do these right."

"Oh, no, not the paddle." He knew that she was aware of the safe word, but there was a gleam of pleasure in her eye as she rose and fetched a wooden paddle from a drawer. He had known all the implements he could want would be somewhere in the room. She knelt before him and presented him with the paddle, eyes downcast. He held it, stroking the smooth wood as Margaret again lay across his lap. He caressed her ass with the cool wood, making circles over her fiery flesh.

"You're making it worse," Margaret whimpered, "making me wait, sir."

"I know," Brad said, smiling. Then he raised the paddle and slapped it smartly on her butt. "Eight," she said.

"Actually, it's nine but we'll accept your count." He delivered the remaining smacks over the sounds of her crying, then he urged her to a standing position in front of him. "Get some lotion and I'll soothe your bum."

From the same drawer from which she had gotten the paddle she pulled a tube and handed it to him. Then she turned around and knelt on the carpet so he could get a perfect view of her flaming ass. He squeezed a large dollup of the lotion onto his palm, and slowly rubbed it over her skin.

"All right, stand up." She stood before him, trembling. "Make me ready." She rubbed her hands over her buns then slid her slippery fingers up and down over his cock, then she quickly opened a packet and unrolled a condom over his throbbing cock.

Rising, she grinned at him, then slipped back into character. Brad placed one hand behind each of her knees and pulled her forward until she was kneeling on the chair, her pussy poised over his cock. "Down!" She lowered her body until he could slide his erection over her hot, slippery ass cheeks. God, he loved the feel of a heated ass against his thighs. She wiggled, allowing her body to inflame him. Slowly, she allowed his rock-hard prick to penetrate her. She felt just right, so tight around him. Her hot cheeks against his groin, her hands on his shoulders, the sight of her fully dressed, her head thrown back in ecstasy all conspired to take his control. His orgasm burst from him as he drove his cock deep into her, thrusting over and over. He couldn't catch his breath or prevent the loud scream that erupted from the depths of his soul. It had never been any better.

Margaret collapsed against his cloth-covered chest, panting as hard as he was. "I'm not supposed to slip out of character," she said, "but that was fabulous . . ." She winked. ". . . Sir."

Eros. It was as it always had been, a totally, unqualified success. He'd be back, whether to Room 21 or to another, he'd be back. Soon.

When she finished the story she was so hungry that she masturbated to orgasm. But it wasn't enough. For the first time she called Zack and invited herself over for the following afternoon. She made it quite obvious that she was coming over for sex. But what kind of sex? she wondered. For the first time she thought about her sex life with Zack objectively. He'd taught her so much about what she liked and what her body was capable of. But what about him? What about what he liked? Suddenly, she wanted very much to know Zack. Could she be brave enough to find out?

The following afternoon she showed up at Zack's apartment and he answered the door wearing only a pair of low-slung jeans. "I guess you figured me out," she said, a bit embarrassed. This wasn't the Marcy she had been just a few months ago and she loved her new attitude.

"I'm pretty perceptive," he said, "especially when you sound so hungry." His eyes glowed with pleasure. "You're fabulous when you're hungry, free of the constraints you had when we first met."

Curiosity was gnawing at her. How could she ask? Maybe she didn't have to, at least directly. She wanted to give him the kind of pleasure he'd given her but she had no idea what to do. She remembered how he'd treated her the first time they made love and decided on a plan. "Let's go into the bedroom so we can make love."

"Pushy broad, aren't you?" he said with a wide, mischievous grin.

Her grin matched his. "You bet."

"Yes, ma'am." They went into the bedroom and she quickly stripped to her bra and panties. Over the past few weeks she'd bought several new pair and today she wore black lace. She knew she was fat, but she loved the look in Zack's eyes. He didn't see her weight, just what was beneath. He seemed to be enjoying her attitude so she pressed on despite the tiny ripples of nervousness that slid through her. "Take those jeans off," she growled.

"I love it when you're masterful," Zack said with a chuckle, then pulled his pants off. He wore nothing underneath and his excitement was obvious.

She was on the right track and she almost giggled. Could she carry out her slightly dominant role? She'd carry it as far as she could. "Lie down."

When he was stretched out on his bed, she sat beside him. "I realized something," she said. "I don't know what you like, so I'm going to find out." She kissed his chest, then his belly. "Which do you like best?"

"I like them both," he murmured.

"Not the right answer. You have to choose." She kissed him again, then nibbled at his skin. "Which?"

"I like it when you kiss me here," he said, indicating his belly.

"Good start. Now here?" She kissed his neck. "Or here?" She nibbled on his ear.

"I like that second one," he said, smiling.

In the next few minutes she found out that he liked being kissed on the mouth better than any other place. She wanted to know about more intimate activities but it was difficult to be brazen. Gathering her courage she looked at his cock as it twitched and seemed to grow thicker. She'd touched him before, of course, but in the heat of passion. Now she wanted information and her brain was engaged, not her body. She slid her palm from the tip of his cock to the base. Then from the base to the tip. "A or B?" she asked.

"C. Both of the above," he said, and she realized that he was finding it difficult to talk.

She was in heaven. Giving Zack pleasure was proving to be a heady experience. "That's cheating, but I'll accept that answer." How much further could she go? She leaned over and lightly licked the shaft of his penis, again once from tip to base and again from base to tip. "A or B?" she asked again.

"Shit, Marcy, I love it all."

"Good," she purred. "So good." She continued to lick his erection as it became still harder, then reached between his thighs and cupped his sac. She'd never done anything like this with a man before but the quick catch of Zack's breath was incredibly rewarding.

She knew she couldn't do the deep throat thing, but she thought she might be able to take part of his cock into her mouth so, while still fondling his testicles, she put just the tip into her mouth. "Do you like that?" It was a serious question and she hoped he would take it as such.

"Baby," he said, panting, "I like it so much that you'd better stop before something happens that I don't know whether you're ready for." He grabbed her, ripped off her panties, quickly rolled on a condom and plunged his cock into her. She was amazed to discover that, although she wasn't really aroused, making love with Zack gave her unbelievable pleasure. Zack climaxed almost immediately.

Later, calm, he said, "You didn't climax."

"True, but I loved what we did and I know that, if I play my cards right, I might convince you to play with me later."

"You bet." He rolled over and cradled her in his arms. "You know, you're an amazing woman." He stopped short of saying that he loved her, but she knew and they had plenty of time.

Chapter
16

Marcy used her key to let herself into Jenna's apartment. Her sister had sounded really bad on the phone and she'd run down the two flights from her apartment to Jenna's. "Sis," she called.

"In here," a small voice answered from the bathroom.

Dashing to the small bathroom, Marcy found her sister draped over the toilet bowl looking absolutely awful. "What in the world is wrong with you?" Marcy asked, turning on the cold water and soaking a face cloth.

"Something I ate, I guess," she said, weakly, rinsing her mouth. "I think it's mostly out of me now."

"Oh, baby," Marcy said, holding the wet cloth against her sister's forehead. "I'm so sorry. What can I do? Do you think you need a doctor or the paramedics?"

"I don't think it's anything serious," Jenna said, holding her stomach. "Let me sit here for a few minutes, then maybe you could help me to my bed."

"Of course, Sis."

About half an hour later, the two women were in Jenna's bedroom, Jenna on the bed, looking a bit less green than she had when Marcy first arrived. "I think I'll live," Jenna said. "Phew. That was awful."

"Can I get you some soup or something? Are you sure you don't need an ambulance?"

"No, sweetie," Jenna said, a slightly forced smile on her face. "I'm really much better. As Mom used to say, 'Better an empty house than a bad tenant.' "

"That always made me so mad when I was sick," Marcy said. "It was as though throwing up wasn't so terrible. And it always was."

"It's pretty awful, but it really did solve the problem, whatever it was. I think I just need to sleep for about three days." She looked at the clock, then grabbed the phone, dialed, listened, then hung up. "She's not home. Let me try her cell." Again she phoned, then hung up. "She's turned her phone off again," she growled.

"Who, what?"

"Chloe. She's about as reliable as the weather. Shit. I've got an interview with a new client at four and it's almost three-thirty now." She swung her legs over the side of the bed and struggled to a sitting position.

"You can't go out," Marcy said. "You're in no condition to do an interview. Call him and postpone."

"It's a her, and we've already had to reschedule twice. She's been vetted and already approved." She reached for the phone and again seemed to get no answer. "I can't reach her." She stood up, but her wobbly legs wouldn't quite hold her and she dropped back onto the edge of the bed. "Shit. I've never stood up a client before."

"Things happen," Marcy said.

Jenna gazed into space, then looked her sister in the eye. "You could do it."

"Me?"

"Sure. You know what we do and how. You're a good listener and it's really not that difficult."

Not a chance. What did she know about other people's fantasies? Actually, she admitted to herself, quite a lot. She'd done interviews, written stories, all based on other people's fantasies. She had to stop thinking like the old Marcy. "I'm not experienced at this sort of thing," Marcy protested.

"I wasn't either when I started Club Fantasy. I just went with what people told me and, well, sort of helped them to talk about what they most wanted. Please, Marcy. How bad could it be? You do all the bookkeeping and note taking. You know almost as much about what goes on at the Club as I do."

"I do, I guess, but I haven't done it. There's so much kinky stuff I know nothing about."

"You know more than you think, but if you really don't think you can do it," she paused, for effect Marcy thought, then continued. "I'll just wait until she calls and apologize."

"Cut it out, Sis. Don't try to guilt me into this," Marcy said. "I'm not biting."

Jenna chuckled. "I'm sorry, Marce. I didn't mean it that way. I know you have your limits." Through her grin, she added, "It always worked when we were kids though."

Marcy couldn't help but smile. "It did, didn't it, and it still does. But what if I louse this up?"

"If she doesn't become a visitor, so be it. It will be good material for the book."

Marcy's laugh was full now. "Okay, you beast, you've got me. Don't push it."

Jenna lay back on the bed. In a weak voice, with a slight moan, she said, "Maybe some soup before you go?"

Marcy slowly shook her head. "God, you're impossible." Marcy got the information about the contact and made the soup.

Twenty minutes later she entered the small bar where she was to meet Caitlin Petrie. She was in her early thirties, with short almost black hair and dark eyes. She was sitting at a small table toward the back of the room, gazing at the door. Her eyes followed Marcy as she walked to her table. "You must be Caitlin," Marcy said. "My name's Marcy."

"I thought I was supposed to meet a woman named Jenna."

"She's my sister and she's not able to be here. I hope we can work together." Was that the right expression?

"That's a good way to put it. I don't know whether I can do this."

"You certainly don't have to."

"But I want to. I've always wanted to."

"Okay. Why don't you tell me what your fantasy is?"

Caitlin sipped her drink. "I'm a bit of a softie. A wuss, actually, and I don't know whether you can make a silk purse out of a sow's ear."

"Let me be the judge of that," Marcy said. "Just tell me about it slowly."

When Caitlin said nothing, Marcy was content to let the silence continue. Finally, struggling for words, Caitlin said, "I want to be powerful. I want a man to grovel at my feet. I want to force him to do my bidding." She let out a large sigh and her voice dropped almost to a whisper. "Is that so terrible?" A deep blush colored her face and she sipped her drink, keeping her head down.

"You know, I was sort of like you not so many months ago. It's not easy to become assertive and I still have a ways to go, but it can be done."

"Assertive. I like that word better than aggressive. I know it sounds really lame, but that's what I want. I don't want to yell and scream, I just want some man to bow to my will." She laughed, nervously, and twirled the plastic swizzle stick from her drink. "I got that phrase from a movie."

Marcy patted her hand. "What was the movie about?"

"It was a cop thing. I don't remember the details."

"How about a cop thing for your fantasy?"

"What kind of cop thing?" Caitlin said, her face brightening.

"At Club Fantasy you can be anything you want. What if

you were a cop, with a prisoner handcuffed to a chair. He'd do anything not to go to jail." Marcy deliberately left the sentence hanging.

"I couldn't do that."

"Why not? In a fantasy you can be anything you want to be." Was she living her own fantasy? She could be the girlfriend of the most gorgeous male prostitute in the world. That would be her fantasy. But what about when she woke up?

"Anything I want to be. Do you think so?" Her eyes widened.

"We've done all kinds of fantasies for all kinds of people. Think about it."

"Yeah," Caitlin said, her voice breathy. "He'd do anything I wanted. He'd have to, wouldn't he. Even really bad things."

"We could make that happen for you. You know the fee?"

"Jenna told me and it's no problem. And expenses, too."

"Actually, I think the expenses will be minimal. Costume rental will be about it."

"A cop? Really? With a gun and everything?" Her disbelief was almost comical.

Marcy lowered her voice. "Yes, Officer. Sometimes we make films of the fantasies for the player to see over and over. Would you like that, too? It would cost extra, I'm afraid."

"A film?" Marcy could see her chest heave. "I'd like that. How much?"

"We usually charge an extra five hundred, but that's for someone to film the event." God, she sounded professional. Actually, she'd written a scene like this for her book and was delighted to find out that it worked pretty much the way she'd imagined. "If you'd just like the hidden cameras to record it, it would be three-fifty."

"You could really do that? That would be great. Then I could watch it later."

"Done. Any requirements for the man involved?"

"Big. It won't mean nearly as much if he's a wimp, too. Some big, tough-looking, gang type." Her voice dropped again. "Can you do that?"

Rock. She'd have to check his schedule, but he'd be perfect. "I've got just the guy. Tattoos and everything."

"Wow," Caitlin said. "You're wonderful. But I'm not sure I'd know what to say. How to act."

Marcy considered. "I could write you a little story that you could use for ideas. Then you would have a starting place and you could branch off whenever you chose."

Caitlin looked relieved. "Could I have it before so I could get an idea of what it would be like?"

"Sure. I could write it and fax or e-mail it."

"Wow. Would you charge extra?"

"I don't think so. What would you like your name to be?"

"I hadn't thought about that. I don't know. How about Callahan? Like Dirty Harry. He's my hero." She grinned and straightened her shoulders. "Go ahead, sucker, make my day."

"Sure. That will work. I'll write a short story all the way through but you can change whatever you want, go off in a different direction if you like. Should I give it to the guy, too? Then he'd know what to expect."

Sitting up in her chair, she said, "No. He needs to be spontaneous, you know. Just react to me and my power."

"Right. Let's coordinate our calendars and see what we can work out." They agreed on a date toward the end of the following week.

Marcy called Jenna, who was feeling quite a bit better, and told her about the interview. "What a fabulous idea," Jenna said when Marcy told her about the story. "We've done that a few times, but since you're writing stories for your book you'd be perfect. However, from now on we'll charge for the stories. Two hundred a pop."

Marcy giggled. "At that rate I'd make more doing that than writing my book."

"Damn straight," Jenna said, laughing.

THE POLICE OFFICER

Caitlin arrived early and sat in the living room of the innocent-looking brownstone, her palms sweating, her pussy tingling with expectation. Finally, at exactly the appointed time, she was escorted upstairs to a small dressing room. There it was, her outfit for the evening. The policewoman costume was amazingly authentic, navy slacks and shirt complete with badge and phony ID pin, heavy leather shoes, a wide belt with its complicated mechanism to hold it up. She had a nightstick, a very realistic gun and holster and several pair of handcuffs.

As she changed from her jeans and sweatshirt, she noticed with a grin that the slacks had the center seam adjusted so the crotch split. Before she put them on she removed her panties. Then she found a note beneath the clothing. "Your prisoner awaits. He's willing to do anything to guarantee that you won't turn him in. Have your way with him and enjoy the evening in whatever way will give you the most pleasure."

By the time Caitlin finished reading the note, the crotch of her slacks was soaked. This would be even better than her dreams. She looked around and spotted a door labeled Entry so she opened it and stepped inside. The room looked just like a police station, with two gray metal desks, folding chairs, file cabinets and bookshelves. Every horizontal surface was covered with papers and file folders. Typewriters, telephones and computer terminals topped the desks. There was an open box of donuts on one bookshelf and a coffeemaker on another. The room smelled of a combination of sweat, burned coffee and very old, lingering cigarette smoke covered with a floral air freshener.

A long wooden bench filled one wall and seated on it was a biker type, with black jeans and a black leather vest over a tight, short-sleeved tee shirt. His boots were huge, with chains dangling from the sides. His arms were thick with muscle, every inch of skin covered with permanent artwork. He even had a tattoo of a chain around his neck. He wore a skull earring in one ear and was completely bald. Although there was a grungy air about him, he was clean shaven with very white teeth. His hands were also clean with well-manicured nails. Nice, she thought. The gang-banger illusion was excellent but if he touches me, and he will, he'd better be clean.

As the man started to rise, she became aware that he was handcuffed to the arm of the bench. Jerked back, he resumed his seat and lowered his head. "I'm innocent," he said.

"We have all the evidence we need," she said. "There's no hope for you. The minimum you'll get is five years upstate."

"Please, Officer Callahan," he said, a slight whine in his voice. "I can't go to jail. I just can't. It will kill me to be in a cage."

"Really," she said, sitting on the bench beside him. "And what will you do to keep me from formally arresting you?"

"Anything. I'll do anything. Just please don't send me to jail." During their conversation, the man had kept his head bowed.

"Anything?" She cupped his chin and raised his head. His eyes were deep blue and, although not handsome in the traditional way, his face had a strength about it that made this humbling still more exciting for her.

"Yes," he whispered.

"I think that's Yes, ma'am."

"Yes, ma'am. What can I do to make this right?"

"An orgasm might make me feel more kindly toward you." She spread her legs and motioned to the floor between her feet.

It took the man several minutes to figure out how to kneel before her with his wrist still handcuffed to the arm of the bench but eventually he managed. Caitlin enjoyed his maneuvers tremendously and the expectation only heightened the experience.

Once he was in position, Caitlin took one of her sets of cuffs and fastened his ankle to the far leg of the bench. Now he was bent slightly, his face in her crotch, unable to straighten or move away. One hand was free to please her.

He struggled to part the seams of her slacks and eventually she felt cool air on her hot, wet pussy. "May I please you?" he asked. "If I make you come will you let me off."

"Maybe," she said. "Let's see how good a job you can do first."

His fingers found her pussy and slid through its deep folds. She leaned her head back against the wall and closed her eyes. His face was forced so close to her that she felt his hot breath on her pussy lips and shivered.

He explored, slowly, and, although she wanted more, she let him set the pace. Finally, one finger found her opening and tickled her inner lips. It was all happening so slowly. The finger penetrated only about half an inch then circled, teasing the outer part of her channel. She pushed her hips forward on the bench, and, taking her hint, he slid his finger deeper. His mouth found her and he licked a heated path from her pubic hair to her inner lips. God, he was good. He licked and fingered her until she was aching with need.

After several minutes of playing, one slippery finger slid backward, toward her anus. She shifted her hips upward so he had better access and the finger slowly entered her rear opening. With one finger in her anus and his tongue licking her clit, she came then, barely able to keep her hips still.

When she calmed, he said, "I'm very uncomfortable in this position. Will you let me go now?"

"Not quite yet. Get to work. I want at least one more orgasm."

She came twice more before she was finally too exhausted to continue. She unfastened his ankle and he scurried out of her way. "I hope I pleased you, Officer," he said as he crouched on the floor at her feet.

"Oh," she said, barely able to stand. "You did. You certainly did."

———

"Got any plans for the first Monday in January?" Jenna said when she arrived back in Manhattan the following Wednesday afternoon after a visit to Seneca Falls.

"Plans?" Marcy asked, only half paying attention. She was doing data entry in Jenna's apartment, something that took quite a bit of time each week.

"Like being at my wedding?"

Marcy jumped out of her ergonomic chair. "You set the date?" she shrieked, dashing across the living room and embracing her twin. "I'm so happy for you and Glen."

"We're going to pick out a ring next week. I'm all in a tizzy. We need a place in Seneca Falls to have a reception the following Saturday, then there's food, a band and I need a dress. Something simple." She stopped, breathless. "There's so much to do and we only have two months."

"I'm the planner. We'll make it happen together and it will be the best wedding anyone's every seen. Where will it be, here or back home?"

Jenna dropped onto the sofa and sighed. "Both, sort of. I told Glen that I actually wanted to be married here, in the brownstone, with you, and Rock, Zack, Chloe, everyone, and he agreed. He wants Rock to be his best man. He's the one who got us back together last winter.

"We have friends in Seneca Falls, so we'll have a party there and one in Ohio, too, I guess." She heaved another big sigh. "Glen has family near Toledo so we'll probably go some-time in the spring. I've never met his family and it's a daunt-ing thought. They're small-town people. What are they going to think of me?"

"They'll love you because he does, I'm sure."

"I guess." She pulled Marcy down beside her. "Will you be my maid of honor?"

Marcy glowed inside. "Of course," she said with a dramatic pause, "as long as the dress is becoming." Her grin was infec-tious and she saw that she was lessening the strained look around Jenna's eyes. "Your dress is of primary importance. Remember that a wedding is all about the woman in the white dress. You will wear white, won't you?"

"That feels kind of strange—the owner of a brothel and pri-mary prostitute wearing virginal white." She grinned. "Yes, I'm going to wear white. I've already been looking through magazines. And thanks for being you. I know, between us, we can pull all this off."

"Why that strange date?" Marcy asked.

"January is usually slow at the Club and it's closed Mondays so everyone can be there. I thought we'd hold it in the living room. You and I could come down the stairs. You know, the grand entrance thing. The room needs to be filled with flowers. Oh, God, flowers."

"Stop panicking, Sis. We'll make it all happen, I promise." Marcy dashed to the computer table and grabbed a pen and pad. "Let's get to work."

Several days later Marcy stopped by the brownstone to meet Jenna for a quick dinner between customers. As she sat in the living room, waiting for her sister, a man was ushered in to wait for his appointment. He looked slightly familiar, of medium height with chocolate brown eyes, a slightly crooked nose and a moustache and tightly trimmed beard.

"Do I know you?" he asked. "You're really quite lovely."

"I don't think so," Marcy answered, glowing from his wonderful words. It sounded wonderful to hear herself described that way. "Although you do look a bit familiar."

His face brightened. "You look a little like Jenna, the woman who runs this place. Wait. I remember. Last winter. We met quite briefly. I never forget a face." He looked her over. "Or a figure."

"I do recall." She'd been terribly upset, a dream making her think Jenna was in some kind of trouble. That was the evening she'd found out about Club Fantasy.

"I'd love to spend an evening with you," he said, "when you're free. I come here often so maybe next time I'll ask for you."

"I'm afraid not."

"I won't push, of course, but I assume you're in the business. Is it me you don't like?"

"Of course not, and I'm in the business only through the paperwork. I don't entertain."

"What a pity. You excite me."

Her face heated and she was sure she was blushing. "Thanks."

"I pay well," he said. He was actually trying to talk her into becoming a prostitute. In the past she would have been deeply insulted. Now she was flattered. "Will you think about it?"

"Mr. Phillips," Rock said, interrupting their conversation, "your room is ready. Second floor, first door on the right tonight."

The second motel room, Marcy realized. "Thank you, Rock." The man stood. "And miss—I don't even know your name."

"Marcy."

"Please think about my offer. Rock knows how to get in touch with me."

Nonplussed, Marcy stared at his retreating form. She found she was tempted, and that shocked her. She hadn't thought about actually doing what Jenna did but it was exciting to know that someone might be interested, even if she was still heavy. Could she do it? She could learn what goes on firsthand and she might enjoy it. But what about Zack? How would he feel? He'd be okay with it, if she decided to give it a try. After all, he had sex with women almost every night. Why couldn't she?

But what about the guy? Maybe, when push came to shove, she couldn't go through with it. If she ever decided to do it, it would have to be perfectly clear that this was her first time and she could call it off at any time. A money back guarantee. Was she actually considering it?

Rock came in and sat beside her on the sofa, taking the place Mr. Phillips had just vacated. He was looking much more relaxed since his father had begun physical therapy after his heart surgery. "I hope he didn't bother you."

"Not at all," Marcy said. "He wanted me to know that he was interested in me."

"I can imagine," Rock said. He was dressed in his usual unrelieved black, which on him looked erotic to the extreme. "He's always asking for *zaftig* women. He says he wants ones with meat on their bones. They're difficult to find in this business. Women think they have to have tiny waists and gigantic breasts to make it here."

"I've gathered that from the people I've met, but heavy women like me?"

"Sure. It goes without saying that lots of men want women with model's figures, but others want different types. Tall, short, thin, zaftig, big breasts, tiny breasts, we try to cater to it all." He looked her over. "You know you've really changed since last winter. When I first saw you I couldn't picture you as Marcy's sister. Now you're as poised and alluring as she is."

Startled, she thanked him. "Don't thank me," he said. "It's your doing. And Zack's."

She knew he and Zack were good friends and wondered

how much he'd told her. "Zack's been a great help in the ego department. He thinks every woman is special and he makes me feel special."

"You are, and he's very taken with you. I hope you know what a great guy he is."

She couldn't suppress her grin. "I know."

"Does his job bother you?"

"Of course not."

"There's no 'of course' about it. You're dating a man who makes love to women for a living. That has to tweak you sometimes." When she kept silent, he continued. "Have you ever considered following in your sister's footsteps?"

"That's just what I've been sitting here thinking about. I don't know whether I could go through with it."

"We could offer him his money back if you decide not to do it at the last minute."

"Wouldn't he be angry?"

"He's a long-standing customer and I think he'd be flattered to be your first. He's really a nice guy. An investment banker with gobs of money to throw around and no family to throw it at. We would refund his money if you didn't—consummate the evening."

She shook her head, suddenly facing this ultimate decision. "I don't know."

"You don't have to decide right this minute. It would be for the book, of course. That way you could experience things firsthand. Maybe you'd learn to understand Zack a little better, too. Just think about it."

She did think about it and two days later, sitting across from Zack at a small neighborhood restaurant, she mentioned it. "Rock asked me whether I'd be interested in playing at the Club some evening. For the book and all."

"You mean entertaining a customer?" Zack's body went quite still.

"I guess so."

"Are you considering it?"

"I don't really know," she said, cautiously, "but it's an interesting idea."

"Phew. That's a switch. It makes me think about what I do and how you must feel. I don't know whether I'd be okay with that."

She was shocked. He was a male hooker and he wasn't sure he wanted her to play, too? "That's chauvinistic and very narrow-minded of you."

"I know, and I can't tell you how my gut is surprising me. You're surprising me, too. Last winter you knew nothing about Club Fantasy. You were a small-town girl with rather small ideas about yourself."

"Ouch, that hurts."

"I'm sorry, but it's true. Now, barely six months later you're considering becoming something that would have been totally alien to you back then."

Marcy's anger was increasing. "I'm thinking about it, but I'm not necessarily going to do anything. And anyway, it's what you do, and what my sister does. Why shouldn't I follow in the family footsteps?"

"You're getting irritated with me." He stared deeply into her eyes. "I'm sorry. It's a bit of a jolt for me, that's all."

"I've gotten used to what you and Jenna do, but considering doing it is a big step and I'm not sure how I feel about it."

He let out a long breath. "I'm so glad you've adjusted to what we do and please forgive me for not wanting you to get too close to that side of the business."

She was totally taken aback by his attitude. "Close? I've talked to a dozen people and learned all about kinky sex, both from them and from you. Why shouldn't I get to play, too?"

She watched Zack's shoulders slump. "Why not indeed? Of course you should."

The subject shifted, leaving Marcy with the distinct impression that he didn't agree at all.

For several days Marcy considered Mr. Phillips's offer. She really needed to experience this for the book, yet she wasn't sure she wanted to. She also didn't like the idea of Zack asking her not to. Why couldn't she do what he did? Damn him. It made her angry all over again.

Marcy and Jenna sat talking over coffee and jelly beans in Jenna's apartment just before Thanksgiving. Marcy hadn't told her sister about her argument with Zack or her conversation with Mr. Phillips. She had done a lot of thinking about his offer but still hadn't come to any conclusion. What worried her more was that although she and Zack still saw each other frequently and made love often, things didn't feel quite the same. *Relax*, she told herself. *It will all work out. If Zack can't deal with the possibility of my seeing Mr. Phillips, to hell with him.* No, it wasn't nearly that easy.

"I think the wedding is getting pretty well organized," Marcy said, returning to reality and crossing another item they'd just discussed off her list. Two months wasn't a lot of time to get everything together but already both the ceremony and the party back home were pretty much planned. Now all they had to do was make it all happen. "We have a few more details . . ."

"Enough for today," Jenna said. "It seems I've done little else these last few days. Glen and I used to have long, sexy talks about love and life when we were apart. Now it seems all we talk about is caterers and whether to have cheese puffs or miniature spinach quiche." She let out an exasperated sigh. "You and Glen plan it. I don't want to know any more." Her breathing quickened. "I'll agree to anything, just do it for me, Sis."

Marcy put her hand on her twin's shoulder. "I'll take care of it all. Just relax or you'll hyperventilate."

Marcy felt Jenna relax. "I know. I'm sorry. Thank God the wedding's done. But for the party back home I don't care whether we have confetti or bubbles. I just want a nice party to celebrate."

"I'm sorry, Jen. I guess I've kind of thrown myself into this whole thing. It's the only wedding I'll ever get to plan this way."

"You'll plan your own." After a short pause, she added, "With Zack?"

Marcy realized that she shouldn't be upset. Pairing her with Zack for a long-term relationship was a logical step for Jenna. "Zack and I are sort of cooling it right now." Cooling it. That was a good way to put it. Nothing seriously wrong, just cooling it.

Jenna's eyes widened. "Now I'm sorry. I've been so wrapped up in this wedding thing I hadn't realized. Did something happen? Can I help?"

Wanting to unburden herself, Marcy told Jenna about Mr. Phillips and Zack's reaction. "He was calm, but I knew he was really angry. How dare he be angry considering what he does? What kind of a double standard is that?" She was working herself up to a serious fury so she stopped talking.

"It's different for him when he thinks about you doing it yourself. Glen and I have had some of the same problems. I know that, for me, being part of Club Fantasy is pretty benign, but it still makes Glen uncomfortable, and I understand that. I know he worries that I'll get involved with one of my clients but I know it's not a problem. I can imagine that Zack feels pretty much the same way about you. He doesn't want to take the chance that you'll get involved with someone else totally accidentally."

"You think that's what he's worried about?" Could it be that simple? Maybe it wasn't that he didn't trust her. But still . . .

"I don't know. Maybe he wants you exclusively, too."

"What right has he? He's never even hinted at something long-term." What would she do it he did?

"Maybe you should ask him."

Since the holidays were approaching, Zack had been quite busy. In addition to writing and working with Club Fantasy's paper work, Marcy had begun to walk around the city, enjoying the Christmas atmosphere and revisiting spots she enjoyed. The last Tuesday of November found her in the crush, watching the lighting of the giant Christmas tree in Rockefeller Center. Then, as the crowd dispersed, she went to a nearby restaurant for a quick glass of wine before heading home.

As she sat at the bar waiting for a table, she heard a woman's voice behind her say, "That was such a wonderful idea. I never expected to enjoy something as ordinary as a tree lighting, but it was thrilling." The voice was cultured, if a bit condescending.

"I thought you'd enjoy it," another, all-too-familiar voice said, "and later we'll show up at your company's party." It was Zack. Her back was to him but the way the sound made her skin feel, it had to be him.

"You certainly know how to make me feel good," the woman said. "Just what I needed before this evening."

"Don't worry. You'll be a sensation. We'll see to that."

"Darling, with you on my arm they'll all drool. Then later we can go back to my place and celebrate." The way she said the word celebrate left little doubt about how. Marcy kept her back turned and soon the couple was shown to a table.

He's working, she told herself, and you know what he does for a living. This must be one of those "keep the lady happy" jobs. He was well paid for it, too, and it wasn't a secret. If she were to have a permanent relationship with him she'd have to get used to the reality of what he did for a living. Marcy quickly headed for the door and grabbed a taxi back to her apartment, her mind frozen.

Back in her apartment, she grabbed a pint of Cherry Garcia ice cream and a spoon and dropped onto the sofa. This was what Zack did. She'd known it all along but somehow, in the abstract, it didn't seem as personal. Now she'd seen him with another woman. Chewing on a piece of fruit, she tried to sort out her feelings. If she couldn't deal with it, she needed to get out. Now. If she sorted it out and decided she could live with it, she needed to let it go. The same went for Zack and his feelings about Mr. Phillips.

She recalled the story of the fox and the scorpion. Standing beside a flooded river, both needing to get to the other side, a scorpion asked a fox for a ride on his back. "But you'll sting me and we'll both drown."

"Of course I won't sting you. If you go, I go, too. I just need a lift. I promise I won't sting you."

The fox thought this was reasonable so he let the scorpion onto his back and began to swim across the flooded river. Suddenly he felt the scorpion sting him on the back of his neck. As he was sinking, he moaned and asked, "Why did you do that?"

"Because I'm a scorpion," the insect said as he fell toward the water. "It's what I do."

Well, Marcy thought as she scooped another spoonful of ice cream from the box, "That's what Zack is and what he does," she said aloud. "I need to make some serious decisions and so does he." For now, maybe "cooling it" was exactly what they both needed.

Chapter
17

The following Monday evening Marcy was still trying to sort out her feelings, both about entertaining Mr. Phillips and Zack, when Jenna called and invited her out to dinner. Slightly surprised at the formal offer, she met Jenna in a small Chinese restaurant they both loved.

They ordered, then, over hot and sour soup, Jenna said, "I'm leaving Club Fantasy."

Marcy almost dropped her soupspoon. "You're leaving?"

Jenna rested her elbows on the table and leaned forward. "After the wedding I'm moving back to Seneca Falls. Glen and I are going to live together like a traditional married couple."

"Where did that come from?"

Jenna took her sister's hand across the table. "I'm sorry I haven't discussed this with you before, Sis, but I needed to think this through by myself."

"I've known you were troubled but I chalked it up to prewedding jitters. I never expected this."

"The wedding is the one part of all this I'm totally sure of. I want to have sex with Glen and only with him. I don't want to do this anymore. It's not right for me now."

"I thought you loved it here. Are you regretting Club Fantasy?"

"Not at all!" Jenna said, vehemently. "I've loved every minute of the last eighteen months but now I'm ready for life, phase next. I want to be there when Glen gets home from work. Every night. I want to be a real wife." She paused, then said, "I want a baby."

"Phew," Marcy said. "That's a big step. What will you do about the club?"

"Nothing much will change, I hope. That's what I want to talk to you about. You've extended your leave of absence twice and I have the feeling that you're not going back. I would love it if you'd take over for me here full-time. Chloe certainly doesn't want the responsibility and never did, so you're the logical choice."

"I don't know whether I can be with clients. I've thought and thought about it and I think I've finally figured me out. I'm not you, Jen. I can't do what you do. Maybe once or twice but not all the time."

"I don't need you to, nor would I ever want you to do anything you're not comfortable with. You know me better than that."

She huffed out a sigh. "Of course I do."

"What I meant was that I want you to keep the books, work with Chloe on the appointments there, and do the interviews."

Marcy had done a few after Caitlin and had discovered that she was pretty good at ferreting out the details of the fantasies people wanted. "I suppose I could do that part."

Jenna squeezed her hand and beamed. "I knew I could count on you. I need to talk with Chloe but I know we can work out the financial arrangements. You'd get a piece of the action, of course."

"You're already paying me for the accounting and stuff. With that and the occasional work for AAJ I'm doing okay."

"The Club will pay you for the interviews and, in addition, you'll get a cut of the profits. If you want to stay here permanently, you can have my apartment and become a rooted city girl."

"City girl." She chuckled. "That's really funny. You're going back to Seneca Falls and I'm becoming a city girl. What a switch." She thought about Jenna living with Glen. "What will you do all day? Until there's a baby at least."

"You're doing some of the contracts for AAJ, but I contacted Ms. Henshaw and she's delighted that I can do some per diem, face-to-face work. They never did replace you and Paula's pregnant. I chatted with her this afternoon. She's due in about five months and is planning to take maternity leave for a month before the baby's born and about six months after."

"She's pregnant? That's great. For both of us." It would mean more faxing for her and more pay checks. Money wasn't going to be a problem. "Pregnancy might even be contagious."

"I hope so. Glen and I have talked about having several and I'm already on the downside of thirty."

Marcy felt a hollow space open up in her belly. She too was on the downside of thirty and had few prospects for the kind of life Jenna was going to have. *That's okay*, she told herself, *running Club Fantasy will be great and I don't need more.* The image of Zack flashed through her mind. She had no idea where she and Zack stood. Maybe it was time to get it all out in the open. "When?"

"After the wedding. Mid-January, if you're ready to make a permanent move."

"I think I am, one way or another." With Zack or without. It was plaguing her; she couldn't seem to make up her mind how she felt, about Zack or Mr. Phillips. She really should take Mr. Phillips up on his offer, if only to spite Zack. No. That was no reason to do anything. The money? For the book? Not good reasons either.

Was Glen's difficulty with Jenna's job part of why she was

moving back upstate and giving up the business? It was more difficult than she could have imagined dealing with the reality of Zack bedding a different woman every night.

Zack must have the same problem dealing with her desire to become part of the staff of Club Fantasy. The past few weeks they had only seen each other about once a week and those evenings were strained and awkward. Everywhere except in bed. Their sex life was the easiest thing about their relationship right now. She wasn't surprised by the fact that she missed him terribly. She knew that he was busy almost every evening because of the holidays, and that bothered her more than she wanted to admit. Sauce for the goose?

To help her understand Zack and to complete the stories for her book, Marcy arranged a meeting with a man named Gerry who worked for Club Fantasy. Gerry was adorable, with brown, curly hair and bright country-blue eyes. He also had the same charming grin as Zack had.

She and Gerry talked for almost an hour, about his clients and about what it meant to be a male prostitute, while she tried to understand what it must feel like to be Zack. She didn't pump him for specific information about Zack, but Gerry did mention that he'd done several threesomes with Zack and a customer. No homosexuality involved, Gerry told her, just two men pleasuring one woman. Probably not, she thought, Zack probably wouldn't be into anything that didn't involve women.

Gerry wasn't as into women as Zack was. To him, Club Fantasy was just a job that fit well with his good looks and natural charm. "I'm looking for stories for my book," she said, not wanting to dwell on Zack. "Got anything unusual?"

"I don't know what you'd call unusual," Gerry said, his blue eyes twinkling, "but several of my ladies are interested in something a bit different. At least I thought it was until it became popular with several ladies." He went on to describe a different use for the exam room. The way he described the game it sounded really hot, but she knew little about it. She dialed into the Internet, searched and read, read and searched for almost two hours. Yes, Gerry's activity was hot and not as uncommon as she would have thought. She began to write one final story for her book.

A NEW EXPERIENCE

Marge had "been there, done that." She'd played with most of the fantasies offered at the Eros Hotel. She'd been going there every few weeks for almost a year and she'd played in every room with every guy they had. She sat with the director and they discussed her problem. "I'm bored with it all," Marge said. "No, don't get me wrong, it's all hot and sexy and I come several times with each visit. But I've run out of ideas for new things to try."

"There are a few things left," the woman said.

"I'm not into any really kinky, heavy stuff. I like all the guys I've been with and we've even done several threesomes. I've been spanked and done the spanking, played with toys and enjoyed your basement a couple of times."

"I know exactly what you've done and what your desires are. Would you trust me to set something up for you that I think will solve your boredom problem?"

Marge sighed. The director, it was funny that she didn't even know the woman's name, had never failed yet. "Okay. I will have the right to say no and get my money back, right?"

"Of course, as always. Why don't you come over around eight tomorrow night and I'll set things up for you?"

Grinning, Marge left. Something new. She could hardly wait.

The following evening she arrived at eight o'clock and was shown into a small room. "You're going to play patient tonight," a note from the director said. "I know you've done this one before but I've got a new twist for you. Roll with it all and I know you'll be well rewarded. Of course, at any time you can say stop and we will either change the scenario or return your money."

A bit puzzled at what the woman might have come up with, Marge changed into a well-washed cotton gown that tied in the front with nothing beneath. She'd played doctor-patient several times so she knew the drill. She entered the "exam room" and settled on the exam table. "Good evening," a cultured voice said from a shadowed corner. "I see you've been here before."

"I have. Shall I put my feet in the stirrups?"

"We have something a bit different for you tonight." He crossed the room. A new guy, she thought. "I'm Gerry." Cute name, cute guy, with a head full of brown curls and bright blue eyes. He looked about sixteen but Marge knew that the Eros Hotel only employed consenting, and well-paid adults.

Marge watched as Gerry removed the stirrups and instead, raised curved pieces of metal that would fit behind her knees and hold them raised and well apart. Okay, she thought, whatever.

"I need you to be perfectly still for what I'm going to do," Gerry said, "so I'm going to use these." He lifted first one knee then the other onto the devices, then said, "I mean perfectly still. I hope you don't mind." He pulled a roll of adhesive tape from his lab coat pocket and began to wrap strips around her knees and thighs to hold them tightly in place. "Remember that if you say stop at any time, I will."

"Of course," she said. She'd played with bondage and, although the situation was a bit unusual, this wasn't very different from other ways she'd played. Okay, a bondage exam?

"Now," he said, "I'm going to wash you thoroughly."

Wash? Didn't he think she was well-groomed?

"It's part of the scenario," he said, "and has nothing to do with your cleanliness."

"Whatever," she said, and settled back against the leather-upholstered table. The soft, warm cloth was deliciously arousing and she felt both excited and pampered as Gerry slowly and sensuously used the cloth on every part of her cunt. "Now I'm going to trim this hair," he said.

"Trim my hair?"

"That's right. It's going to make everything feel so much better."

Marge felt the cold scissors against her hot flesh, then heard the snick, snick as he closely trimmed her pubic hair. Eventually, he said, "Now for the shaving."

Marge struggled to sit up but her legs were fastened to the braces. "I don't think so."

Gerry came around the table and gazed down at her. "It will make all of you feel so different that you'll be amazed. I've done this with lots of women and no one has ever been dissatisfied."

"Won't it itch and stuff later on?"

"I've got a lotion that will just about eliminate any such problems, whether you want to keep your bush shaved or let it grow out. As I said, no one has ever complained."

She took a deep breath. She'd asked for something new and the director had kept her word. Was she ready to try this? Sure. Why the hell not? "Okay, go for it," she said.

Gerry smiled then moved around to the foot of the table. He moved a light so he could see, but the heat on her wet tissues made her pussy spasm. "Try to keep as still as you can," he said.

"I'm a statue," she said, deciding to trust him with a razor so close to her pussy.

"I've got one of those shaving cream heaters so this should feel really erotic." She heard the unmistakable sound of an aerosol can and felt Gerry's talented fingers spreading the warm foam over her flesh. He was right. The warmth of the light and the heated goo spread throughout her body.

"That's wonderful, even without the actual shaving," she said, barely able to keep her breathing even and her hips still.

"Just don't move," he purred.

There was something extra exciting about having to hold perfectly still despite the needs of her body. The razor slid over her outer lips, then her inner ones. She could hear water sloshing as he continually rinsed the razor.

It must have taken more than ten minutes for him to be satisfied with the job. Then he spread lotion over her, slowly and carefully covering every inch of the newly shaved area. Then he blew a stream of cool air over her. "How does that feel?" he asked.

She'd never felt anything like it. "Amazing," she said. Air was flowing over areas that had never been exposed to it before.

"How about this?" he asked as he leaned closer and flicked his tongue over her now fully exposed clit. "And this?" His tongue stroked her now naked pubis. His tongue and fingers were everywhere and it was as though a veil had been lifted, allowing her to feel with an intensity she hadn't ever experienced before.

"Oh, God," she panted, "it's so different. So alive somehow." Her heart was galloping and she could barely function. When one finger tickled her anal opening and three more filled her, she climaxed. "Oh God, oh God, oh God, do it, do it, do it, don't stop, don't stop, don't stop." He didn't stop, bringing her easily to two more shattering orgasms.

Fabulously, deliciously exhausted, she finally began to come down, Gerry moved to the side of the table and pulled off his shorts and briefs. She looked at his erect, shaved penis and scrotum and salivated. She loved sucking a man's cock, but the hair did sometimes get in the way. Now she could try it with a totally naked dick. "Come here," she said, opening her mouth. "I've never sucked a naked cock before."

The table was at the perfect height so when he moved nearer his cock slipped easily between her lips. She used her hand to stroke him as her tongue licked the length of his oh-so-smooth erection. Her fingers cupped his balls and she scratched just behind gently. Shaving her must have been an erotic experience for him too since it took only a few minutes for him to brace himself on the table and let out a long groan as he filled her mouth with semen. While he came, she milked his cock and squeezed his balls.

Eventually he dropped into a chair, naked only from the waist down. He presented a handsome sight, his now-flaccid penis fully visible against his thigh.

When they were both calm, he brought a mirror and showed her how her groin looked without any pubic hair. "You're so beautiful down there," he said. "You should keep it this way all the time."

"How often do I have to do it?"

"Every few days if you want to keep it smooth. I can give you some of the lotion too."

"No need," she said, slowly sitting up. "I'll make an appointment with you for three days from now and you can, let's say, touch me up."

"Touch ups are the best," he said, chuckling. "The very best."

As she pulled on her panties and jeans, she realized that the new sensation from her naked pussy would keep her hot and wet until her next visit. She couldn't wait.

Marcy printed the pages and saved the story on the hard disk and on a floppy. She'd used Gerry's name, but she'd do a global change before she incorporated the story into the book. This would be the ultimate, final story. The heroine was fully into the world of the Eros Hotel.

Marcy had been weaving the main plot around a woman who'd come to the city and been drawn into the world of prostitution. At the beginning Meg, the heroine of her novel, had been as innocent as Marcy herself when she first arrived in Manhattan the previous summer and now, at the end of the novel, she was wiser and more understanding about this previously baffling world. Meg could deal with it all, but could she?

The evening before the wedding the Club was closed and, while Rock, Zack, Gerry and a few other men took Glen out for a bachelor fling, Marcy, Chloe and several of the other women took Jenna out for a celebratory evening. All of the women knew that Jenna was moving back upstate so this was a combination bachelorette and farewell party. They visited several of their favorite night spots, drank quite a bit of champagne and enjoyed each other's company.

At one point in the evening, Marcy sat beside Jenna, her mind freed by the number of glasses of bubbly she'd consumed. "Jenna, I've been meaning to ask you. Is you decision partly based on Glen's difficulty dealing with Club Fantasy?"

Jenna looked Marcy in the eye. "No. Not really. I know Glen will be happier with me not doing what I do, but he had already told me that he would cope with whatever I wanted to do. He trusts me and knows I'd never do anything to hurt him or lie to him about anything. I'm moving back so I won't have to take birth control pills anymore, so we can try to have kids. I would never do that while I was still having intercourse with other men."

Marcy had finally decided that she couldn't have sex for money with anyone. She wasn't going to spend an evening with Mr. Phillips and that was that. Although it was obviously fine for all the men and women who worked at the Club, she thought, looking at all the wonderful people around her, it wasn't right for her. But it was right for Zack and she'd live with it. He was more than worth it. She would learn to feel

about it the way Glen felt about Jenna. She needed to talk to
Zack and clear the air.

The wedding was planned for four in the afternoon and
there would be a sort of cocktail party afterward for the two
dozen people attending. Rock would be best man and Marcy
was to be maid of honor. She and Jenna had selected an ankle-
length dress of rose wool for her that was amazingly becoming.
Of course, next to the bride, Marcy was a poor second.

Jenna's dress was demure: ivory satin overstitched with lace,
in the style of the 1920s, with a slender, calf-length skirt, long
sleeves and a modest neckline. Instead of a headpiece, she
wore a large, ivory picture hat. They dressed in the motel room
on the second floor of the brownstone. Tears threatened both
the women so they tried to avoid topics more serious than
whether they were wearing the correct color panty hose. "I'm
going to miss you like crazy, Sis," Marcy finally said as they
prepared to head downstairs. "We'd just gotten back together
and now you'll be so far away."

"No farther away than we were while I was here last year.
It's only a brief plane ride, train trip or drive. We'll visit often.
Glen and I have managed to see each other almost every
week."

"I know," Marcy said, blinking hard to keep from bawling.

"Let's not get blue now." Jenna grinned through eyes filled
with tears. "I'm marrying the best guy in the world."

Best next to Zack, Marcy thought.

After a long, slightly tearful hug, Marcy opened the door
and slowly started to descend the stairs to the strains of the
wedding march. The ground level of the building was filled
with flowers, mostly off-white lilies and pale pink roses. Marcy
carried a bouquet of the same roses and Jenna, she knew,
carried lilies. The planning had been hectic, but as she gazed
at the area below her she knew it had been worth it.

Her eyes found Zack, handsome in his dark suit. His gaze locked on her and he winked. They could work it all out. They must, or she'd lose this fabulous man. She almost wept at the thought that they might not be able to.

When she was halfway down the stairs all eyes moved to Jenna, who quickly made her way down to walk beside her sister. The two women, arm in arm, descended the remainder of the steps.

At the front of the living room, Glen waited, looking a bit uncomfortable in his tux, with Rock beside him. As the two women approached, Glen's expression softened and, as he took Jenna's arm from Marcy, he grinned.

It took only a few moments for the minister to say the words that united Glen and Jenna, after which they pledged themselves, each to the other, with wonderful words they'd written themselves. One sentence rang in Marcy's ears. "Separately each of us is a formidable force; together we're dynamite." Separate, yet together. Could that work for her and Zack?

Then it was over and everyone milled around, offering congratulations to the obviously happy couple. Marcy didn't have to turn around to know that Zack was behind her. "That was lovely," he said in her ear. "I think we need to talk."

She turned. "Weddings do strange things to people and I don't know whether this is the best time."

"Now is the best time. Please. Let's go somewhere a little more quiet."

They ended up back in the motel room where she and Jenna had dressed, sitting side by side on the bed. They spoke simultaneously. "Marcy."

"Zack." They laughed, awkwardly, then dickered as to who'd speak first. Finally, Marcy said, "I saw you with an attractive brunette the night of the Rockefeller tree lighting. In a little place on West Fifty-sixth."

Zack thought a moment. "That must have been Belinda." When he started to explain the circumstances, Marcy held up her hand. "That's not the issue. It's just been difficult for me to come to grips with the reality of you with other women and my feelings about it. I knew what you did from the beginning, and I tried to keep myself from getting too involved with you but it didn't work. At that moment, seeing the actuality of what you did hurt me more than I could have imagined."

Zack started to put his arms around her but she stood up and moved across the room. "I've thought about it for six weeks and I've come up with this. I love you." Again she held up her hand to forestall any comment from him. "Please let me say this all at once." He stopped trying to talk. "I'm afraid that, in the end, all my warnings to myself didn't make a bit of difference. I fell in love and that's a total thing for me, and it scared me to death. But once I accepted my feelings, I had to figure out what to do about what you do.

"You are what you are and I love you the way you are. If you're as interested in a future with me as I am with you, I'll deal with everything. I'll only ask that you hold me and tell me that you love me. You're worth it to me." She stopped, and, when he didn't respond, she continued with a watery smile. "You can talk now. And if I've made a complete fool of myself, please let me down easy."

"Marcy, oh God, love, you haven't made a fool of yourself at all. I've been having the same sort of arguments with myself. I'm a male prostitute so I didn't think I could ask you to be with me, to trust me. I want to spend my life with you more than I've ever wanted anything. I looked at Jenna and Glen and, well, I hope that if they can make it, we can. If you want to take up where Jenna is leaving off, I'll adjust and shut up my protective voices. If it will make you happy, I'll also slowly get out of the business. I don't want anyone but you, and, if the whole Club Fantasy thing makes you uncomfortable, I'll do something else, anything else. I'll even flip burgers."

Marcy felt the tears flow freely down her face. "You don't have to flip burgers and I'm not going to follow in Jenna's footsteps. I can't do it. You and she can, I can't. I was going to make a date with Mr. Phillips on spite, just to show you that I can do anything I want, but that's a truly dumb reason to make love with a man. I want you and only you."

"I want you," Zack said, crossing the room and enfolding Marcy in his arms, "and I love you more than I've cared to admit, even to myself. Marry me? Whatever we do from here on, I want you as a permanent part of my life."

Marcy swallowed hard. She hadn't expected a proposal. Marry him? "Weddings do strange things to people. They make you want the flowers and music. It's not all magic, Zack. Are you sure?"

"Are you trying to talk me out of this?" He held her tightly. "Because I've never been more sure of anything."

"Even flipping burgers?"

"If that will make you happy."

"I'll marry you on one condition," Marcy said, resting her head against his chest and listening to the firm beating of his heart. "Just be what you are. That's what I love."

"Can we go downstairs and tell everyone? I'm so happy I want to share it."

Tears and smiles confused her facial muscles. "Let's wait a few days to tell everyone. I don't want to intrude on Jenna and Glen's day. Then we'll have a celebration."

"Then we'll have a wedding. I don't want to wait."

Hand in hand, Marcy and Zack walked back down the stairs at Club Fantasy. As she descended, Marcy's gaze caught Jenna's and the two women smiled.

It was spring sixteen months later as Zack maneuvered a rental car off the New York State Thruway toward Seneca Falls. "I feel like I haven't seen Jenna and Glen in years," Marcy said from the passenger seat.

"It hasn't been more than three months, love, and you two talk on the phone every day. Just relax. We're almost there."

"I can't imagine why I'm so nervous."

Zack reached over and squeezed his wife's hand. "It's probably the babies. You two will be comparing notes for hours while poor Glen and I get quietly toasted."

"I guess." Marcy and Jenna had gotten pregnant at almost the same time and had delivered within hours of each other, Jenna upstate and Marcy in the city. The only difference was that, while Glen was with Jenna during the birth of their little girl, Zack had coached Marcy through the delivery of twins, two perfect little boys who now slept in car seats behind their parents. Marcy turned back and watched seven-week-old Patrick and William sleep. Named for Zack's father and Marcy's, the boys were amazingly easy, both now sleeping for four or five hours at a time. Marcy was beginning to lose her haggard look. Zack was wonderful with the babies, giving a bottle to one while Marcy nursed the other. Their friends couldn't tell the two apart, but neither Zack nor Marcy ever had any trouble.

How far they'd come in the past year. Marcy was now running Club Fantasy and business was thriving. Most of the rooms were booked every evening. Rock still lived in the downstairs, but he had also hired a friend to be there the nights he wasn't so the Club could stay open seven evenings a week. Marcy kept the books and had done almost all the interviews until she was so pregnant that she turned the public face of the Club over to a reluctant, but willing Chloe. She'd return to doing everything when she could get good, reliable child care. Several of the women involved with the Club, who'd become close friends of the couple, had volunteered for the job until a more permanent solution could be found.

She and Zack had been married two months after Jenna and Glen's wedding, in an almost identical ceremony. They'd had the two dresses altered so Jenna wore Marcy's matron-of-honor dress and Marcy wore her sister's wedding dress. The same minister married them as had married Jenna and Glen, with Rock and Glen standing with Zack, each giving a small speech afterward as they toasted the happy couple with champagne.

"It's been a tumultuous road that's led us to this wonderful day," Zack said, raising his glass toward his wife, "but I know that what Marcy and I have found is better than any fantasy I've ever had."

"You're the only fantasy I'll ever want," Marcy had added.

Zack had continued entertaining for only a few months after their marriage but then decided to see what was available in the corporate world to utilize his psychology degree. To everyone's amusement, he was now a rising star in the human resources department of a major brokerage firm. Every time he came home with a story about one of the employees, Marcy couldn't help but think of Ms. Henshaw.

Marcy's book was being published and she had received a modest advance against anticipated royalties. Called simply *The Eros Hotel*, it was due out that summer and her editor had assured her that it should sell well. She was even discussing with her agent the possibility of doing a sequel, more or less based on her life rather than Jenna's. How honest could she be about herself remained to be seen.

As the rental car turned the corner Marcy saw Jenna and Glen sitting on the glassed-in front porch of their house, staring down the street for a first glimpse of the approaching couple. Marcy watched Jenna bounce up when she spotted the car and hand little Isabel to her husband. Then, almost jumping up and down, Jenna waved wildly.

Marcy rolled down the window and waved back. Two women, twins, both incredibly happily married and now mothers, had used their similarities and their differences to become fast friends.

As the car pulled to the curb, Marcy unfastened her seat belt, leaned over and kissed Zack on his cheek. "I love you."

"I love you, too," he said, his wicked wink still able to increase the heat in her belly. Thank heavens the six week wait after the twins' birth was finally over. "We've got it all, haven't we?"

Marcy looked at the two car seats in the backseat, then at her sister and her husband. "All, and more."

Dear Reader,

I hope you've enjoyed reading *Night After Night* as much as I enjoyed writing it. When a book is done I always find I miss the characters and I know I'll miss Marcy, Jenna, Zack, Glen and all their friends. Of course, as you've probably realized, characters do tend to return for guest appearances in later books.

If this is your first visit to Jenna and Chloe's world, pick up my earlier novel, *Club Fantasy*, and learn how it all began. Courtesans, Inc. was the centerpiece of another earlier book, *The Price of Pleasure*. Erika's story is another novel of erotic romance.

Please let me know whether you've enjoyed this book and what you'd like to read in future novels and please visit my website at *www.JoanELloyd.com*. You can poke around in the advice, letters and erotic short stories, learn about me (and Ed) and read excerpts from all my past books—and there are lots. You can write to me from there, or directly at *Joan@Joan ELloyd.com*. You can also snail mail me at Joan Elizabeth Lloyd, P.O. Box 221, Yorktown Heights, NY 10598. I answer all my mail; although snail mail takes a bit longer.